Tunnel Vision

Dave Amonson

Publisher's note: This is a work of fiction. Names, characters, places, and incidents either are the product of the author's imagination or are used fictitiously. Any resemblance to actual events, locales, or persons, living or dead, is entirely coincidental.

Printed by Create Space
Designed, formatted, and edited by Kristen Corrects
Cover art design by Bella Faccia Photography

First edition published 2015
10 9 8 7 6 5 4 3 2 1

Amonson, Dave
Tunnel Vision / Dave Amonson

ISBN-13: 978-0-9940597-0-3

Dedication

To those who wonder and aspire to improve situations.

Chapter 1

Two captains in dress whites emerge into the sunshine. Youths from every nation follow. The nearest ocean is two thousand kilometers away.

Twelve years earlier, drizzle fell on the remnants of a graveside service. Mourners moved toward their cars. A father and both daughters, hand in hand, lingered by the grave.

After the funeral lunch, as the sky lightened, Elaine asked Brett, "Will you walk with me in Bowness Park?"

"Sure, let's go by the house and change clothes on our way."

The sunlight reflected off the water in a pond. A glint of light caught Brett's attention.

Could a tiny spot of light change the trajectory of a life?

Elaine sensed his mood. "What're you thinking?"

He pointed to the far bank. "Do you see that spot of light?"

Elaine leaned closer to him. "Yes, I see it."

"I wonder whether I might provide a speck of light to deflect a person's path toward a better life."

"You do that all the time."

"Marjie occupied our circle for twenty-eight years. She missed the light; she's dead."

She turned to him. "Are you responsible for everyone?"

"No, but there're lots of Marjies in this world. Do you think we could help a bunch of them?"

"We're near retirement. I have visions of times with the children and grandchildren, quiet times in the garden, sorties to visit friends and relatives, a peaceful golden age. Are you going to shatter my dream?"

Chapter 2

Beth approached Brett's café table. "Hi, old friend, good to see you."

"Hi, Beth, it's been awhile. How're you doing?"

"Fine. I'm busy and enjoying life's little challenges."

"Remember when we worked through the weekend until one-thirty Monday morning, so we could accommodate the customer's final inspection on time?"

"Do you remember my words to you? Next time, let me manage the job. Mac was angry because I missed his parents' anniversary party. He went alone."

"Was that the last straw for Mac?"

She shrugged. "No, he viewed marriage as a joint endeavour but I ran it. He ran."

"I'm sorry I caused one more rift. Your ability to manage projects was a lifesaver but we should've accommodated our families more. Still, Mac wasn't the only guy in town."

"No, but I prefer TV. No drama when I turn it off."

He smiled. "You must have been born after the Romantic Period."

"And you're the perfect marriage partner?"

"No, not perfect. That's why I invited you to lunch. I've got an idea; Elaine doesn't like it. I want to run it by you."

"I'm supposed to help you sell an idea that Elaine doesn't like. This should improve things."

He sipped his coffee. "It's a tunnel from the mouth of the St. Lawrence to Whitehorse; it'll provide material for a multipurpose transportation-utility corridor across the northern expanse of Canada with townhouses along each side. I want to use labour plucked from youth that choose not to integrate in conventional settings. The project will be a viable alternative to welfare."

Beth ordered coffee and looked at Brett. "I spent school breaks at my uncle's cattle ranch. One spring, Uncle noticed a cow in trouble. As we chased her toward the corral, she charged me. I ducked behind a tree. Uncle got his horse between me and the cow. She was delirious from her dead calf rotting inside her. The vet wasn't available for several hours, so Uncle shot the cow, ending her misery. As you described your idea, I considered whether a hallucinating geezer could be shot. Probably not. Tell me about feeding young blood to mosquitoes and draining Lake Athabasca."

"I want to convince my family I can make this project work. Elaine wants to relax, share time with the children and grandchildren, travel, and socialize. I'll go crazy. I hope you'll help me consider the possibility that I could make this happen. Outside of my family, you're my best friend."

"They'll shut this joint's lights off before I recite all that's wrong with your idea. There're hundreds of interest groups lined up to thwart any project. The Indian situation has been screwed up for a 150 years. The national and provincial parks, Indian reservations, wetlands where a trumpeting swan lands every twenty years, half a dozen provincial and territorial governments, and thousands of individuals will resist any idea, even if it's a good one. It takes money to build a tool shed—try building two townhouses 4,400 kilometers long. A professor tried to teach me negative numbers. I never noticed a need for the concept. Now, I see negative numbers could illustrate the probability you could make this work."

"So you think it might not work?"

She waved her hand. "Oh, I think it'll be as easy as getting an ice cream at the dairy bar. Don't you see it's impossible?"

"Did the Wrights learn how to fly? Did Bell get a phone to work? Did Watt figure out how to improve steam engines? You might be talking to the next great innovator."

"I might be, but I like my odds better than yours."

"Will you come to the grand opening when my project is finished?"

"Of course, my TV will escort me."

Chapter 3

Monday evening, Elaine and Brett ate dinner at home.

Brett raised his glass of water. "I want to lead a change in our social welfare system. What evening could we set aside to talk it through?"

She wiggled her fork. "Don't you listen? I don't want to be involved in obligations. I want us to slow down in retirement."

"I know, but I also know that our serenity must consider our individual interests, and I know I won't be happy line dancing on Tuesday and playing Bingo on Thursday."

"And, if you're not happy, I'm not happy. Is that it?"

"It's not a threat, Elaine. I hope to have a purpose most days, and I don't see satisfaction in idleness."

"Let's have our discussion now and get it over with."

"No, I hope we'll come to some consensus rather than pick at each other forever."

"How will I prepare? I long for a slower pace," Elaine said. "Now, when it's within sight, you go off on some ridiculous tangent."

"I have a suggestion." He put down his fork to indicate his seriousness. "Let's each make a list of the main things we plan for ourselves for the rest of our lives: where we want to live, how much we want to travel, how often we want to visit the grandkids, how much yard work we want to do, where we want to winter, what kinds of hobbies we want, etcetera. We each make our own lists and then we integrate our lists so that each of us gets forty-eight percent of what we want and leave the last four percent for Murphy."

She glanced at him. "Who's Murphy?"

"Murphy's Law, where anything that can go wrong, will go wrong, but we'll plan this so well that nothing will go wrong, right?"

"Wednesday night. You make dinner. I'll sit at the counter, with a glass of wine, and describe my vision and list of wants. I'll clean up the dishes while you tell me your vision and list of wants beyond sex every twenty minutes."

Brett grinned, gave her a thumb up, and rose to pick up the dishes.

Elaine loaded the dishwasher. "What do you plan to do tonight?"

"You've suggested the first forty minutes, then I expect to sleep 'til breakfast."

Chapter 4

Wednesday, Brett brought in the groceries.

Elaine's greeting was abrupt. "Hi."

This'll be piece of cake.

Brett set the bags on the counter. "I bought five minute rice because I didn't want you to have too much time to present your list of hopes and wants."

"And I chilled a bottle of Barolo because I like red wine a tad chilled. It should pair nicely with my shoulder."

He grinned. "Come here, babe. Give me a kiss and let's make this a great evening."

Brett placed two candles on the counter and lit them.

Elaine joined him in the kitchen. "This is a fight to the death. These must be memorial candles?"

"No, the flames will reflect in your eyes until we have a plan that will cause a real spark for the rest of our lives."

"Perhaps you can bottle your crap and sell it door-to-door. It'll give you a reason to get up in the morning. You can call it Bretth Mint, a special blend of dreams and drivel that will dampen every hope and fuel every disagreement. It should sell well."

He faced her. "Forty-seven years ago, I met a spunky little lady who saw potential in me. She has persevered, so far, and I hope she doesn't give up in my remaining thirty years."

Brett began to prepare a meal of wild salmon and stuffed peppers. "So what's on your list?"

"I want you to love me all the time."

"That's easy; I do love you all the time. More than you know."

"Yes, but I want you to demonstrate that love all the time."

"I've worked on that since I met you. You multi-task and thrive on it. I focus and thrive on it. I'll demonstrate my love when I'm focused on it but that won't be often enough to meet your expectations."

"I hope you'll have more time in retirement and you'll have more time for me."

"I'll be around more, but it'll provide more opportunities for you to notice I don't focus enough on demonstrating my love for you. We're a great match. We have similar values. We've raised great kids—they have fine mates and one child. We've not burdened family or society. Why can't we continue to support people and causes we believe in, love each other, and demonstrate our love in ways that match our psyches?"

"You see, the list is hopeless because you never change."

"Is it just me? Do you change? Can we try to find common ground so we can do things that allow each of us to grow and feel fulfilled?"

"I want to live in Calgary. I don't want a home in Phoenix or Timbuktu. I want to be near the kids and grandkids and go to their sports and recitals. I want to continue family dinners on Sunday. I want to have the family together on special occasions."

"I want that, too. We agree one hundred percent."

"How will you do it from your hovel near the Arctic Circle?"

"Perhaps you misunderstood when I said I'd like to lead the initiative, not be the person on site."

"I know, Brett, but there'll be meetings in Ottawa, New York, Vancouver, Whitehorse, Sept Isles, and a trillion other places." She waved her hand in the air in exasperation.

"Have we agreed that Calgary will be our home forever?"

"Yes."

"Do you expect me to be home Friday through Sunday on a regular basis?"

"Yes."

"Does your list allow me some time on Monday through Thursday?"

"Yes, but I don't want you away most of the time."

"That's fair. However, I expect to ask people to commit resources to the project and I'll visit them on occasion. You're welcome to travel with me."

"Yeah, I look forward to hours in the lobby of a hotel in Iqaluit while you schmooze with some government rep."

"Would it help if I find an office within a ten minute walk from here? I can come home for lunch. I'll schedule work and travel for Monday through Thursday. I'll integrate other commitments with you."

"What about the grandchildren's activities? Will you show up to support them?"

"Yes, but probably not as often as you prefer."

She looked at him, a stern expression on her face. "Are you serious about a tunnel clear across Canada?"

"Yes."

"Will it work? When I hear you talk with friends, they laugh and challenge your sanity. What happens when you ask people like that for money and help?"

"Do you remember when we started the construction company? Few people gave us much chance of success. We built the business, we succeeded, and we secured our retirement; why can't we use our skills and contacts to help a bunch of people find their way?"

"Who's we, big boy?"

"I thought you promised to support me, in every little whim that I dreamed up, as long as we both shall live. Will you keep your vows?"

"Only as long as we both shall live; how long will this project consume our lives?"

"About twelve years. Maybe we'll go 'til we drop."

"I can picture you, steadied by your walker, on a rock outcropping in the Yukon. You explain life to some thug from the rough part of Vancouver. He has tattoos all over and seven piercings. You explain to him how you can make him into a young Brett. This has to work out well, don't you think?"

"He might push me off the cliff. I'll die trying to help someone or…he might buy into my approach and become a producer in society, a leader amongst his peers. Either way, I'll have tried."

"I don't want to face life without you."

"It might not be so bad; there're a half million guys waiting for you to emerge from the mist and anoint him as your chosen one. He'll appreciate his libido stored in the deep freeze to be defrosted whenever you put tenderloin on the menu. He'll remember, maybe even care, what dress you wore to the company Christmas party three years ago. He'll come equipped with an early warning system that'll allow him to know how to respond to whatever text, tone, and tenor that bubbles to the surface from the brew that represents your real and imagined life experiences."

She burst into laughter. "Is it that bad?"

"No, but I don't need a higher dose."

"Is supper cooked yet?"

"You're not allowed to change the subject."

"I'm not, I'm multi-tasking."

Brett arranged a garnish of sliced apples, bananas, and grapes, then dished out fish and rice-stuffed peppers, refreshed the wine glasses, and offered his glass. "I love you."

"I love you, too. The salmon is dry."

"On the seventh day, God assembled a woman. She turned out to be complicated. By the time she laughed, the salmon was dry."

Elaine cleaned up the dishes. "It's your turn."

"My list is identical to yours except we differ on the path we'll follow to achieve our continued happiness. You expect me to be more intuitive about situations. When I fail to meet your expectations, you react and widen the chasm. I step back and widen the chasm. We narrow our differences. Each of us can continue to strive to do better, but I'm certain that more opportunities for disconnects will be part of the problem, not the solution."

She held out her hand. "Your stupid tunnel has led to our best discussion in a long time. Come with me; the chill has come off the wine."

Chapter 5

Jeremy, Jacquie, and Simone arrived on Sunday evening. Brett took the bassinette from Jeremy and welcomed little Simone. "Where's King?"

Jacquie took off her jacket. "He threw up this afternoon so we didn't want him to cause a mess in your home or the car."

Erika arrived; Brett took her jacket.

As they gathered around the kitchen counter, the doorbell rang. Sherry stepped in. "Sorry we're late."

With everyone seated around the table, Elaine said, "We have an announcement. Are you ready for a new episode in the Larson world?"

Jeremy looked at her. "Mom, is this charades? Is it good or bad?"

Elaine shrugged. "Ask your father."

Jeremy turned to Brett.

"Elaine and I attended Marjie's funeral some weeks back," Brett began. "I thought about the waste that's caused by young folks losing their way. I want to develop an alternative to social welfare that'll save more troubled youngsters."

Erika asked, "What's this alternative?"

"I want to attract thousands of struggling young people to dig a large tunnel from the St. Lawrence River to the Pacific Ocean and create enough tailings from the tunnel to build a surface transportation-utility corridor across northern Canada that will contain a highway, freight railroad, high speed train, pipelines, townhouses, bicycle paths, and pedestrian walkways."

"Why the tunnel?" Sam asked.

"Two reasons," Brett said. "One, I want to use the tailings to build the raised infrastructure on the surface without damage to the terrain beyond the right of way, and two, I have a secret reason for the tunnel."

Jeremy looked up from his plate. "You intend to dig a tunnel across Canada without full justification. Who's gullible enough to listen?"

"I envision a village, every kilometer along the route, of about 150 individuals who have chosen to develop on this project as an alternative to conventional schools, work experience, and relationship building. These individuals will have decided something has to change to make them happy."

Erika said, "Dad, you describe anarchists. You can't put them all in one place and expect it to work more than three days."

Brett turned to her. "Do you think they are anarchists or are they similar to each of us but less inclined to accept rules that they see as invalid?"

"Mom, this is mad," Erika said, turning to her mother. "Why have you agreed?"

Elaine smiled. "I've talked it through. He wants to try. Haven't we all benefitted from his vision and tenacity? Don't we support each other's dreams?"

Erika said, "You wanted more free time. This sounds like a big job for the old one. Are you sure about this?"

"I'm not sure it will work, but I'm sure we'll try to make it work and I'm hopeful that our kids will support it," Elaine said.

Jacquie smiled and looked at Sherry. "This conversation wouldn't happen between my parents and me. The chemistry is one of Jeremy's attractions. But I see where my life might take some wild turns. I haven't been trained to soar to uncharted heights."

"Or scary depths," Erika added.

"Sam appreciates the latitude he was granted," Sherry said. "My parents support us but they don't exhibit the pioneer instincts visible here tonight."

Jeremy sat up. "Will we let Dad go off on a wild adventure and not talk a little sense into him?"

Elaine refilled Jeremy's glass. "Did we care for you as a baby, did we buy you skates and put you into a hockey league, did we help you learn to read and write and communicate, did we leave you room to choose your own path, did we make room for you to find your mate?" she asked. "Did we do all this because you are more special than your father? I think we did it because it was the right thing to do. Now, your father wants to pursue his mission. Is it too much to ask that we'll support him?"

Erika rose, walked around to her mother, and hugged her. "I love you, Mom."

Elaine anticipated a focused discussion so she put food out after the discussion moderated. Through the meal, the family talked of the opportunities and challenges apparent in Brett's proposal.

After dessert and coffee, Brett said, "I'll try to develop a project that'll be meaningful to each of you while I support family activities. Thanks for your support."

Jeremy shook his dad's hand. "You're lucky you found Mom."

Brett gave him a thumb up. "I know; I hope I'll live up to her faith in me."

Chapter 6

The Larsons gathered at the family home. The guys watched the football game between the Calgary Stampeders and the Montréal Alouettes. The gals made Christmas cards.

The Alouettes scored three touchdowns and a field goal before the Stamps realized the game had started.

Bored and disappointed in the game, Sam asked Brett, "How can 4,400 sponsors be attracted to commit ten million dollars per year for ten years? Didn't you say that the tunnel might cost $100,000 dollars per linear meter?"

Brett lowered the volume on the TV. "And will they see value in the investment?"

Jeremy watched the kick return and surfaced. "There are ways to capture attention, fewer ways to maintain attention, and even fewer ways to sustain it over ten years. It's like a marriage: attraction, passion, trust, respect, and commitment."

Sam feigned shock. "Well, meet my brother, the philosopher."

Brett pushed down on his feet, moving the recliner back to its original position and sitting up. "I assume forced labour built the pyramids of Egypt and the Great Wall of China. I can't support force."

"The migrations that settled the prairies of the US and Canada might work for your tunnel," Sam said.

Brett looked at him. "I like that. We could start with merchandising to capture the imagination, enough daring to challenge the spirit, enough structure to allow development with patches of anarchy, enough front-end commitment to encourage most to persevere to the finish, all leavened with goodwill and spiritual content to ease the soul."

Jeremy said, "Pass the soul food."

Sam glanced over. "What're you talking about?"

Jeremy smiled. "Dad's talk of easing the soul made me think a bottle of beer might help until the Stamps wake up."

Brett stood and paused by his chair. "Now that you guys have brought up the tunnel, I want some help in choosing a name. One restless night, I decided the project should be called Soul Star. What do you think?"

Sam looked at his dad. "I think it's perfect, Father Larson. You should turn your collar halfway around."

Jeremy saluted with his beer bottle. "Sam can tease if he wants, but I think Soul Star's a beautiful name. You done good, Dad."

Sam watched the Stampeders miss a field goal. "Where do a million individuals live for ten years? What do they eat? Who teaches their kids? Who watches out for their safety? What animals migrate through the right-of-way? How is the environment affected? How does one address the issues? How does one manage a project this big? How does one let creativity and imagination thrive?"

Brett turned away from the game. "The answer is chunking, extreme chunking."

Sam glanced at Brett. "I thought a chunk was a poor golf chip."

Brett laughed. "I see chunking as a way to break big challenges into manageable pieces."

Jeremy adopted a theatrical pose. "But once chunked, how do you put Humpty Tunnel together again?"

Brett punched his son's shoulder. "The last resort will be all the king's horses and all the king's men."

Elaine brought down a platter of nachos. "How's the game?"

Sam groaned as he reached for a chip. "The Stamps are getting their butts kicked so we're building a tunnel. We've chosen a name—Soul Star."

Elaine turned to the stairs. "Brett's folly has evolved into a family conspiracy. My dream retirement is morphing into a soulful flight to the North Star."

Brett brought out a batch of sketches showing cross-sections of the tunnel, cross-sections of the roads, pipelines, rail lines, underpasses, bridges, and living quarters. He showed the sketches to his sons. They added ideas, challenges, angles, and risks.

Brett looked up from the sketches. "Do you two remember our trip to the Yukon? We talked about the hardships, the cold and loneliness. You guys enthused about the excitement of the dance hall girls and adventures. Erika dreamed of rich miners competing for her attention. The range of perceptions covered death, drudgery, cold, greed, treachery, excitement, promised riches, and fresh country."

Jeremy said, "I remember the river valleys where gold dredges scarred the channels with mounds of gravel."

Brett handed a cross-section sketch to Jeremy. "The tailings from the tunnel will yield an average surface berm 213 meters wide by 30 meters high, clear across the country."

Sam looked over Jeremy's shoulder. "How do you justify such a scar on the landscape?"

Brett bundled up the sketches. "I pondered that for days. I generated perspectives and justified the surface effects. Nomadic civilizations don't flourish. Societies built on permanent residences tend to mar the natural landscape. The more dense the population, the more intrusive are the structures on the surface."

Jeremy drained his beer. "Seismic lines mar the forested areas for generations. Forestry, power lines, dams, wind farms, roads, and bridges have impacts on the environment. Individuals throughout the world have accepted some level of infrastructure."

Brett put the sketches in his filing cabinet. "The route of the tunnel crosses sparsely populated areas. Few individuals have ventured into the areas near the right of way. Many more will take the route once the road and rail lines are built."

Sam glanced at his dad. "The natural resources will be exploited, though. Clear cutting of trees will generate criticism."

Brett returned to his recliner and said, “These considerations come down to a question of development or no development. We’ve chosen development.”

Sam went back to his chair to watch the end of the game. “I wonder how the world will react.”

The Stampeders scored two touchdowns in the second half. The guys climbed the stairs and looked at the girls’ Christmas cards. A gold star shone in the top right corner of every card.

Maybe Elaine’s protests camouflage some tiny support for my dream.

Chapter 7

Keith Zisemo answered his phone. “Hello.”

“Howdy neighbour, how you doing?”

“Hi, Brett, it’s been awhile.”

“Too long, I’m lousy at keeping in touch. What’s new in Mexico?”

“Cheryl and I just returned from a hike along the Cuchumatanes Mountains. We’ll stay in Taxco for two months and then snorkel in the Grand Caymans.”

“It’s a tough life.”

“Yeah, I’m enjoying retirement.”

“That’s the wrong answer. I have an idea.”

“I can’t hear you. The cell reception is bad.”

“You can hear me and you’ll be hooked.”

“Okay, what’s on your mind?”

“Well, I want to build a utility and transportation corridor across Canada from the Pacific to the Atlantic and I want all the vested interests to accept the results.”

“So give God a call.”

“I’ve got him on the line.”

“Yeah, right.”

“I have an idea, will you listen?”

“Sure, but no promises.”

“My concept involves a comprehensive set of utility-transportation corridors on a hundred kilometer grid across the entire country.”

“Your grid should hit every Indian Reservation in the country.”

“I know; that’s why I called you.”

“What can I do?”

"I want all vested interests on side. I have an approach but I need some expertise."

"Can this magic be described in two sentences?"

"Maybe half a dozen."

"My cell will die after a while."

"I think of an open collaboration on the internet where a map of Canada is set up so that anyone can review the data up to the moment. We'll encourage anyone to record the coordinates of every conceivable spot that should be protected from the corridors and adjacent activity. From that data, the most appropriate corridors will emerge. But we'll still need to address all of the concerns of natives, environmentalists, landowners, and political factions. New issues will be raised as the probable corridors become evident and attention is focused on specific sites."

"It'll have to be easy enough to use so that a casual internet searcher won't give up. Do you have a solution?"

"Yes, I want to design a website that'll allow open collaboration—along the lines of Wikipedia. It'll have to impress anyone who opens it so that we start a stampede to help solve the corridor issues. We need a launch position in which any participant should see the potential."

"Will this website flutter down from the stratosphere?"

"No, you'll build it."

"Good night, Irene. Good night, Irene. I'll see you in my dreams."

"Come on, Keith, you have skills. You're a few months into retirement. You have a chance to do some good. Pay it forward."

"I told Cheryl I'm so thankful that I don't have to tolerate all the crap involved in business. Now, you ask me to dive in again. Do you think I'm insane?"

"The symptoms are there."

"Let me think on it for a bit. I'll call you next week."

"Thanks, Keith. I appreciate it." A thumb up punctuated his gratitude.

Chapter 8

Early morning, the phone rang. "Brett here."

"Good morning, Brett, it's Keith."

"Have you decided to pull your sombrero over your face and forget I ever existed?"

"No; I like the corridor idea. I want to play a part. However, I don't want to give up all the plans that Cheryl and I've made. I'm fed up with Canada; I want to spend most of my time in Mexico."

"Thanks, Keith."

"I know a guy in Calgary who's capable of the day-to-day operations. The guy would need a salary but the Zisemo Foundation will provide an annual grant large enough to support a core office, salary, and computer support."

"Do you need the board's approval for the Foundation support?"

"Yes, but I have made enquiries and I expect the board will approve the project."

"What happens next?"

"I agree to be a mentor to the project. We need to ensure I can stay in the loop from Mexico or wherever our travels take us."

"What can I do to move it along?"

"I suggest you sponsor a weekly coffee party that'll include you and six guests. The guests will rotate out after three sessions. Out of these sessions, you should build a base of ideas. If you video those sessions, you can make the videos available to all current and past guests so each participant can see what evolves and submit further written feedback."

"Yeah," Brett said, "I can make that happen. Anything else?"

"You could find a sketch artist with exposure to highways, railways, bridges, and bullet trains. Invite him to watch the videos and sketch various designs. These sketches will be available to every coffee party participant."

"Okay, what about all the interest groups?"

"I think we should engage researchers to seek out detailed information on the demands of interest groups. Have you made a list of the factions?"

"Yes, First Nations land claims, environmental concerns, political platforms, land owners, and existing laws."

"Okay, we need to figure out how to gather that information."

"What if we issue a challenge to all departments of all universities, colleges, technical schools, and high schools in the world to provide suggestions?"

"That should work. There are opportunities for consideration by engineers, environmentalists, sociologists, psychologists, philosophers, anthropologists, actuaries, and a bunch of others. While the focus of the challenge is the Canadian example, the spin-off of the concept is applicable in every country. The British former colonies have many similarities including British influence, native populations, adherence to the rule of law, and democracy. The rest of the developed world has parallel challenges with variations. There are advantages for the less developed countries where built infrastructure is less dominant."

"We could arrange public recognition for effective design solutions," Brett offered.

"Projects never end unless there are target dates. What timeframes do you see?"

"The public launch of the website might be on Christmas day as a Christmas present to every Canadian. I've thought of a name for the project. The rights-of-way could be called Ribbons and the protected sites could be called Jewels. Do you like the name, Ribbons & Jewels?"

"Yeah, I like it."

"Once Ribbons & Jewels is announced to the public, it will be in the public domain and have a life of its own. I'm excited now; don't tell me to get lost!"

"Keith, you've made my day. Thanks a bunch."

Brett wondered, *This appears too easy; is Canada ready for rational approaches to issues that have festered for years?*

Chapter 9

Myrtle Murdoch, publisher of the Prairie Sentinel, sat in a coffee shop in Winnipeg. Rosie Savard joined her.

"What credentials do you bring to your position as manager of the Healthy Habitats project?"

"I grew up with my native Indian mother on a trap line in northern Manitoba. At six, I went to live with the Yudzik family in Winnipeg. They helped me get an education. I have an anthropology degree and I'm committed to the environment. I decided I'd make environmental sense out of development initiatives in northern Canada. As I cast about for an opportunity, I ran across the initiatives of the Zisemo Foundation. It seemed like a good fit, so I hired on as the researcher for the First Nations aspects of Ribbons & Jewels. Keith Zisemo noted my enthusiasm. We perceived the project as neither pro nor anti-business and needed to raise more publicity. Keith asked me to help find a sponsor to further the effort. The Foundation agreed the Healthy Habitats Society could best carry Ribbons & Jewels to the public. It fell to me to convince Healthy Habitats to sponsor the project. My experience, passion, and reputation led to my appointment as the manager of Healthy Habitats' Ribbons & Jewels project. This is a wonderful opportunity. I'm determined to succeed."

"I want to do a feature on your story in my paper," Myrtle said. "Is that okay?"

"Yes."

"May I take your picture for the article?"

"Sure, but the picture you need is the photo Jack Yudzik took of my mom when she realized I'd have a chance in the white man's world."

"How do I get that photo?"

"You need to ask two people: Jack Yudzik and Hymie Friedenberg. Both of them have rights to the photo."

Myrtle wrote down the names she mentioned. "We could visit a long time, but I believe I have the substance. If I need more clarification, I'll be in touch. Thanks for your help."

"You're welcome."

Chapter 10

Myrtle sent a copy of the Prairie Sentinel article to Jack and Hymie.

Jack read the article. It carried him back twenty-one years.

He couldn't sleep. The opportunity accorded with his convictions. He encouraged individuals to do the right thing. Cecile could have perceptions on this opportunity that could wreck his family, maybe his life. The easy course would be to forget about Rosie.

Are good and bad things random, part of a plan, or pre-ordained?

He recalled stories where individuals prayed for God's intervention, failed to act on opportunities presented, questioned God, and heard God say, "Three times I came to you and three times you rejected me."

In the damp chill of his autumn camp twenty-one years earlier, Jack had decided to act. He would go to Cecile and ask for her support. He'd also explain to their daughter, Theresa, who would soon be seven years old. Jack packed his gear and headed for the designated lake where the chartered Cessna would take him to Flin Flon, where he would pack his Land Rover and head to Winnipeg.

A wealthy New York hotelier commissioned Jack to photograph a unique image of a caribou. No more instructions than that.

On his first trip into caribou country, he found caribou and studied their habits for six days but found no memorable moment. He told Cecile of his fruitless trip and encounter with Young Eagle and Rosie. Cecile covered the spectrum from amusement, to concern, to anger before she trounced off to bed.

Not the envisioned welcome home.

Two days elapsed with scant thaw in Cecile's demeanour. She explored her feelings toward Jack, the threat of a woman in Jack's targeted territory, and the disruption that a Métis girl would cause in their midst. But she also thought of Jack's kindness, his love of nature and people, his drive to do the right thing, and his love for her. She arranged a sitter for Theresa and prepared Jack's favourite meal. When Jack came home, Cecile greeted him.

"Will you be okay if I try to understand?"

Tears welled in Jack's eyes as he hugged her.

"Come, I've prepared dinner; tell me about Rosie and how we make this work."

Jack explained how their family might provide a home and hope for one little girl. Cecile warmed to the possibilities. She trusted Jack. On selfish and superficial levels, she could bite. Jack picked up Theresa at the babysitter's by eight-thirty. As they walked home, Jack asked Theresa, "Would you appreciate a good friend that could become a sister?"

Theresa looked up at her dad. "I'd like a sister that's blonde, knows about princesses and famous places, and imagines travel to faraway places."

Jack laughed. "What if the little girl didn't know any of that, but she knew lots about surviving in the north, hunting, fishing, and watching the night sky?"

Theresa hesitated. "Maybe, but it seems strange."

Jack and Cecile couldn't afford to hire a plane to search for Rosie. Jack called his New York client and described the situation. Jack's goodness and the opportunity shone through. The New Yorker offered to pay for a charter plane large enough to carry Jack, Cecile, and Theresa to the trap line to search for Young Eagle and Rosie. If Young Eagle and Rosie agreed, they would fly back to Flin Flon and drive to Winnipeg where Young Eagle could stay for a few days and Rosie would start her new chapter.

The bush pilot said, “You’re going to pick up a native girl who’s never been off a trap line and take her to live with you in Winnipeg. Are you crazy?”

Cecile raised her voice over the noise of the plane. “That was my first reaction, but we’ve decided each individual should try to make the world a better place.”

Jack had discussed the options with the girl’s mother, saying she should move to a small town where the girl could go to school, but the mother concluded that she couldn’t be happy off the trap line and couldn’t see a way to make a living. Besides, she felt her daughter would fare better if she learned to live in the white world.

“Jack’s philosophy is in tune with this project,” Cecile continued. “Theresa and I are committed to make it work.”

The pilot glanced back at Cecile. “I’ve been around natives all my adult years. Their culture is so different from the middle class in Winnipeg. I can’t see this working out.”

Cecile leaned forward in her seat. “Do you check the fuel and instruments before you take off in this plane?”

“Of course.”

“Do you know about a snag, frozen in the ice and covered by a skiff of snow? That snag is going to catch the skis when you land and topple this plane, end over end. Our lives will be different than before.”

“I know there are risks. I’ve heard the truism that there are old pilots and there are brave pilots, but there are no old, brave pilots. We’re trained to be cautious and alert. I’m confident in my abilities.”

“You have a little advantage over us because of pilot school. We go into this as caring individuals who have parented one child for seven years and observed life in Winnipeg for thirty odd years, but we have not gone to school to learn how to integrate a half-breed six year-old into our Winnipeg culture. We plan to be cautious and alert but we will fly.”

As they flew into the trap line area, all watched for signs of Young Eagle and Rosie. On the third pass over the area, they spotted a woman, a child, and a sleigh pulled by a dog. The pilot made two low passes over the woman and then landed on the nearest frozen lake. The Twin Otter came to rest near the shore and all scrambled out. The pilot gathered twigs and branches and started a fire. Jack readied his camera and noted the light conditions. The trappers emerged from the trees. They moved with purpose but no hurry to this unknown rendezvous. As Jack came into Young Eagle's focus, her jaw tensed but she made no move to welcome him.

Cecile stepped forward. "You must be Young Eagle and Rose Mary. Jack has told us of your dream, so our family—Jack, Theresa, and I—have come to offer Rosie a home so she may get the opportunities you seek for her."

Jack focused his camera on Young Eagle's face. As the enormity of the offer entered her consciousness, Young Eagle's face lit up in a way that's seldom captured on film.

Young Eagle demonstrated genuine appreciation but she refused to go with the group back to Winnipeg. She asked Jack to write their address on a piece of paper and to describe how to get to their home. Then she walked away from the fire with Rosie and explained what was about to happen. Rosie faced separation from every familiar thing: her mother, her home, her territory, her comfort zone. Six years old, stoic, familiar with risk, heart beating rapidly, Rosie stifled her sobs and stood by the plane. Cecile began to question the wisdom of this endeavour. Theresa grappled with the clothing, smells, and sounds of these apparent family members. Jack wondered whether the right thing is the right thing. The pilot busied himself with the plane.

Chapter 11

Twenty-seven years of age, Rosie stood in the boardroom of the Healthy Habitats Society and presented the outline of a feature series on Canada's environmental fabric that she believed would inspire the readership and provide impetus for effective environmental controls. For every "but," Rosie responded. The board asked her to stay in town for two more days. During that time, they'd do some due diligence and decide if they could commit the Society's resources to this task.

They summoned Rosie to the boardroom.

The evasive faces telegraphed failure.

She turned to leave. "I expected more."

The chairman stood. "Ms. Savard, we want to do your project but we haven't found a way to fund it."

Rosie turned. "Give me your plan and your budget and I'll find the funds." She left.

The chairman gestured with both hands. "Comments?"

One director shifted in his chair. "I like the Ribbons & Jewels idea. I think it's a good project for Healthy Habitats, but I don't see how we can work with that dynamo."

Another director looked up. "Dynamos are in short supply."

The chairman settled back in his chair. "There seems to be enough merit in this situation for us to schedule a special meeting to discuss it further. Can we meet two weeks from today?"

They scheduled the meeting.

Chapter 12

"This meeting is called to order. We consider the potential sponsorship of Ribbons & Jewels as offered to us by Rose Mary Savard. Aaron volunteered to organize information for this meeting. Aaron, go ahead."

"Several capable individuals have developed this project. Keith Zisemo is an accomplished executive who has retired to Mexico but is a mentor for Ribbons & Jewels. Brett Larson owns and manages a prominent development and construction company in southern Alberta. They organized focus groups in which several experienced individuals produced a series of videos that illustrate the magnitude of the issues. They hired a sketch artist who prepared hundreds of sketches inspired by the ideas emerging from the coffee parties. The group decided a reliable database is required to make sense out of the many angles. This database is already developed with masses of data from available sources. The database needs more attention to design the website capabilities before Ribbons & Jewels is announced to the public. The Zisemo Foundation hired Rosie to research the First Nations aspects of Ribbons & Jewels. She's well regarded by all of the individuals that I contacted in the last two weeks. We already know Rosie's capabilities. In my opinion, the Ribbons & Jewels initiative is solid."

"Do you have the videos and sketches?"

"Yes; they're set up and ready to run."

The board watched the videos and sketches and discussed the issues.

The chairman straightened his papers. "I believe the last couple of hours have demonstrated this board is interested in sponsoring Ribbons & Jewels. Am I correct?"

The directors murmured assent.

"I detect general approval. Aaron will inform Rose Mary Savard that the board has authorized her to work with Healthy Habitats' management to develop a plan and budget with mutual expectations that Healthy Habitats and Rose Mary Savard will find adequate funds before significant expenses are incurred."

The chairman called the question. "All in favour?"

"Carried, unanimously."

Chapter 13

Three thousand delegates assembled. Rose Mary Savard waited in the wings. The emcee strode to center stage. The crowd cheered, then stilled.

"Ladies and gentlemen, the moment has arrived: Healthy Habitats presents Rose Mary Savard."

Rosie walked to the podium, smiled, and waited.

When the audience silenced, Rosie began.

"Passionate friends, welcome!

"Today, together, we launch a bold experiment.

"Each one of us comes here with an agenda.

"That agenda has evolved from our backgrounds, cultures, commitments and perceptions about big business, politicians, and tree huggers.

"Our experience has taught us to distrust other factions in our society.

"We're here today to lead a fresh, positive, cooperative process.

"We bring commitments to specific causes but we recognize that others have alternative views, and we will reach compromises.

"We will protect elements of each environmental issue and we will allow for other considerations that are important but less critical.

"We will build a consensus and we'll promise to abide by the spirit of that consensus.

"We must not fail! We will not fail!

"We are familiar with prominent corridors in our great land: the Yellowhead Highway, the Queen Elizabeth Expressway, the CN and CP rail lines, the Confederation Bridge, the St. Lawrence Seaway, the TransCanada Highway, to name a few.

"We know that service corridors are essential in our final plan.

"We expect all submissions will concede that service corridors will exist.

"We choose to call the corridors ribbons, a symbol for the concept of corridors for utilities, vehicles, trains, boats, tourists, and other situations where unfettered human and commercial movement is warranted.

"Development near appropriate service corridors is an economic reality.

"Our challenge is to design a system in which such development coexists with the whole environment, including those issues for which you are passionate.

"Canada will have human habitats.

"We will design models that minimize the negative effects on the environment and protect habitats and unique sites.

"We must not fail! We will not fail!

"Each community has sites that are precious to the local population and, often, to the broader population.

"We think of Niagara Falls, the national parks, the provincial parks, the municipal parks, the Plains of Abraham, the site of the Duck Lake Rebellion, the Medicine Tree, cemeteries and burial grounds, rare animal and plant habitats, the paths of migrating animals and birds, the spawning runs of fishes, and the feeding traits of wild animals, fishes, and birds.

"Each of you endeavours to keep these sites and concerns in focus as well as issues that are of particular importance to you.

"We want you to use your passion but we want you to recognize that the universe involves balancing forces, even when humans are absent.

"You will achieve more for your cause with a degree of collegiality than you will with, 'It's my way, or no way.'

"We choose to call all these sites and special issues jewels. You can think of jewels along the lines of Crown Jewels, Marilyn Monroe's diamonds, costume jewels, birthstones, horseshoe nail rings, dandelion necklaces, whatever.

"The jewels have different importance to different individuals.

"The environmental and historical jewels that will be protected will be those that have broad support amongst the human population.

"Most of us will protect unique jewels.

"Your challenge is to put your jewels in a light that will allow them to survive the many compromises that we will face.

"There are infinite perspectives concerning the jewels in Canada.

"We will publicize the identification of the jewels so every discovered issue is taken into account when the plan is published.

"We recognize there are elements of many environmental issues that are not well understood. One of Healthy Habitats' commitments is to continue to encourage the discovery of new issues and promote improvements in habitats, protect unique sites, and future development in concert with current knowledge of environmental issues.

"Each of us recognizes that humans will impact our environment.

"If we adopt a 'stand still' approach until every environmental risk is discovered, researched, and publicized, we know that human initiatives will continue to erupt in unpredictable, confrontational, wasteful episodes with the vocal, best funded, most strategic interests able to carry the day.

"This is not the way to protect the environment, nor is it the way to manage our human endeavours.

"Some of you are guilty of enjoying the game.

"You may start with a legitimate environmental issue but end up addicted to conflict and one-upmanship. Individuals who thrive in this milieu are recruited into various environmental causes. Such gamesmanship must be managed so we get the 'best solutions' with minimal friction.

"With your diligence, permeated with goodwill, many thousands of Canadian jewels will be protected.

"We must not fail! We will not fail!

"Every project benefits from milestones.

"We have prescribed such milestones.

"Initial submissions will be submitted by December 31 this year.

"There are several intermediate milestones to propel the project, but suffice to say a final plan will be published in the December issue of Healthy Habitat magazine a year and a half from now. It will be a Christmas present to every Canadian.

"It will feature a map of Canada, show the identified Ribbons & Jewels, discuss the issues, and promise to publicize jewels with attention to advocacy of 'doing the right thing' for the environment. The printed maps will be supplemented with a digital set of layers that will show the suggested ribbons and the identified jewels. This will permit individuals to identify jewels that will be protected, vulnerable, compromised, and lost if the ribbons remain as chosen.

Where habitats are compromised, the maps will suggest where similar habitats could be developed nearby. This effort might apply to wetlands and forests.

"Canada is a wonderful country.

"We can provide effective environmental protection in concert with human endeavours.

"Canadians, and humans the world over, count on us.

"We must not fail! We will not fail!

"Passionate friends, do it well!

"Thank you."

The activists operated in confrontational systems where they perceived business did the bare minimum and publicity often involved civil disobedience and obstructionism.

How would this new dynamic unfold?

Chapter 14

Gaston Tribolski went for a beer with a teammate after the hockey game.

Josh poured his beer into a glass. “You seem reserved. What’s up?”

“My job’s frustrating me. I’ve got to get out of there.”

“Is it the job, or is it you?”

“Who knows, my supervisor’s ill-suited to his role. He resists innovation, emphasizes cost control over results, and dwells on due process. The place breeds frustration.”

“It sounds like you want a project where you can be in charge.”

“But I don’t have management experience.”

“You won’t learn to manage by following…especially your supervisor.”

“Where’ll I find a job that suits me better?”

“I read an article about the Ribbons & Jewels initiative in the north. I’ll find the article and bring it to work tomorrow. We can meet for lunch and talk about it.”

At lunch the next day, Josh handed Gaston the magazine. “The article describes the extraction of information from every published article in every Canadian newspaper, relevant autobiographies and biographies, published speeches, Hansard transcripts, environmental studies, and court cases…all done by volunteers. The Healthy Habitats Society adopted the cause as a cornerstone of its commitment to healthy habitats.”

“I remember something about it. A woman gave a speech about a system of corridors throughout Canada.”

“Yes, her speech triggered a deluge of submissions. Healthy Habitats recognizes that the volume and variety of Ribbons &

Jewels responses demands more from its data management system."

"Maybe my provincial health ministry experience would be useful."

"The woman is named in the article. Give her a call."

Rosie returned Gaston's call and discussed the issues with him. She liked Gaston's potential. She arranged for the lead IT guy at Healthy Habitats to join her in a meeting with Gaston. The meeting went well. When Rosie determined that Gaston would accept a position with Healthy Habitats, she asked the chairman of the board what step to take next. The chairman arranged for the entire board to meet with Gaston so that each of them could judge his suitability.

Chapter 15

Rosie and Gaston entered the boardroom and accepted coffee. The chairman informed the group that Aaron Woodman, the vice president of the environment, would lead the discussion. After introductions, Aaron directed questions to Gaston.

"How do you see any interested party getting access to the data we've already gathered and the data we will gather?"

Gaston described his ideas in detail.

Aaron asked Gaston to explain how he saw the submissions being integrated into a coherent design.

"It appears to me that some system must be developed where the front end information is neutral and subjected to quality control but any participant can point out errors or improvements. These suggestions must be available to all who wish to review the validity of the front-end information. This will require qualified manpower."

"How do you see the corridors emerging from this mass of data?"

Gaston explained his ideas and answered the questions that arose.

"What do we do with the impossible and the passionate responses?"

"This is where Healthy Habitats will lead. We'll maintain neutrality. We'll request civility. We'll encourage compromise. We'll shift the corridor to reflect consensus. Through much iteration, a democratic solution will emerge. Healthy Habitats must not stop there. We must reach out to the advocates of jewels that are compromised by the corridor. Collegial, compassionate, genuine consideration of the advocates' submissions must shine through. Maybe overpasses or tunnels or some other solution will emerge. The result must be transparent, thorough, and fair."

"I thought you came here as a technical wizard; what's with all this empathy and philosophy?"

"Rosie asked me what would happen if my employer let me out of a locked room in the basement. I told her. She liked it. Here I am."

"I do too. Are there further questions from the board?"

The vice president of humanity asked, "Should we discuss First Nations issues and how to manage those issues?"

Aaron turned to the director. "I considered that line of enquiry and concluded that none of us have enough information to reach a decision. Therefore, I've decided to focus on Ribbons & Jewels. We must develop a strategy to deal with the First Nations issues, but that's a task for another day. I hope the board will accept my approach."

No other questions or comments arose.

The chairman walked around to Gaston. "Mr. Tribolski, we thank you for meeting with us today. I feel certain that the board would ratify your appointment today. However, so much depends on this appointment that I want to ensure that each board member considers your appointment over the next three days. Then we'll meet, debate, and decide. Once we've decided, we'll inform Ms. Savard and ask her to convey our decision to you. Whatever the decision, I want to complement you on your approach to life and this project. Thank you."

Gaston and Rosie thanked the board and left the room.

Out in the hallway, Rosie said, "That was beautiful."

Gaston blushed. "Thank you."

Each wondered what to do next.

They said goodbye and parted.

Chapter 16

Ribbons & Jewels published the viable corridors for major infrastructure from east to west and north to south.

The Ribbon most suited to Soul Star stretched from the St. Lawrence River mouth near Bersimis to the southwest corner of the Yukon. A short stretch of Alaska lay ahead, then the Pacific Ocean.

How do we get access to the Pacific with Alaska in the way?

Chapter 17

Brett decided to mine the knowledge and imaginations of a bunch of bright individuals. He wrote a letter to his contacts that followed a parallel pattern, customized for each addressee. One letter read as follows:

Howdy Neighbour:

I trust you have nothing better to do in the next couple of days than help me formulate an alternative to the welfare system in Canada. My focus is a pioneer camp housing 150 misfits who want to try to improve themselves. These people might be as young as thirteen or as old as ninety; the median age might be nineteen. Some will have spouses, some will have children, some will have addictions, some will have chips on their shoulders, and some will lie (even to themselves). With this crew, how could we assure that most of the individuals will emerge in ten years with an education, a marketable skill, a financial net worth of $100,000, and a respect for their own metamorphosis?

Since your passion is carpentry, I hope you'll provide insight into those initiatives that will nurture a young individual to be a skilled woodworker with sufficient education, discipline, gumption, and tenacity to be the head of a self-sufficient household. I recognize the success of the endeavour depends on a multitude of nuances, so let your thoughts wander.

I'll send similar letters to others with the expectation that suggestions and truths will emerge to help me articulate a village with a dynamic to warm the hearts of most responsible individuals.

Your prompt, thoughtful response will help salvage many lives.

Thanks.

Brett Larson

Chapter 18

Passion often plants a patina on a person. Oscar de Lona got his passion fix at sixteen—fourteen of those years in Canada, when one of his social studies teachers determined learning ought to be intense. She found an opportunity for her class to study a band of Indians in north-eastern British Columbia. The study focused on the history of the band, the lifestyle, the relationships with government, the vagaries of the Indian Affairs administration, treaty terms and rights, and the swap of one reserve for another. During the summer, the students travelled three weeks with the Indian Band. The Kelowna, middle-class kids, experienced different living standards, language, customs, smells, tastes, comforts, and relationships.

Oscar observed the imbalance between the aspirations and resources of the Indians pitted against the forces of commercialization, exploitation, and bureaucracy. He decided to pursue a career in law with emphasis on Indian concerns.

Oscar went to UBC, graduated with distinction, articled with a large law firm, and then started his own law firm in Fort St. John, BC.

His combination of brilliance, tenacity, goodwill, and sense of fair play allowed him to move in all circles with respect and influence. Through Oscar's life as a student in university and at law, he noticed the waste invested in crafting documents. He watched lawyers charge for drafting one-of-a-kind agreements from precedents. Then he saw disputes arise as to the meaning of individual words, of clauses, of whole agreements. He saw lawyers, expert witnesses, and judges struggle with the interpretations. He solved the bulk of the waste with "one page" agreements. He became known for his insistence on these one-pagers. He distilled the body of laws into current grammar and vocabulary and then included those rules into his one-page agreements by reference.

The non-legal fraternity came to insist on one-pagers in most commercial transactions.

As Oscar marked his sixtieth birthday, he received an invitation from the chief of the Fort St. John Indian band.

When Oscar and Louise arrived in the village, they noticed many people appeared attentive and waved as they passed.

The chief greeted them at his home. "Oscar, it's my honour to recognize you as an honorary band member. We've organized a ceremony for you."

Oscar swallowed. "Why me?"

"Because you're a true friend and advocate. Come, the band members gather at the ceremonial grounds in a few minutes."

As the crowd settled, the chief raised his hand. "This is a special day. We appreciate Oscar's work on our behalf. Our council decided to recognize Oscar de Lona."

As the applause receded, the chief presented a beaded, fringed jacket. "Oscar de Lona, on behalf of the Blood Tribe, we declare you Oscar One Page, an honorary member of our band. Please wear this ceremonial jacket as a symbol of our respect for you."

Beaming, Oscar donned the beaded, fringed, buckskin jacket and waved to the crowd. He shook the chief's hand. "Thank you."

The celebration carried on into the late evening.

While comfortable with his career, Oscar curried no favour with the establishment. Some of his commentary reflected his distaste for the approaches of many of his fellow lawyers. None of his peers initiated the Queen's Counsel honour for him.

Louise took it all in stride. "Congratulations, Oscar. You deserve this recognition."

"Thanks, I was surprised."

"I wasn't; you're a diamond, even if imperfectly cut."

Chapter 19

Erika asked Brett to help her set up her booth at the art show in Bragg Creek.

On the drive out, Erika turned to her dad. "Sometimes the path seems long. Do you notice that?"

"Yes, I notice it most when the road's unfamiliar. A drive going somewhere seems longer that the return trip."

"Do you remember when we drove the Alaska Highway to the Yukon? The white posts with the mileage in black numbers."

"Funny you mention that; I'm working on an addressing system for the line. I expect each section will name its village. I think back to the villages placed every nine miles along the railways to provide service centers for horse-drawn teams to make a round-trip to a siding in one day. Folklore has it that trains steamed west and threw a pioneer off every nine miles and the pioneer settled the area, named the village after the family, or village in the old country, or whatever whim occurred to the founder. This freedom appeals to me and fits the Soul Star philosophy."

"Do you have an idea for the addressing?"

"I've been thinking about those mileage signs along the Alaska Highway. During the Second World War, the American military built the road from Dawson Creek, BC to Alaska. They planted mileposts every mile along the ditch. The local population relied on the mileposts in their day-to-day communications. The service station and truck stop at mile 54 was known by most people as '54'. So it was with the village at mile 101, which was called Wonowon. Locals knew Fort St. John was at mile 49 and Fort Nelson was at mile 250."

"How does that integrate with villagers choosing a unique name for their village?"

"The line, from coast-to-coast, will be called Soul Star Trail. Each kilometer chunk will be street named X Soul Star Trail. Then each housing unit will have a house number. The family that lives in one home will have the address: 248, 3114 Soul Star Trail, Swimmer, Alberta. This means Swimmer is the village located at kilometer 3114 in northern Alberta and townhouse 248 is in the village of Swimmer. Canada Post will tack on a postal code."

"You've told me you want to preserve as much individuality as possible. Does one numbering system for the whole line do that?"

"The village names will be part of the address. We need an addressing system that's idiot proof. Lots of people will rely upon addressing. A coherent system will contribute to clear directions."

"I can see that. Where would the numbering start?"

"I think the south-east end of the line, near Bersimis, Quebec."

"Why not the west end?"

"Because it seems more natural to have the numbers increase as the line goes farther north. Also, the surface structure will end at the foot of the mountain range in south-western Yukon. That's not as distinct as the water's edge on the Quebec end."

Erika watched the flickers of the sunlight through the trees. "I can't think of any improvement to your addressing system. On another topic, how do you plan to document the arrangements that are required to keep your project manageable?"

"I've heard of a lawyer who advocates simplicity. I think his nickname is One Page."

"Why can't Beth pay attention to the administration? You trust her."

"I do trust Beth, but she has her business to run and she hasn't admitted that she'll pay attention to Soul Star. I can't let events go too long or they'll get out of control."

"What if this One Page character turns out to be a jerk?"

"Haven't I been able to select better than jerks, at least most of the time?"

"Yeah, but I worry about you."

"You worry, hon, but I'll do my best."

Chapter 20

As Brett drove to Fort St. John, he recalled a segment in Naked Gun where the military intended to recruit a prominent American Indian for some adventure. They approached this man's home, a traditional tepee with overstated padlocks, chains, and security paraphernalia.

Would One Page turn out to be an eccentric?

One Page's home was immaculate with a veranda, flowers in planters, and trees framing the home.

How could this be the home of the radical One Page?

A woman, about sixty, answered the door. "Hello, may I help you?"

"Yes, I'm Brett Larson. I arranged to meet Oscar today."

"Oh, Brett, I've looked forward to meeting you since Oscar told me about your call. Oscar's in the backyard; please come through."

Oscar rose from his lawn chair. "Brett, I feel like I've known you for ages. Your conversation on the telephone intrigued me. I practice reading individuals' characters and assume every individual has flaws; many are profound. I intend to discover yours before you leave."

Brett extended his hand. "Pleased to meet you, Oscar."

Oscar signalled Brett to a lawn chair. "What do you think of Fort St. John now that you've driven through it? Many folks call it foreskin John."

Brett grinned. "It appears to be drawn back, ready to be thrust into full production."

Oscar cackled and took his chair. "I like your humour."

"Life has enough ups and downs." Brett settled into his chair. "I don't take things too seriously."

Louise brought out iced tea and home-baked raisin cookies. All three enjoyed the refreshments. When Louise went inside, she said, "Brett, please stay for supper."

Brett smiled in acceptance.

Oscar sipped his tea. "Please describe your vision from start to finish without dwelling on the positives or negatives."

Brett recited the basics and acknowledged many factors would influence Soul Star as it progressed from a spark of an idea to a completed transcontinental corridor. Oscar listened and fiddled with a yellow wooden pencil. He often stuck the eraser end in his ear.

Maybe One Page isn't as normal as he first looked.

Oscar sat there awhile. His pencil antics continued as he assimilated the concept and the roadblocks that would be thrust in Soul Star's path.

Visionaries gloss over obstacles. Could he count on Brett to overcome, or circumvent, every impediment?

Louise called them to supper.

One Page bowed his head over his plate. "Father, we thank you for opportunities to influence the lives of millions. Help us pursue Soul Star with dedication, flair, skill, fairness, and faith. Help us appreciate this food and fellowship and pay it forward in meaningful ways. Amen."

Brett sensed well-being that would sustain him through the challenges that would persist through his remaining days.

The birds chirped a new day as Brett stood on the porch. "Thank you, for your enthusiasm and hospitality. I'll strive to use your one-page approach. Please thank Louise."

"You're welcome, Brett, I've enjoyed it."

Brett gave One Page a thumb up as he walked to his car.

Chapter 21

Brett remembered a television documentary featuring the Silver Valley and some of the mining issues.

He drove down to Silver Valley's town, Burke, Idaho, to gather insights for Soul Star.

The valley is quiet now. One can listen to the gurgle of the creek. It wasn't always so. Three and four generations ago, this valley throbbed to the beat of a thousand miners and their families. A combination of heavy snow and poor transportation meant living quarters crammed into the narrow, steep valley. Care for the environment seldom surfaced. Outhouses built over the creek let sewage flow without clean-up. Chemicals used in the mining operations leached into the creek. Most of the mines are closed; a road and a few houses remain but the abuses of the environment have healed themselves.

The narrow valley, the remnants of old mines and houses, and the stories of environmental abuse festered in Brett's consciousness as he stood on the foundation of a deteriorated building. He listened. He sensed someone nearby. Then he saw him, an old man beyond some trees.

Brett walked over and greeted him. "Howdy neighbour, I'm Brett Larson."

"Hello, Brett, I'm Oats Wolf."

"Pleased to meet you, Oats. How long have you lived in Burke?"

"Sixty-three years. I came here as a seventeen-year-old, looking for a job."

"I want to tell you about my dream, Oats. Will you listen and spend the day with me?"

"Well, how do I know you're not some axe murderer who'll kill me and take both my dimes?"

Brett said, "You have lived a long life here in Burke; I offer you a diversion and a job. If I murder you and take your money, your epitaph can read 'Here is planted rolled Oats' and…you'll never again have to pull up your pants. Maybe the press will label me a cereal killer."

Oats looked at Brett. He hesitated, then he grinned. "Thank you, Brett. I'll spend the day with you."

Brett gave him a thumb up. "How'd you get the name, Oats?"

"My name is Otis. When I arrived here in Burke, friends nicknamed me Oats. I told people my name but when I spelled it, Otis, they asked me to spell it again. So I spelled Oats and saved trouble for all."

Brett described Soul Star and his hope to benefit many lives. Discussions filled the day to the point Brett asked Oats if he would ride to Wallace with him and share supper.

The sunlight flickered through the trees.

Brett glanced at Oats. "Would you consider appointment as an advisor to the Soul Star project?"

Oats shifted in his seat. "I'm a simple, uneducated, old man. How could I help you?"

"I expect you're a wonderful resource for Soul Star. You've experienced the reality of mining with manual labour. You've emerged from your shift wet and dirty, with none of the conveniences the miners enjoy today. You've lived in a community with no electricity, no piped-in water, no sewer, no refrigeration, and few modern conveniences. You've seen how miners resolved their disagreements with their fists. You've watched the pollution of the creek. You've watched fires race up the valley. You've watched managers push miners to take risks to optimize production. You bring unvarnished perspective to a project that might, at first, seem easy to many of the individuals attracted to the project. I hope Soul Star will allow each individual to experience some of the challenges of rugged pioneer conditions but grow to modern living conditions as the project develops, all the while conscious that our primary focus is each individual. If a productive capital asset for Canada is a fringe benefit, so much the better."

Brett's fluency impressed Oats. He wondered whether he could be a productive part of Brett's vision. He recognized that his experience would be useful to the project, but he lived in Burke. An inner spark harkened; Oats found himself intrigued by the possibility that he could make a difference.

Brett noticed Oats' revitalization. He invited Oats into the lounge for a nightcap.

Oats accompanied Brett but ordered coffee. "I watched alcohol trap men and I want to avoid that fate."

Brett looked at Oats. "I envision Soul Star free from alcohol, cigarettes, drugs, and gambling."

During the car ride back to his home, Oats asked, "Will you come back in the morning and spend another day with me?"

Clear, warm weather welcomed Brett as he made his way up the valley, confident that Oats was a valuable source of information and guidance as the first few crews embarked on sections of the tunnel.

When he pulled up, the door stood ajar and Oats appeared. "Come in for coffee."

Brett noted the tidiness of the home. Oats mentioned his concern that no one cared how he lived or looked. It appeared that Oats took good care in spite of his comments.

Chapter 22

Brett phoned a friend in Ottawa. “Hi, Gerard, how’re you doing?”

“Is this Brett? Is there some calamity in Alberta? I don’t hear from you unless you want something.”

“I’m so glad you appreciate my call.”

“No problem, what’s up?”

“I’m launching a big project with political nuances. I want to position the head office where the pushback should be minimal. Where do you suggest?”

“What kind of project?”

“It’s a transportation-utility structure stretching from Quebec to the Yukon.”

“I thought you said big, not impossible.” The sarcasm was thick in his voice.

“I leave the petty problems to the peons in Ottawa.”

“But you call me when you have a little problem about locating the head office of a project that will upset every thinking Canadian.”

“No, just the select few whom Ottawa defines as thinking.”

“Most national projects set up an office in Ottawa.”

“I don’t want that; my focus is on non-government participants and I don’t want to brush shoulders with politicians any more than necessary.”

“Have you considered Thunder Bay? It looks benign to most regional factions.”

“Do you know anybody there who might help me find a leader for the project?”

“No, I think you should look in Hollywood or Mumbai.”

“I’ll call you when the leading man is contracted. Thanks for the vote of confidence.”

"You're most welcome. Not even Ottawa can put a positive spin on your proposal."

"Don't you have a legendary politician who said, 'Just watch me'?"

"Yeah; he didn't die from his scars, but he did die."

Brett retrieved his luggage in Thunder Bay and walked out to the taxi queue. One taxi stood at the curb. The driver, dressed in a purple turban, grey suit, white shirt, and purple tie, walked around to take Brett's bag.

Brett climbed in the front seat. "Howdy, neighbour. The Crossroads Motor Inn on Arthur Street, please. How long have you lived in Thunder Bay?"

"I came here in 1972," he said as he pulled away from the curb.

"What caused you to move to Thunder Bay?"

"A few months after my family tried to force me into an arranged marriage, my siblings helped me leave Bombay and come to Toronto. My parents and extended family shunned me. I got a job as a shipping clerk, in a warehouse. After a few weeks, a co-worker told me he'd decided to move to Thunder Bay. I hated my job, so I resigned and went with this guy to Thunder Bay. He soon got a job in a mine at Ignace, west of here, and I got a job as a gas station attendant. Many of the local taxi drivers fuelled their cars at my gas station. Through the East Indian drivers, I found a job as a taxi driver. I like my work."

Brett nodded, then directed the conversation to his purpose. "If I asked you to name the most influential person in this city, who would it be?"

The cabbie looked over. "There're several individuals who contribute to our city. Why do you ask?"

"Well, I want to find an inspirational leader for a national project and I want the project's public face to be in Thunder Bay."

"Maybe you should consider Thompson Miller."

"Why him?"

"I've hauled every businessman, city councillor, provincial politician, federal minister, Indian chief, union leader, grain buyer, architect, and miner who has visited Thunder Bay and I know that Thompson Miller is the person who makes things happen."

"Why so formal? What's this Thompson Miller bit? Wouldn't Tom be more appropriate?"

"I don't know, sir, everybody says Thompson, not Tom."

They had arrived at his destination.

"Thanks for the ride, bye," Brett said. He gave the driver a thumb up as he headed into the hotel.

Two o'clock in the afternoon. Brett rented a car and toured the city. He entered a jewellery store; a woman in her thirties greeted him.

"Howdy neighbour, I'm from out west. I hope to find a trinket to take home."

The clerk led Brett to a display of spoons, lapel pins, and Christmas decorations. None of it struck Brett's fancy. "How long have you lived in Thunder Bay?"

"All my life."

"Who do you think is the most impressive local leader?"

"What a strange question."

"I'm sorry, I'll explain. I plan to set up the head office of a national project here. The locals sometimes suggest great leaders that don't show up on head-hunters' rosters."

"Then you need to talk to Thompson Miller."

"Is he a saint?"

"No, but he's closer than many."

I must meet this guy.

"I don't see any gift that strikes my fancy. I'll look up Mr. Miller. Thanks for your help."

He gave her a thumb up.

He came to the grain terminals and railway sidings. He sensed no vibrancy. Back in the business district, he noticed a restaurant on Algoma Street. He entered. The waiter shuffled over, a Chinese man, gaunt and hunched over.

"Howdy neighbour," Brett said, "I'd like some pie and coffee. What kind of pie do you have?"

"Apple and laison; laison all gone; what kind you like?"

"Apple à la mode, please."

When the pie and coffee came, Brett asked, "How long have you been in Thunder Bay?"

"Eighty-two years. My parents started this café. An Asian stork delivered me upstairs."

"Who is the most important leader in this town?"

"Why do you ask?"

"I want to open a national business with its head office here and I want it to be accepted by the locals."

"Well, I like Thompson Miller's approach to business."

"Where do I find Mr. Miller?" Brett asked.

"His office is in a bronze-coloured office building on Simpson Street. He's the owner-manager of Miller Transloading."

Brett finished his pie and paid. "I enjoyed the pie. When do you get more raison pie?"

The old head lifted, a toothless grin spread across his face. "I never have laison pie, I can't pronounce it."

Brett gave him a thumb up and went back to his room, looked up the number of Miller Transloading, and dialled.

"Good afternoon, Miller Transloading, may I help you?"

"Yes, I'm Brett Larson from Calgary and I'm in Thunder Bay to open an office. Would Mr. Miller have time to see me?"

"Let me check his calendar. Mr. Miller is due back in the office at 5:15 this afternoon. He has to be out of here by 6:15. Can you be here at 5:15?"

"Yes, thank you."

"Okay then," and the line went dead.

Brett wondered how this would unfold. He decided on business casual. He drove down to Simpson Street, found the bronze glass building—the most upscale property in Thunder Bay. He punched four, the top floor. He stepped into a tidy but plain lobby.

"Hi, I'm Brett Larson, here to see Thompson Miller."

The receptionist smiled. "Mr. Miller just phoned; he's on his way; would you like some coffee or juice?"

"No thanks, I'm fine."

Thompson Miller came in and approached Brett. "Welcome to Thunder Bay, Brett. I'm Thompson Miller. Come in. I have a few minutes."

Seated in soft chairs on either side of a coffee table, Brett described Soul Star and why he picked Thunder Bay as the head office.

At 6:15, Thompson said, "Brett, please come with me to a bakery opening. On the way, I'll call two guys who should be interested in Soul Star. They might meet us for coffee after the ribbon cutting."

Brett appreciated why the locals put Thompson Miller top of mind when asked about their best leader. Thompson arranged for two men to meet at the Miller home at 9:30 that evening. As they settled in the den, Thompson went to the kitchen and made coffee. He brought it with some of Marie's date squares.

The meeting broke up at two in the morning. Thompson agreed to meet for a full day session and a dinner on Tuesday, three weeks hence. One of the guests dropped Brett off at his car on Simpson Street. Brett drove back to his hotel and went to bed satisfied Soul Star now had a public face—Thompson Miller.

From the departure lounge, Brett phoned Beth Ragouski and Oscar One Page and asked them if they'd attend a meeting in Thunder Bay, Ontario.

Beth asked what planet he was on and One Page said he already lived in a remote place; he didn't have to go to Thunder Bay.

But both agreed to go. Brett gave a thumb up to no one in particular.

Chapter 23

The Thunder Bay Shield Club, established in 1918 on High Street as an elite business club, sported dark mahogany wood, plush carpets, and attentive staff. It started out as a stuffy establishment. It barred women during the business day. Through the decades, other luncheon clubs emerged and attitudes changed to the point the Shield Club became ordinary.

Beth, One Page, and Brett, in business attire, stepped into the Shield Club and met Thompson Miller. He led them to a room with a conference table in the shape of a circle, hollow in the center, inlaid leather on the surface, mahogany galore.

"I chose this city to build my business because I found Toronto, and my own family, insufferable. Even with my family's faults, I inherited skills, money, and confidence. I know I can accomplish much and I'm excited about Soul Star. Brett met me three weeks ago and introduced Soul Star. He also described you two. Brett is enthusiastic about the project and the people involved. Brett is known to all three of us but Beth and Oscar do not know me, so let's take a few minutes to get to know each other. Beth, tell me a little about your background and your interests."

When Beth finished, Thompson said, "Oscar?"

With the preliminaries out of the way, the group worked through the issues. The walls wore flip chart pages taped to them, lists of must haves, wants, investors, safety concerns, organization structures, a morass of disparate ideas and concerns.

Beth looked around the room. "Let's figure out who'll do what."

Thompson took charge. "One Page, demonstrate your claim to fame and lead us to a single page for each of us to execute."

They made “to do” lists for Brett, One Page, Beth, and Thompson. As Thompson moved to take down the flip charts and roll them for future reference, Beth asked him to wait a minute while she took digital pictures of each of the sheets. “I’ve proven to myself that actual, documented information at my fingertips is better than undocumented ‘he said, she said’ vignettes from memory.”

Dinner lightened the intensity of the day and each individual relaxed as rapport developed.

Beth sat at dinner with three men; they were exuberant, smart, and unwary of the problems ahead. She thought about the obstacles that she imagined and the many more that she knew would emerge.

The perceptions of what could be accomplished varied but every individual recognized the others expected performance. Beyond that, Soul Star represented a contribution to mankind.

Brett thought, *Circumstances like this are never experienced by most of humanity—a gulf that leads to frustration, akin to the gulf in perceptions between woman and man.*

Chapter 24

Hymie Friedenberg stared out of his New York office window.

What does the future hold?

The Statue of Liberty stood out there, a symbol of individual risk and reward in a country that Hymie appreciated.

But what did lie ahead?

When Hymie arrived in New York, fresh from his escape from East Germany, he got a job as a night clerk in a crummy little hotel in a rundown area of the Bronx. The hotel owner noticed his reliability, astuteness, business ideas, and persistence. As Hymie mastered each new task, the owner continued to throw new responsibilities in his lap.

On Hymie's thirty-fifth birthday, the owner came to him and offered to sell his business empire to Hymie. Hymie accepted and assembled funds and capable people to manage a real estate group that covered the eastern seaboard. An array of bankers, lawyers, brokers, and entrepreneurs appreciated Hymie's nineteen years of attention to the business. Many doors opened for Hymie to arrange his financing, but strings were attached to every door. Hymie designed payouts, performance incentives, and innovations that allowed him to pay out all his creditors in ten years.

Hymie was wealthy when he celebrated his forty-fifth birthday. His business acumen combined with flair, genial personality, and desire to pay it forward to people who wanted to help themselves combined to cause a group of bankers in New York to ask Hymie to tour western Canada to find real estate investment opportunities. One of Hymie's friends planned to attend a Bat Mitzvah in Winnipeg in June. He invited Hymie to come to the celebration and start his voyage of discovery in Winnipeg.

Hymie spent a few days in Winnipeg and then headed for Regina. Both Winnipeg and Regina lacked the necessary vibrancy, so he went to Calgary. He got there on the last Friday of the Stampede. One of his contacts took him to the rodeo and walked him through the exhibition grounds. Hymie happened by a photography display that captured his imagination. He marvelled at the photos and singled out two photographs by the same man—one of a wolf and one of a doe and fawn. The images stuck with him; he knew not why. After a corn dog and a Big Rock beer, Hymie went back to the photo display. He recorded the name and town of the photographer: Jack Yudzik, Winnipeg.

When the real estate excursion ended, Hymie went back to New York and reported that Calgary and Vancouver showed potential but he sensed business culture differences in both cities, as compared to each other and as compared to New York. He advised the New Yorkers to find a transplanted one of their own already assimilated into one of those two cities prior to making any investments.

Some weeks later, Hymie came across a slip of paper in his pocket. The paper held the name and city of the photographer whose work he noticed in Calgary. Hymie phoned. Cecile answered. She took Hymie's number and told him that Jack would phone back in about two hours. When Jack returned the call, he agreed to a caribou photo commission.

Chapter 25

Rosie visited the Yudziks in appreciation of their kindness and their friendship.

Rosie gathered the dishes. “You won’t believe this, Cecile.”

“What?”

“I met with Brett Larson, the brains behind Soul Star. He asked me to become Soul Star’s environmental monitor.”

Jack folded his napkin. “Is that wise?”

“I don’t know. I may alienate a few environmentalists but I see merit in the project.”

As Cecile and Rosie put the dishes in the dishwasher at the end of the evening, Cecile learned that Rosie would be a Soul Star consultant committed to protect the interests of the environment.

Jack and Cecile stood in the doorway and waved goodbye to Rosie.

Cecile told Jack of Rosie’s confession. At first he wouldn’t believe it. After a night of contemplation, he realized Rosie could take on this task. He discussed the plan with Rosie and learned funds would be needed for the pilot project.

Jack called Hymie and told him about Rosie’s latest endeavour and asked if Hymie might consider financing the pilot section of the tunnel. Hymie listened to Jack’s version of the project. It sounded wonderful, but he knew facts often differed from perceptions.

Days later, Hymie sat in a meeting room at the Petroleum Club in Calgary, bemused by the assembled cast: Oats Wolfe, Brett Larson, Oscar One Page, Beth Ragouski, Thompson Miller, and Rosie Savard. From a Jewish millionaire’s perspective, this dysfunctional set of egos could not endure. Each person spoke for a few minutes, then Brett played a Power Point presentation. Hymie saw the substantial thought but he knew it could fail.

Hymie left Calgary, hooked on this project.

If I piss away money, it's good that the wind isn't blowing in my face, isn't it?

Chapter 26

Elaine put a hand on Brett’s arm. “What's wrong, Brett? You’re moody; the slightest thing irritates you.”

“I’m sorry; it’s time to create mass excitement to attract crews for Soul Star and we haven’t found a viable way to do it.”

“Well, think of examples that might capture the imagination of rebellious youth.”

“Hitler's youth, both World Wars, the Klondike Gold Rush, the hippie movement, women….” He trailed off. “I don't know.”

“For thirty seconds’ thought, that’s an insightful list. What’re the common denominators in those examples?”

“Youth, leadership, focus, urgency…. How come you’re so smart?”

She grinned. “I guess because only a few men got in the way of my education.”

He gave her a thumb up.

The window blind clicked against the jamb as a breeze stirred through the open window. The clicks symbolized time slipping by, thoughts turned in each mind, the inevitability of life, opportunities missed.

Youth—leadership—focus—urgency. How might Soul Star create an epidemic, use these ingredients to benefit the project and the participants?

Chapter 27

For several days, Brett talked up this theme with everyone who crossed his path.

One evening at a benefit dinner for the Inn from the Cold organization, Brett described his dilemma to the other dinner guests at his table. A young man with a ponytail showed enough interest that Brett recorded his name and phone number and arranged to meet him the following day.

Hal Eastman showed up at Brett's office—thirty-seven minutes late. Hal paid no attention; he placed a large portfolio case on the conference table and removed nineteen graphics. For two hours, Hal talked and showed graphics that represented ranges of the human condition. For two more hours, Brett described Soul Star, his values, the personalities and the idiosyncrasies of Oscar One Page, Beth Ragouski, Oats Wolf, Thompson Miller, Hymie Friedenberg, and Rosie Savard. Hal asked many questions about Brett's convictions concerning drugs, alcohol, cigarettes, violence, and bully tactics, commenting that these topics formed the epicenter of rebellion against parents, authority, status quo, and rules. In a good-natured tone, Hal asked Brett why he couldn't start on level ground instead of at the foot of a steep mountain.

Hal left Brett with the assurance he'd create a fresh, dramatic movement that would cement Soul Star in the lexicon of five generations. While Brett liked Hal and marvelled at his creativity, his thirty-seven minute tardiness foretold a thirty-seven year wait for the pandemic to take hold.

Chapter 28

The following Monday afternoon, Brett received a call from Hal Eastman.

Wonders never cease.

Hal said, "I worked on your project all weekend. I finished my proposal at four o'clock this morning. Do you want to see what I've got?"

"Certainly; I didn't know whether you'd pursue this project with a vengeance."

"Artistes don't always project the correct message to guys who're so straight they can't bend over to smell a flower."

"Am I supposed to fight back?"

"No, just kidding. But I'm excited about my proposal; can I bring it over?"

"My wife Elaine galvanized my thoughts on youth, leadership, focus, and urgency. Would it be okay if I asked her if she'd make dinner for you, me, and her so she can share in what I anticipate will be a red letter day?"

"Bachelors do not turn down home cooking. Tell me where and when."

"I'll phone Elaine to get her okay and make arrangements. I'll let you know the time. You probably don't get thanked enough by old guys…thank you."

"Well, Brett, I know a fellow who always says thanks for dinner before he eats because he can't lie if he doesn't like the meal. Your thanks before you have a clue what I've developed is a bit much but it feels good. I'll see you tonight. Bye."

The doorbell rang at two minutes before six. Brett went to the door and said, "Howdy, neighbour. I expected you to be thirty-seven minutes late."

"Food is way more important than some guy's sense of propriety."

"Come in, I'll introduce you to Elaine. Elaine, please meet Hal Eastman, Soul Star's creative genius."

"Pleased to meet you, Hal. Dinner will be a few minutes. Please have a seat at the counter and tell us about your experiences before you met my hopeless husband."

"I'm the son of a nurse who worked night shift for many years. She refused to take promotions to day jobs because she wanted to be available to respond to my needs. My father left when he discovered Mom's pregnancy. All these years, Mom has refused to strike up new relationships because she wanted me to be sheltered from the vagaries of a flotilla of men. While I believe Mom erred in her decisions, I'm touched by the love and sacrifice that she's provided to me."

He continued, "My interests tend toward art, nature, and creativity. I excelled in school so I helped other students do their projects. I'm different than most of the boys; I got teased but I protected myself with dry wit and occasional anger that left bullies bleeding. My uncle started a computer shop. I experimented with computer graphics while other kids played ball, stood in front of the Mac store, and discovered how far girls would go. In university, I studied computer graphics and marketing. I didn't want to be a further drain on my mother's resources. Last week, my mother attended my graduation ceremony and we ate an early supper so she could go to work by seven. I promised a friend I'd use his ticket to go to the dinner where I met Brett. While I plan to use my talents to get what appeals to me; I admit that meeting Brett soon after graduation got my attention. It's not every day one happens on a world scale project. I feel I must help make Soul Star a success."

Elaine looked at Hal across the counter. "You may think your mother erred but I think she nurtured a precious boy. Regardless of how the Soul Star project goes, I want you to check with your mother and suggest a day when she can accompany you here for dinner with Brett and me. Dinner is ready; please take a seat and enjoy."

After dinner, Hal retrieved his case. "Can we use the kitchen table for my presentation? I see symbolism in the kitchen table as the center of family discussions."

The first graphic took the breath away: a young man stood straight and tall, able to thrive in any situation.

Hal turned the sheet toward Elaine and Brett. "This young man might be the poster boy who'll inspire a generation of young people as they rebel against unfairness. Think about the examples of unfairness that occur around us: in family life, in gender situations, in race, in religion, in government, in taxation, in business, in education…everywhere you look. Fighting unfairness will inspire young people. They'll rebel against many genuine examples of unfairness sanctioned by authority figures outside the family.

"When we start an epidemic along these lines, elders will acknowledge the youth are indeed better people than their forbearers.

"While Soul Star will incubate the virus, this movement must sweep the world. Kids in the Arab states, sub-Saharan Africa, South America, Europe, Greenland, every corner of the globe can find unfairness to correct. Mild mannered and polite kids can pursue projects. Firebrands and zealots can find causes. Peer pressure can drag the masses along. But we must harness the destructive attributes of any emotional cause. That's why Soul Star is a fine place to start. We'll find pressures of big business, government interference, greedy participants, thieves, and drug salesmen. Our challenge is to position the right answers to be the force of the youth fairness movement. A powerful way to lead is to allow the exuberance, conviction, and energy of youth to decipher the right answer and then propel the population toward that answer.

"I expect young individuals will show up who're unhappy with their circumstance and itch to find better solutions. They can't see how to achieve their goals in their home environment. Without a valid direction, they rebel and cause friction, anguish, and disruption. Brett has happened on a model that provides a viable alternative for many of these folks. But rebellious youth will not go where they're told. They'll make their own decisions. Our opportunity is to present Soul Star as one viable alternative in place of drugs, gangs, and debauchery.

"Many will end up respectable, in your eyes, because they won't deviate so far from authority that the path back is impossible. I believe you want to engage the swath of young people who have deviated and don't want to find their way back. On the other hand, they sometimes admit their current paths are less than perfect. Perhaps out of brilliance, luck, or divine guidance, you two happened on four words to drive my recommended strategy for Soul Star. Youth, leadership, focus, urgency; thank you for these words. Here's my plan.

"Kids adapt well to unconventional names like The Naked Ladies, The Grateful Dead, and ABBA. Maybe we'll come up with a better name, but I've hit upon what I think is a great name…Sparks Rock. I think young instigators will invent symbols that coordinate with Sparks Rock. The sports teams in each village may be rock bands. The mentors that I believe will emerge as necessities might be called Flints because they can cause sparks when struck, they're tough, they're predictable, they require action on the part of others before they're noticed. All of these traits will serve young people well. Each young person may be a Spark. Maybe the prized work shift will be 10:00 PM to 6:00 AM, the hours when youth are at their peak. Maybe the Sparks will choose their own work crew leaders. Maybe people like Thompson Miller and Beth Ragouski are too set in their ways to adapt to this line of thought, but I picture Brett, One Page, Oats, and Rosie as personalities who will accept successful, untraditional methods. Maybe the Sparks will find their own Flints. Maybe the Sparks will find their own financiers."

All paused for a time of contemplation, then Brett said, "I think you're onto something. However, your plan's so far removed from my perception of how things get built that I want to reflect on all the repercussions. You've centered your attention on youth. That's good. But urgency and leadership seem uncovered?" His last statement was posed as a question.

Hal straightened his sheets. "The Royal Bank says it builds its customer base one at a time. Can we take a few days to refine the leadership and urgency models? I like the pursuit of fairness as a focus for rebellion. In terms of rebellion against authority and rules, I hope Soul Star imposes no rules at all. I know that anarchy can't be tolerated, but whose anarchy? If clothes are strewn on the bedroom floor, if parties go on all night, if loud music plays, why do you care? If a person dies, if a psyche is wrecked, if blood flows, everybody cares. So let's design a contract with few rules but profound consequences. You've suggested an accidental death on the tunnel project may mean the expulsion of many villagers. Why don't you expand that thought to an unnatural death caused by a villager—or an action by the village members—in any element of their existence: domestic, fights, cars, horseplay, drugs, suicide?"

"One of the risks that we run," Brett said, "is the probability that a young person with incurable flaws shows up in one of our villages, and, whatever the villagers do, the individual isn't manageable. How do we protect the villages from this situation while being open to most salvageable lives?"

Elaine spoke up for the first time since Hal's presentation started. "It seems to me that a small village is the best possible setting for a person like that. It gets the person out of an environment that's the cause of the strife. Where you may run into problems is if you get too many troubled folks in one village. With a little guidance from the Flints, the young villagers ought to include, cope with, and develop two troubled individuals in each village. With something like 4,000 villages, it seems that a paradise for 8,000 youngsters with challenges is laudable. It appears the young people who can't be assimilated into a village are the ones that need professional, daily attention. This is a more inclusive model than the bunch of brats from middle class homes I pictured as your source of villagers."

Brett thought back to the movies that touched him over the years: *To Sir With Love, Good Will Hunting, Radio, Pay It Forward, Forrest Gump,* and *Freedom Writers*. It reaffirmed a mentor who clicks with a kid is the answer to many of life's challenges.

Hal changed the subject. "The urgency you seek can be managed by a first come, first accepted policy for manning the tunnel crews and finding financiers. If we tie the crews to two responsibilities, person power and committed funding, and let the crews that are ready choose their preferred section of the tunnel, we'll create a sense of urgency similar to a gold rush mentality. On the fairness initiative, I suspect the way to create urgency is to find a way for large blocks of young people to get inflamed over some unfairness and get it fixed. To me, this is a wonderful way to educate young people. It'll involve research, analysis, teamwork, writing, debating, adapting to other points of view, maturing as the steps are taken, and being embroiled in a cause that fuels itself."

Elaine placed After Eight mints on the table. "How will you protect kids under eighteen and ensure they're not exploited in the villages?"

Brett finished his mint. "I think we'll be able to arrange a guardian individual for each under-age youngster in a village. I expect individuals with nurturing tendencies will be noticeable. We can arrange the schedules with lots of learning, participation in skits, and village chores so the kids have the opportunities prevalent on family farms a couple of generations back."

The discussion went on until 1:00 AM. Then Brett stretched and yawned. "Well, Hal, my preferred shift is not 10:00 PM to 6:00 AM. I'd like to stop for tonight. I appreciate what you've developed. I think it'll be the base on which Soul Star is populated. You've widened my perspective and, probably, the perspectives of the other individuals who support Soul Star. I'll call you next week and we'll figure out how to move this along. Thanks."

He gave Hal a thumb up.

As they walked to the door, Elaine held Hal's jacket for him. "I enjoyed our evening. Come again."

Hal grinned. "Food attracts me almost any time; attempts to adapt to your husband gives me indigestion. Thanks. Bye."

Hal strapped his portfolio to his motorcycle and drove away. His bike made more noise than the community expected at one in the morning.

Elaine turned to Brett. “How do you find these people?”

“You have to be in the game, generate some offence, watch for opportunities, and act on the opportunities you see. It adds up to high satisfaction.”

Chapter 29

One Page waited his turn in traffic court. He drove in winter conditions for years in northern British Columbia. The driving infraction angered him.

One slippery winter evening, One Page looked for a residential address. As he rounded a curve, the reflective stripes of a policeman's safety vest caught his attention. The officer stopped him as part of a murder investigation. Divided attention caused One Page to hit his brakes too firmly. His car slid over to the curb, bounced a bit, and stopped, quite close to the policeman's car.

The policeman, frustrated by this extended assignment, ticketed Oscar for careless driving. Oscar expected to get the ticket quashed in traffic court. As he waited, his thoughts turned to his Soul Star task. He'd agreed to design a good person model for Soul Star individuals.

Chapter 30

Days later, Oscar attended a birthday party. "Gary, what makes a person good?"

"What—in bed, in politics, in sports, in business, in heaven?"

One Page grinned. "I want to design a model for a village where most of the villagers are there because they've made poor choices in the past and are committed to better choices from now forward. They'll have fragile foundations on which to base good choices."

Gary acknowledged a passing guest, then turned back to One Page. "Do you remember the movie *Schindler's List*? As I recall, Schindler was a bit of a reprobate prior to his decision to help the Jews escape. His lawyer dedicated the rest of his life to search for what makes people good. He wanted to develop a curriculum that would teach people how to be good. I don't think he's found the answer yet."

"Yes, I want to build on it and try to find a model that'll reinforce individual responsibility in a defined environment. I expect broader implementation will have a good chance if our controlled model works."

"What do you have in mind?"

"Well, in traffic court, I thought about the driver demerits system that keeps habitual traffic violators off the road or, at least, without a valid driver's license. Then, I thought about the industrial safety standards that load most of the legal responsibility on the employer. Trade unions hold employers responsible for safety issues through grievance mechanisms. The business examples put the obligation on the employers instead of the individuals involved. I think the emphasis is wrong in principle and confrontational in practice. I want to find a balanced model that will place primary responsibility on the individual involved and on the supervisors most able to influence the immediate safety issues."

Gary raised his eyebrows a bit. "Do you always choose the path of most resistance? Don't you see that they are responsible, not I am responsible?"

One Page nodded. "I hear you, but I want to try in the controlled environment. I want to include both work and non-work activities in the same model: bullies in school, unfair teachers, coaches who push too hard, domestic partners that don't know when to quit, parents who have agendas…whatever makes an individual afraid."

"Whew, I just came to a birthday party, now I'm changing the world."

"Sorry, Gary, sometimes my missions become too central. I'll leave you alone now."

"No, I like your idea. I'll think about it and get back to you."

Chapter 31

The following Wednesday evening, Oscar checked his e-mails.

From: Gary Stavolski
Sent: May 17, 2012
To: Oscar de Lona
Subject: What makes a person good?

Oscar:

Your idea captured my interest. I think it can work in the closed village.

Here're some ideas:

- Set up a demerits system that is well known in the village, included in all contracts, taught in school, publicized in the local paper, and reported when villagers are assessed demerit points.
- Set the limit for a family and each individual where the cumulative demerits will cause expulsion of the individual and/or the family from the village and the project.
- Make the perpetrator absorb the most points.
- Make all of the individuals around that key person partially responsible, and
- Make the supervisors in a relevant chain of command partially responsible.
- Once an individual has reached the maximum individual demerits, that individual is expelled from the village and the project.

• Once a family reaches the maximum family demerits, that family is expelled from the village and the project.

You'll need a system to gather evidence and hold dangerous individuals. A tribunal will decide the demerit points and expulsion. A jury will decide on appeals of expulsion of individuals and/or families.

Please let me know how your model develops.

Good luck! Gary.

Chapter 32

Louise came out of the bedroom at five in the morning. “Oscar, what’re you doing?”

“Brett asked me to design a good person model.”

“When will you be done?”

“When I die.”

“Which will be when I lose my last ounce of patience.” She went back to bed.

Later that morning, Oscar showed Louise his draft of the Good Person Act. Despite her irritation with Oscar’s willingness to ignore everything around him when he embarked on a mission, Louise forced herself to pay attention to One Page as he read his draft aloud. She listened and became enthused with the engine for good that might be unleashed with the Good Person Act.

Chapter 33

Hymie set his coffee aside. “I’ve owned my own businesses for more than thirty years. I’ve taken risks, relied on staff, advisors, and business associates. But, I never dreamt I’d be sitting here in a coffee shop in Fort McMurray, Alberta, Canada, with another old codger from the United States. It’s a strange world, isn’t it?”

Oats finished his toast. “At least you have business experience. I’ve no business background at all.”

“It’s strange that he convinced you to come up here, isn’t it?”

“You know Brett. He told me his story, kidded me a bit, gave me a thumb up, and I decided to sign on.”

“Can you teach a bunch of brats how to mine safely? It’s a challenge, isn’t it?”

“I can teach them. Whether they’re able to pass on their skills without killing each other, time will tell.”

“What’ll you call your training village?”

“Oats’ Patch.”

“Oats’ Patch; that’s weird, isn’t it?”

“Well, Brett teased me about rolled oats and I’ve often associated my nickname with a field of oats. I want to recognize the graduates of the mining program. I want to hand each graduate an embroidered emblem for his or her jacket. So, I’ll call the village Oats’ Patch, and the symbol of each graduate from the school will be a chenille Oats’ Patch crest. Perhaps the Oats’ Patch will become as recognizable as the engineers’ iron ring; perhaps not.”

“How can Soul Star get enough trained miners to populate the thousands of villages along the line?”

“I see exponential growth. We’ll teach 150 students here every semester. We’ll select the best 15 of those to lead training crews in new villages of 150 workers, and then their best 15 will lead training crews in new villages until we have a full complement of trained leaders in every village. We'll continue to train villagers, with leadership potential, here at Oats' Patch so that we continue to improve the skills of the miners and the depth of trained personnel throughout Soul Star."

"You sound like a guy with business sense."

"Thanks."

"At your tender age, can you lead a bunch of characters to be safe, diligent, responsible, and productive miners?"

"I have a plan to recruit some experienced miners who're retired but younger than me. Soul Star has done much for my zest for life; I might see the tunnel completed."

"Maybe Brett will have to change your epitaph to read, 'Here Lays Bold, Old Oats. The Best in the Patch'; isn't it?"

"He'll have to live longer than me to have any say at all."

Chapter 34

Two soldiers finished their furlough in the hill country of central Sri Lanka. On their way back to the Tamil struggle, a combination of youth, exposure to atrocities, alcohol, and ignorance caused the troublemakers to accost a woman. When they moved on, a raped, near naked woman lay dying in the ditch.

When the pregnant Phoan did not come home, her husband looked for her. George Zhong walked into the village. He enquired of Phoan's whereabouts. George walked in the ditch; he did not see any sign of Phoan. So, he walked back toward town in the other ditch. He came upon Phoan's dead body.

His wails filled the air.

He'd learned to farm with his parents, found a wonderful wife, and expected their first child. Now she was dead. His hopes gone.

After the funeral, George gathered his meagre possessions, bid goodbye to his parents and siblings, and headed for Colombo.

Chapter 35

George searched for a job on a ship. After a week around the docks, he got a job as a stateroom attendant on a cruise ship.

One of George's co-workers, Ole Yaglund, haled from Watson Lake, British Columbia. When Ole discovered George's farm experience in cold, high-altitude climates, he told George about a truck garden near Watson Lake.

Ole phoned the owner of Great Northern Plants Inc., Ivor Knetson.

Ivor agreed to arrange for George to move to Canada to work at the Watson Lake gardens and earn his Canadian citizenship.

George transferred to a ship that worked the Pacific shoreline and cruised near the glaciers along the Alaska Panhandle. When his contract ended and with work visa in hand, George left the cruise line in Vancouver, cleared immigration, and bought a bus ticket to Watson Lake.

Ivor had not prepared for the arrival of an immigrant. He had no accommodation for the young man. An old, wooden granary stood in the corner of the yard. Ivor led George to the granary and told him he would find a bed for him to use.

Bewildered, George slumped on the doorsill of his new home, his head in his hands.

Could this be the life I've chosen?

He heard footsteps.

A woman approached. "Are you the young man from Sri Lanka?"

"Yes, I'm George."

"Welcome, George. My name is Sarah Knetson. I'm Ivor's wife and I'll help you get set up here."

"Thank you. I not know what to do when Mr. Ivor leave me here."

"I'll drive you to town and get you a bed, stove, refrigerator, and utensils, cutlery, and food to get you started. We'll need to get electricity over here. I'll make sure you're okay. If you don't know what to do, please come and ask me."

"Thank you, Miss Sarah."

George bought his food and made his own meals.

He built an outhouse behind his home.

The summer weather allowed George to be comfortable in the granary. However, he needed better protection in the winter.

George asked Sarah if she would help him find heating systems for greenhouses. George decided that he could learn about greenhouse heating systems and then adapt that knowledge to heat his home. Sarah took him to the library in Watson Lake and helped him enter searches in the computer. A self-contained boiler in the farmyard that supplied hot water heat to all the farm buildings intrigued him. Sarah printed the pages that illustrated the design of the commercial system. George took the papers home and studied them. The words didn't help as much as the illustrations. Then he asked Sarah if she would help him find an electric pump and a thermostat-controlled switch for it. She found these parts in a shop that installed in-floor heating systems and George used his savings to pay for the parts.

George wondered how to keep the cold from seeping under the floor. The granary sat on two skids that held the floor joists up enough that air circulated under the floor. More searches at the library introduced George to spray foam insulation. He ordered the spray foam kits through the hardware store.

With tools from Ivor's shop, George levelled the granary and dug a six-inch trench around the circumference. Then he used treated plywood as exterior sheathing on the bottom four feet of the walls so that the plywood extended down into the trench. For the rest of the exterior, he used untreated plywood.

George removed every third floorboard in the granary so that he could inject the foam spray insulation under the floor to fill all of the space between the ground and the floorboards. He sliced off any excess foam that expanded above the floor with a handsaw.

Ivor observed.

With the floor fully insulated, George sawed plywood into twelve-inch strips and nailed them to the insides of the studs and rafters, leaving a three-inch gap between each strip. Then he sprayed the foam into the wall and rafter cavities and let the excess foam expand through the gaps. He sliced off the excess with the handsaw.

A weatherproof cabin provided a chance against Watson Lake winters.

George laid out water tubing on the surface of the floor and placed two-by-fours on the flat between the tubes. Then he hand mixed sand, cement, and water and filled the spaces around the tubes and between the two-by fours with mortar.

George built an addition big enough for a water tank, shower, and toilet with aisle access from a door in the back wall of the granary. Just beyond this room, he built a heater that would heat the water in the tank. He would put wood in the heater at six in the morning, noon, six at night, and ten at night. He hoped the wood replenishments would allow the heater to keep the water hot for all except the two hours from four in the morning until six. If that worked out, the hot water tank would have enough hot water to help warm the home in the two hours when the heater might not have enough fuel to heat the water.

For backup, George installed an electric heater that would protect against cold even if the boiler failed.

With Sarah and Ivor's help, George finished the interior with gyproc walls and laminate flooring.

George went to work at seven every morning except Sunday and didn't leave work until six at night. He took an hour at noon to replenish his heater wood and have dinner. He paid attention and worked diligently. He showed Ivor how vegetables and flowers grew in the hills of Sri Lanka. He built terraced gardens: easy to till, water frugal, and efficient in using the heat stored in the rock.

Ivor came to appreciate George's innovations, skill, and diligence.

Sarah offered to drive George into Watson Lake on Wednesday evenings so that he could attend night school to improve his English. One night, his teacher asked him to tell a story to his class about his work. George described his terraced garden.

Cal Boychuk, the teacher's boyfriend, sat in the back of the class. Cal and his girlfriend planned to drop in on a friend's birthday party after the class. George's story caught Cal's attention because it meshed with his idea for a robotic farm implement. Cal worked as a heavy-duty mechanic but he innovated as a hobby.

After the class, Cal called out to George and told him about a project that would complement George's terraced garden. George did not know how to react to this situation, so he looked to his teacher for guidance. She, Cindy Gallimore, introduced Cal to George and assured George that it would be okay, and safe, to discuss business opportunities with Cal. George agreed to go over to Cal's home on Saturday evening.

"Hi, George; glad you came," Cal greeted George.

"I'm not good at English so I'm afraid."

"I watched your talk in class last Wednesday; you do just fine. Let me show you my robot."

Cal led the way to a Quonset in the backyard. George wondered at the hodge podge of tools, parts, wheels, wires, and junk. *Could Cal's mind be as cluttered as his shop?* Cal described the robot that hovered near the ceiling. As George focused, he saw that it hung from an overhead square frame, made of pipe. Wheels carried it on a track.

Cal pointed to the unit. "I've designed a robot that can be programmed to work unattended. It's controlled with software that will cause it to respond to the implement attached to the engine and it'll control every aspect of the intended operation: cultivation, seeding, irrigating, spraying, and harvesting. The robot is designed to cultivate a six-inch width of soil at two miles per hour. So, the robot could cultivate a sixteen and one-half foot stretch of farmland, one-half mile long, in thirty-three passes of six inches per pass. So the one-acre field could be cultivated in eight and one-quarter hours. All other field operations could be performed at this speed—or faster, if the task required less torque. When I heard you describe your terraced garden, I assumed that my robot would suit the terraced garden because conventional farm equipment is too large for the plots. I've encountered problems when I deliver granular materials to the robot. Water and liquid chemicals work well but seed and granular fertilizer applications need refinement."

Cal launched the robot with a rototiller attachment that worked the soil into a five-inch thick bed of fluffy loam. A plastic shield around the rototiller protected observers. George grew up in a labour-intensive environment where high tech translated into shellacked horns on water buffalo.

Cal continued, "I want to power the robot with solar energy. I use a solar panel on the roof of the Quonset. It'll drive the robot for demonstrations but it doesn't generate enough power to allow the robot to work under full load. I've observed that a little additional protection from the elements will increase the frost-free season and growth. Homeowners cover their flowers to prevent frost damage and ginseng farmers cover their crops all summer. This tells me that some sort of awning is feasible for many farm situations. I've toyed with an awning over a sixteen and one-half foot by twenty-six hundred and eighty foot garden that would be a solar panel, plus protect from rain, snow, hail, frost, birds, and whatever else threatens the crops. I've thought of a name for this type of agriculture. I want to call it fawning: farming under awning.

"When I heard you describe the warming effect of the daytime sun stored in the soil and rocks, I thought about an awning with solar power capability plus a radiator circulating a liquid that would warm in the sunshine and release heat at night. This should increase growth and lengthen the season."

George's eyes shone with the potential of Cal's ideas. He thought back to the chill in the high altitudes of Sri Lanka. He knew that terraced gardens could flourish in harsh climates.

George spent many evenings with Cal in the Quonset. Their friendship flourished. George added knowledge of plants and soil to Cal's innovations.

George became a Canadian citizen.

Chapter 36

One evening, Cal said, “Cindy and I have broken up. I move to southern British Columbia in ten days.”

“How can you do that? You’re my only friend.”

“You’ll do fine. You’re a great guy, George.”

A subdued George went back to his home.

Will I make it here, alone?

He continued to go to night school.

After the last class of the semester, the teacher organized a little graduation ceremony. At the end of the evening, George approached and thanked her.

She smiled. “Well, thank you, George. I’ve enjoyed our time in class. Would you consider having supper with me on Saturday evening?”

George looked at her. “I don’t understand.”

“I’d like to be your friend, not your teacher.”

“You mean woman-man friend?”

“Yes.”

“Saturday is far away.”

She laughed.

Chapter 37

"Mr. Miller?"

"Yes."

"I'm Scott Beaumont, Deputy Minister for Northern Development. Please come in."

As Thompson Miller and Scott Beaumont entered the boardroom, Beaumont turned to the people in the room. "George and Sarah, please meet Thompson Miller, President of Soul Star."

"Mr. Miller, this is George Temple in charge of wildlife and Sarah Reid in charge of forests."

"Hello, Sarah and George." Thompson shook hands.

Beaumont indicated all should sit. "Mr. Miller, please update us on the Soul Star project."

"Thank you, Mr. Beaumont; we have all government approvals in place, except yours. I'm here to learn what can be done to expedite your approval so that we can build Soul Star."

"In that regard"—Sarah opened her folder—"we have concerns about the spread of the spotted beetle, which attacks the leaves of black poplar trees in some areas of New Hampshire and the Eastern Townships of Quebec. We want to be certain that the infestation does not become a problem in our jurisdiction."

Thompson stared at her. "How could Soul Star exacerbate the risk of infestation?"

"We understand you attract individuals from across Canada to work on Soul Star. Some of these individuals could have traveled through the infected areas of Quebec and New Hampshire; we require assurance that Soul Star won't contribute to the spread of the spotted beetle."

"What kind of assurance do you require?"

"We await your suggestions, Mr. Miller."

He fought to control a level-toned voice. “Well, I’ll discuss your concerns with my team and respond on Thursday; Mr. Temple, do you have open issues?”

“None that we wish to table today, sir. However, we reserve the right to restrict Soul Star’s activities in the future should we become dissatisfied with Soul Star.”

Thompson was taken aback. “Is that a threat, Mr. Temple?”

“Absolutely not,” Temple answered. “This department administers Northern Development in this province; you’ll do well to recognize the significance of our mandate.”

“Are we done here?” Thompson rose from his chair.

Beaumont stood. “The formal segment of our meeting is concluded; however, I’ve reserved a table for lunch at the Shepherd’s Crook restaurant down the block. Please join me for lunch.”

“All right, my plane leaves at three-thirty, so I’ll have time for a quick lunch. Thank you.”

Seated in a quiet corner of the restaurant, Scott raised his glass in a mock toast. “I have a small farm in Switzerland where I plan to retire. My present focus is the assembly of 200 North Country Cheviot ewes at 500 US dollars per head. As soon as I complete the Soul Star approval process, I’ll move on to the next segment of my retirement plan.”

Thompson glanced around the restaurant. “How did this place get its name?”

“I asked the proprietor. He told me that a painting of Jesus as the shepherd of his flock inspired him. I enjoy hosting people here, as I serve a flock of wonderful people.”

Thompson shrugged. “Life is full of ironies.”

“I'm pleased you get my drift, Mr. Miller. Please take this pen from the North Country Cheviot Society of Switzerland as a memento of our meeting. It’s been a wonderful day, thank you. Good day.”

He went on his way.

Thompson reached for his own pen in his shirt pocket and clicked it once.

Back at the Thunder Bay air terminal, Thompson telephoned Brett.

"Brett Larson here."

"Hello, Brett, Thompson here."

"How'd your meeting go?"

"He wants a $100,000 US dollar bribe; his Swiss bank account number is enclosed in the barrel of the souvenir pen he gave me."

"We don't do bribes; get it approved without a bribe."

"I do politics, I go with the flow, and I don't know how to get it approved without a bribe."

Silence.

"Are you still there, Brett?"

"Yeah, I'm here." Brett's voice on the other end was strained. "I wonder whether we can function with a president who condones immoral activities."

Anger flared up within him. "Now you've made me mad. I agreed to work with Soul Star because I know I can smooth many of the potholes along the way. I've perfected how to get along with everybody. I work hard at relationships. My specialty is alliances, not change. If you want to stop bribery in provincial government, you do it because I won't. We've come a long way in Soul Star; I want to be there at the end. I promise to continue to work hard, within my abilities and my circle of influence. When it comes to stronger means, I'll stand aside and help in areas where politics will work."

"I'm sorry, Thompson. I, and all the team, appreciate what you do for us, and we function well with you as our president. However, we won't pay bribes. Beyond that, we won't tolerate Beaumont in a government job when we're done with him. I assume you taped your discussions with Beaumont. Please make copies and place them in at least two safe places and send a copy of the tape and the transcript of the tape to me by courier as soon as you can."

"Okay, Brett."

"I'm sorry, Thompson. I was too critical. We just can't tolerate corruption."

"Well, Brett, you really pissed me off…but I'll get over it. Goodnight."

Chapter 38

Beth heard the phone as she walked into her office. "Beth Ragouski here."

"Howdy, neighbour."

"Hi Brett, what's up?"

I have a forensic challenge you might help solve. The deputy minister, Scott Beaumont, wants a $100,000 bribe to approve our permits in the province. We won't pay a bribe but we'll get our approvals. Can you take this on?"

"Do we have evidence of what Beaumont asked for?"

"Yes, I have a transcript and a copy of the tape."

"Okay, I'll see what I can do."

As Beth got a coffee, she mulled over the Beaumont implications. Solutions might reflect on Soul Star's reputation. She decided to find out how Beaumont fit into the government hierarchy—not his position but how he came to be there and why Soul Star needed to fix the situation. She made some calls. Premier Robbie MacDonald had appointed Beaumont as the deputy minister of Northern Development. Since rumours in politics have elements of substance, Beth looked for the levers Beaumont might've used to secure his position. Two lines of inquiry yielded tidbits. Beaumont used the approval process to get bribes on large projects. This provided Beth with an avenue to keep Soul Star out of any publicity that might erupt as the facts emerged. The second facet relied on DNA.

More enquiries revealed that the premier's mother-in-law, Naomi, embarked on a one-year sabbatical, two years before the premier married her only daughter, Barb. The sabbatical was characterized as a recovery from mental illness, which caused doubts amongst close friends.

The detectives found evidence of the birth of a boy in Victoria. The baby was adopted by the Beaumont family from

Regina. Scott Beaumont, thirty-five years old, showed up in MacDonald's face as the premier approached his limousine for his drive home to dinner. A few words caused the premier to return, with Beaumont, to his office where he learned of Beaumont's intention to secure a permanent government job for the next thirty years and gain a full government pension.

Chapter 39

Out of the blue, MacDonald's mother-in-law received a telephone call from a stranger. The stranger laid out a scenario that could not be ignored. She called Robbie and told him to meet her at her home, immediately. When he got there, she told him of the detective's call and the facts assembled so far.

MacDonald slumped in his chair. "I'll tell Barb."

"You'll ruin your marriage."

"Perhaps, but it may save my soul." The premier walked out.

Three hours later, he phoned back and suggested he and Barb would come over for dinner and Barb and Barb's father would be told.

Naomi tried to reconcile, one more time, her indiscretion compounded by so many years of unconfessed guilt. She remembered the combination of circumstances that led to her actions. She had been unhappy with her husband. Barb had mistreated Robbie the previous evening when he expected better. When she woke on Saturday, Harold had gone to play golf and Barb was out for breakfast with Sherry. Naomi dressed in an erotic outfit, made breakfast for Robbie, and called him to breakfast. She wanted to experience everything so she ignored any kind of protection. While in Victoria, she indulged herself repeatedly, but she realized she was the cause of her unhappiness at home. She later became more considerate of Harold and he responded well. Their marriage recovered.

Still, the ache of betrayal coloured everything she did.

The dinner atmosphere spelled discomfort; father and daughter knew of nothing untoward but sensed tension; mother and son-in-law endured. As they finished the main course, Naomi said, "Barb, Robbie and I have a devastating confession. Be prepared. One Saturday thirty-six years ago, I seduced Robbie. During that tryst, I became pregnant. I went away to Victoria for a year, alleging mental illness, and gave up the baby for adoption. While your father knew of the pregnancy and my infidelity, he didn't know who fathered the child."

Barb slammed her glass on the table, spraying wine and shards of glass everywhere. "Mother, how could you?"

"I'm sorry. I didn't have the strength to tell you, even now, but Robbie insisted."

Barb's father chewed on the new pieces of the story.

Then Barb turned on Robbie. "Why didn't you tell me?"

"Until Scott Beaumont showed up at my office, I didn't know I caused a pregnancy. As for the seduction, I failed to gather enough courage to tell you. I've tried all these years to put it out of my mind but it still hurts. I'm sorry I betrayed you. I hope—and trust—you'll forgive me and your mother."

Barb gathered some of her wits. "I'm outa here. Robbie, you can find your own way home, or you can bed down here for the night or forever."

Chapter 40

National news, the next morning, reported the premier's resignation.

Scott Beaumont's career needed an overhaul.

Soul Star received the last of the required permits.

Thompson Miller observed.

Chapter 41

Gord read the letter.

Between Ewe And Me, Inc.
1141 Banner Lane
Okotoks, AB T4C 1X7

Attention: Gord Rempel
Re: Pasture Management

You've been recommended to us as an innovator in farm fences. We wish to develop a pasture management system for the Soul Star project in Canada's north from Quebec to the Yukon.

We envision a controlled enclosure that will allow domestic animals and birds to graze on fresh pasture at all times from spring through fall.

The contemplated pasture area is in the order of 50,000 acres arranged, bead-like, along 4,400 kilometers.

We operate on a spartan budget, so the solutions we choose must be cost-effective.

If this opportunity is attractive to you, please contact the undersigned at your first opportunity.

Kindest regards,
Soul Star

Per Brett Larson
cc Rosie Savard

Gord re-read the letter. Should I chuck it?

He called a friend who administered grazing leases for the Alberta government. “What do you know about Soul Star and Brett Larson?”

“I know a fair bit. We have two people dedicated to the repercussions of the project in northern Alberta.”

“I just received a letter from Brett Larson. He asked me to design an automated pasture rotation system for Soul Star. Should I pay attention to his request?”

“Yes, you should pay attention. That initiative will make you the authoritative pasture management guru on the planet.”

“Has this Larson turkey bought you?”

“Soul Star amazes me. You’ll be bowled over by its plans.”

With endorsement from his taciturn friend, Gord arranged to meet with Brett and Rosie.

As Gord left the meeting, he wondered if the Soul Star vision would fly.

Chapter 42

The following Friday evening, Gord went to the Bishops' College alumni pub night. He described the Soul Star request to his fellow alumni. Their comments dominated the chatter.

"You say the pasture fence will rotate around a central pivot?"

"Yep."

"What causes it to rotate?"

"A solar-powered motor."

"How big is the enclosure?"

"About 150 feet in radius. The outer edge of the wedge might be 50 feet."

"What happens if the ground is uneven?"

"I picture a preparation module that could be used to work up the ground, smooth it, and plant it to grass. When the construction module is moved off, the pasture would be ready for a conventional pasture wedge that would have wheels at the outer perimeter to follow the terrain."

"What keeps predators such as coyotes and eagles out of the pasture?"

"It looks like the pasture wedge would be covered with an animal and bird-proof mesh."

"Will the pivots collide?"

"We'll need software to control the rotation so that no wedges collide as they complete their rotations."

"I see—Gord is the caller for a square dance. One lady stands in the middle in a full skirt with solar panels. As she twirls, her skirt flares out and catches the sun's rays, the captive animals dosey-do, and the fence wedge allemandes left or right in step with the political stripe of the day."

"What happens at mating time?"

“It looks like the females will be in the driver’s seat.”

“What’s new?”

The banter continued until the bar closed. Gord knew he impressed his friends with the potential of his opportunity. He took a cab home.

Chapter 43

After oodles of sketches and chats with anyone interested, a possible approach emerged. What about a quarter section comprised of 160 one-acre plots with a pivot on each one-acre parcel? But square pegs do not fit in round holes. So Gord decided to enlarge the circle so that it nipped the four corners of the square acre. This would work as long as the pivots did not occupy the same space at the same time.

How about a wedge-shaped enclosure that pivots around the centre of a 209 foot square piece of land?

The wedge would contain a cow and her calf, sheep, goats, chickens, ducks, geese, and turkeys in numbers that would utilize the forage produced in the parcel. Variations could include milk cows separated from their calves, horses, goats, and other grass-fed animals. Gord suspected that pigs would not be suitable because they root into the soil.

The small scale of the pivot would allow each village to find suitable land, clear it, and install pivot wedges in well-managed modules.

How do we get water to the animals and to irrigate, how do we grow winter feed, and how do we manage reproductive programs?

Pioneer experiences across the world indicate that innovative solutions to most problems will be found. Gord developed the prototypes for beef, dairy, and poultry and let the villagers innovate the rest.

Aaron Wood, a villager in Bent Hill, heard of the pivot wedges and lobbied to be the manufacturer. As each wedge went into service, Aaron inspected the installation and developed a relationship with the operator. Out of this dialogue, Gord continued to improve his pivot wedges.

As news of the system spread beyond Soul Star, farmers around the world installed pivot wedges.

An article in The Economist came to Gord's attention. He realized his innovation would change the perception of aircraft passengers as they observed farm circles, reminiscent of pixels on a computer screen.

Chapter 44

Engineers littered the conference table with documents as they presented various perspectives on solar energy and hydrogen fuel. The engineers diagnosed insanity as Soul Star management's key attribute.

Brett and Thompson watched Rosie discuss the challenges with the specialists.

Rosie gained experience on the Healthy Habitats project that culminated in the environmental guidelines under which Soul Star was the largest project that stood to benefit from, and impact on, the northern Canadian environment. "Gentlemen, I have a lifetime of experience filed under 'why things can't be done'. Individuals in Canada—and around the world—assume the Soul Star project will fail. We've found, and we'll continue to find, substantial participants who help us accomplish our mandate. Our society uses resources faster than new resources are discovered. We don't accept that our conventional practices are appropriate. We will do better. We've identified solar energy as an acceptable source of sustainable energy and hydrogen as an acceptable storage vehicle. Our goal is to develop the best solar energy and hydrogen storage model. Soul Star asks, 'Do you wish to be part of a team to develop the technology for the benefit of Soul Star and mankind?'"

Visibly upset with Rosie's comments, the engineer who represented a large firm gathered his notes, placed them in his briefcase, and said, "Our firm will not participate in Soul Star." He left.

The second engineer, Kerry Kelly, looked at Rosie. "I'm a professor at the University of British Columbia. Professors are expected to research and publish. The Soul Star project appears to be a wonderful incubator for solar energy and hydrogen technology. I want to be part of it, however, I have a concern: my wife and kids will get cold and hungry without my income. If I can earn sufficient money to keep my family alive, I'm in."

The third engineer, Scott Shadle, hair untouched by grey, had launched a one-man firm two months prior. With no wife or kids to support, he sensed the dynamics of the project and jumped to the conclusion that it could work. "I'll put my heart and soul into this project."

Scott Shadle woke in the middle of the night, drenched in sweat. His parents encouraged him to get an education that would provide him with a livelihood as well as job satisfaction. At 3:30 AM, he believed he had bet his livelihood on a pair of deuces.

Chapter 45

The night crew saw the traces of silver and excited murmurs transmitted the news. Tom Cairns grew up in a tough part of Vancouver. He chose to exploit the situation.

At shift end, he described how the crew could keep the find a secret and then come back at a later time and sink a new shaft to mine the silver. He sloughed off questions about ethics and integrity and assumed the crew accepted his scheme.

Most of the members experienced many wrongs in their short lives, but here they found a new start and, now, they regressed. The group of youngsters, with strong survival instincts and weak role models, chose to follow Tom's lead even though they knew it was wrong.

Glen Aspol walked home, showered, and changed. He didn't feel up to breakfast at his girlfriend's home. The conspiracy wore on his conscience. When he knocked on Sally's door, she welcomed him with a smile. But then she saw his face. "Glen, are you okay?"

"Sally, I've agreed to do something wrong."

"What's happened?"

"We found traces of silver tonight and Tom got us all to agree to keep it quiet. He plans to exploit the find later outside of Soul Star."

"Glen, how could you agree to that? Don't you remember your pledge to Soul Star, to yourself, to me? Soul Star is designed to help us all be good citizens."

"I know, Sally. It seemed like the easy way but I feel lousy."

"Well, Glen, this can't continue. How'll you make things right?"

"I must go tell Tom to report the find right away."

"And if he refuses?"

"Let's take it one step at a time."

"No, let's think this through. Maybe Captain Tchir will help you."

"But Sally, if I tell the captain, Tom will be sunk. I must be loyal."

"No Glen, you must be good. Tom will get a few demerit points if he declares the find right away but he may drag lots of people down if this continues. Please go discuss this with the captain. I have stuff for breakfast but this can't wait. Please go see him now."

Glen found Captain Tchir in the coffee shop and asked him to go back to his office. Ole Tchir almost made light of Glen's request when vibes told him to comply without comment. When Glen finished his story, Ole shut off the tape recorder and instructed Glen how to proceed.

Tom answered the door.

"Glen, what brings you here this fine morning?"

"Tom, I realized after my shift that I can't condone concealment of the silver find. I want you to report it to Jerry Gage at once."

Tom grabbed Glen by his shirtfront and dragged him inside. "You lily-livered, non-grate; I offer you a way to fortune and you pretend you're in Sunday school. You're in this right up to your neck. One word about this and your mangled body will be found along the trail and that pretty little girlfriend of yours won't be so pretty. Now get out of here and shut your trap."

Glen stumbled out the door and headed for Sally's home. One of the assistant captains emerged from the shadows and walked with Glen, still rattled by his confrontation.

With Tom Cairns' words recorded on tape, the captain developed a plan. Thirty-seven people worked that shift, including Tom. The captain called Jerry Gage, the manager of the tunnel crews, informed him of the allegations, and asked Jerry to find all of the crew members except Tom Cairns and Glen Aspol. Jerry wondered how a nice kid like Glen Aspol could've got caught up in this mess. The captain admonished each person to be discreet about the allegations.

Tom opened his door a second time within the hour and saw Captain Tchir. He didn't link Glen's visit with the captain's but a crook can put two and two together. He calculated his options.

Should I pull my switchblade on the captain?

The captain's words changed his mind: "Two of my assistant captains are outside the door. They've been informed that you may be treacherous. I carry an activated tape recorder. I request that you come with me to my office. You are under arrest for allegations of breach of trust, advocated breach of trust, and two separate charges of uttered threats against individuals. You are aware of our demerits system; a tribunal will be called to consider the allegations against you. You will be held in custody until the tribunal has made its decision."

The two assistant captains walked behind and paid close attention to Tom's actions.

With Tom in custody, Captain Tchir went to the village hall and interviewed each crewmember, one at a time, as they arrived.

Captain Tchir started each interview: "Our conversation is being recorded. Anything you say may be used against you. Is this your signature? Did you break your contract with Soul Star this morning? Do you wish to explain what happened? Do you wish to remain on the Soul Star project?

For those shift members who admitted the truth, the captain said, "Integrity is the key to all facets of life. You took a huge step forward in this meeting. You'll have your hearing before the tribunal but your integrity should serve you well."

For those shift members who did not admit the facts, the captain said, "Integrity is the key to all facets of life. You took a huge step backward and have threatened your right to continue at Soul Star. You'll have your day before the tribunal but your demonstrated lack of integrity will affect your reputation. Steady integrity, in every aspect of life, from here forward may salvage your character."

Chapter 46

The dais held three tables. At the table near the back sat three tribunal members. Stan Hislop was in the middle. He received the most votes for tribunal members in the annual elections. Along one side was a table designated for the prosecution. Captain Ole Tchir sat alone at the prosecutor's table. Along the opposite side was a table designated for the accused. Tom Cairns sat alone at the defendant's table.

The chairman said, "Ladies and gentlemen, this tribunal hearing is open. The tribunal is recording the words spoken in this hearing. Would the captain please present the allegations?"

Ole rose from his chair. "On the morning of September 14, 2007, Thomas Joseph Cairns gathered the night shift of workers in the Gronson Fjord section of the tunnel and informed them about traces of silver. Mr. Cairns induced the thirty-six other members of his crew to keep the silver find secret for future exploitation outside of the terms of the Soul Star contract. Every member of the crew signed the Soul Star contract. One member of the crew, Glen Aspol, agreed to the breach of trust but reported the incident to me on the same morning.

"In order to substantiate the allegations against Mr. Cairns, I planted a recording device on Glen Aspol. Mr. Aspol went to Mr. Cairns' home and informed him that he could not follow through on the secret plan. He urged Mr. Cairns to go to the manager, Jerry Gage, and inform him of the silver find. Mr. Cairns reacted by saying, 'You lily-livered, non-grate; I offer you a way to fortune and you pretend you're in Sunday school. You are in this right up to your neck. One word about this and your mangled body will be found along the trail and that pretty little girlfriend of yours will not be so pretty. Now get out of here and shut your trap.' One of my assistant captains escorted the shaken Glen Aspol to his girlfriend's home and stayed with them until we took

Mr. Cairns into custody and charged him with breach of trust, advocated breach of trust, and two charges of uttered threats against Glen Aspol and Sally Ann Fenn."

Ole sat down.

The chairman turned to Tom. "Mr. Cairns, please respond to the charges."

The chairman waited.

Tom bowed his head. "When I was three years old…my father beat me unconscious…because I told our neighbour that Dad stole a bottle of rum from him. When my mom tried to stop Dad, he beat her too, broke her teeth and her ribs. I never saw him again. Mom worked two jobs to get us by…but she wasn't home much and my friends were wild. Through it all, I tried drugs, liquor, pickpocketing, armed robbery, pimping, arson…anything for a thrill. I came to Soul Star because I needed a fresh start. While the structure of Soul Star left little room for treachery, I did okay…but the silver find brought back my survival instincts. I did what I did."

The chairman let Tom's story linger. Then he asked the captain to describe the recommended demerits.

Ole rose. "For breach of trust, five points with a gravity of three for fifteen points; for advocating breach of trust, five points with a gravity of two for ten points; for uttering a threat of bodily harm against Mr. Glen Aspol, five points with a gravity of three for fifteen points; and for uttering a threat against Miss Sally Ann Fenn, five points with a gravity of three for fifteen points. I recommend fifty-five demerit points for Mr. Thomas Joseph Cairns."

The chairman looked at Tom. "Do you realize the recommended total demerits approach four times the expulsion limit?"

"Yes."

The chairman turned to the captain. "Mr. Tchir, please explain your logic for the recommended demerits."

Ole stood. "I've studied the Soul Star model and understand that each village is to be a safe haven for those who commit themselves to a better life. I meander through this village an average of fifteen hours every day. I get to know each person and try to be a mentor to all. Most of the individuals in this village have experienced bad things. The Soul Star model has congregated a high percentage of fragile personalities. Each individual came here under specific contract. That contract promised that each individual would receive a chance for an education, an independent source of income, a substantial net worth, and a safe place to live. In return, each individual promised to honour the Good Person Act. Each step of the way, the village has emphasized the importance of trust and safety. Tom Cairns has been through this experience, as have all the others. He made a commitment to meet the ideals expounded by Soul Star.

"Tom Cairns is a bright man. He knows the rules. He rose to foreman because he's capable. He knows how to manipulate. The tape of him threatening Glen Aspol would frighten the toughest of us all. The meek and hopeless speech he delivered today tears at our heartstrings. Soul Star set the demerit point system to achieve speedy removal of incorrigibles but provide a second chance for individuals who demonstrate commitment to the Soul Star model but make mistakes along the way. The demerit points fall off in three years. Tom Cairns can flourish in the outside world. He may even come back after three years and demonstrate that he is a reliable person. In the meantime, he's proven he's not Soul Star material."

The chairman asked Tom, "Mr. Cairns, do you have further submissions?"

"No sir."

The chairman invited questions from the tribunal members. After questions and answers, observers concluded Tom Cairns committed the alleged actions and failed as a good person in the context of the Soul Star project.

The chairman called for a short adjournment and the tribunal members retired to the village manager's office. The tribunal members debated the gravity of the offenses. No doubt Tom

Cairns committed all four offenses. Expulsion loomed without consideration of the gravity factors.

The tribunal deemed deterrence important so other villagers would know that first offenses would be considered grave, as appropriate. The tribunal decided that the gravity of advocated breach of trust should also be raised to three to take account of the thirty-six individuals exposed to Tom's advocacy.

The tribunal chairman reconvened the hearing and read the decisions.

The guilty decision did not surprise, but the order that Tom Cairns be escorted to his home to pack for immediate transport to Winnipeg startled the villagers. Some wondered whether Tom Cairns received a fair chance of appeal with his immediate expulsion. The chairman clarified the tribunal's position: "We recognize that immediate expulsion is dramatic, but we view Mr. Cairns' threats of bodily harm to be so detrimental to the villagers' peace of mind that we do not wish to have the villagers exposed to Mr. Cairns from here forward. We have therefore ordered Mr. Cairns' immediate removal. He shall have the right to appeal to an expulsion jury hearing. We have determined that Mr. Cairns will not be allowed in any Soul Star village without the captain's supervision. Should Mr. Cairns appeal his expulsion, he shall be in the custody of the captain whenever he is in any Soul Star village while his expulsion is in effect.

"This hearing is closed."

Chapter 47

Of the thirty-six individual crewmembers, thirty-one admitted what happened, four denied the allegations, and Glen Aspol blew the whistle. Three tribunals dealt with the charges brought by Captain Tchir against the other villagers on the shift.

One tribunal heard the charges against the thirty-one villagers who admitted the allegations when asked. These villagers received four demerits, based on a gravity of one, on the premise that each encouraged the breach of trust by original acceptance of Tom Cairns' proposal. All thirty-one villagers left the meeting with four demerit points for the next 1,100 days.

A tribunal who heard the charges against the four who initially denied the allegations, but later admitted loyalty to a co-worker, received more demerit points than the captain recommended. Captain Tchir recommended assignment of nine demerits on the basis of one charge of encouraged breach of trust and one charge of lying to the captain. The captain recommended a gravity index of one for each offence. However, the tribunal increased the gravity of the lying charge to two. These four villagers entered the next three years with fourteen demerits with no demerit room before consideration of expulsion. This decision rang harsh in the eyes of the villagers and considerable dissatisfaction ensued. Since there was no expulsion ordered, the fourteen demerit points stood.

Glen Aspol's tribunal hearing caused more controversy. The captain recommended Glen Aspol be spared any points because of prompt disclosure of the conspiracy. The tribunal determined Glen committed the same offence as the other thirty-one villagers and assigned the four demerit points. Many villagers thought that the tribunal sent the wrong message because honesty deserved more consideration.

Chapter 48

Glen Aspol and Sally Fenn married later that year and proved pillars of their village. They never incurred another demerit point.

On the day that Glen's demerit points fell off, the village celebrated.

Louise de Lona described One Page's nightlong drafting binge and her excitement when she recognized the force for good represented by the Good Person Act.

She presented inaugural One Page Citizenship pins to Glen and Sally Ann.

Chapter 49

How do you keep track of a project this complex?

Beth Ragouski mulled this over as she stared at her Thunder Bay task list. She knew that a detailed business plan would be essential to Soul Star's development. No other founder would manage the database to monitor the forecasts and actual results.

Beth could continue with her professional practice and stay aloof from Soul Star—a sane, businesslike thing to do—or she could exit her practice and place her faith in Soul Star. The thought of this radical, pie-in-the-sky project stretched her powers of reason but she believed in Soul Star. This brought her back to the question: How do you keep track of it all? Brett hooked her with the sketchiest of real plans but with vision, passion, and justification that stirred pioneer spirits, even in those individuals with no visible pioneer spirit.

Beth opened an unscheduled meeting with her senior assistant on Monday morning.

"Molly, how would you like to buy this business?"

"Do you have terminal cancer; did all your smarts escape on the weekend? What's going on?"

Beth smiled. "You know I discussed the northern Canada project called Soul Star, with Brett Larson. I want to be the person who keeps tabs on Soul Star. You know how anal I am about details and systems. Well, Soul Star is already full of visionaries and can-do characters who'll pay attention when events hit them in the face. I want to be the one who is responsible for Soul Star's reports."

"That's nice, but you're the key person in this business. Who runs it, who finds the projects, and who generates the funds to pay the bills?"

"You do, Molly."

"How do you get paid for this business?"

"I believe my goodwill is worth sixty percent of one year's gross fees. I propose that you buy the business for $240,000, payable at ten percent of the gross fees collected until you have paid me $240,000 without interest. If gross fees continue at current levels, you'll be the one hundred percent owner in six years."

Molly thought of the downsides. "What if I fail?"

"I know you. You won't fail. I've decided to go to Soul Star full-time, so things will change around here. The changes will be significant. You might as well be the player as the pawn. Think about it and we'll talk again tomorrow. I don't have to make immediate arrangements but I have an agenda and I'll follow through."

Molly had worked with Beth for eight years. She knew the business and the systems but she didn't have Beth's skill, incisive commentary, and business drive. Molly gathered her thoughts.

How do I find projects? How do I figure out the issues and provide valuable advice? How do I replace the gross fees that Beth generated? Who does the administration when I'm doing the projects?

A plan emerged. Molly developed a perspective that would allow her to accept this proposal with enthusiasm but she recognized the challenges.

Beth made her decision without input from Brett Larson, Thompson Miller, or One Page. On Tuesday evening, she called all three and told them. They expressed their appreciation consistent with their personalities.

Brett appreciated assurance of solid administration.

Thompson assumed he could have found an individual to fill the role.

One Page recognized his "one-page, keep-it-simple" model would be strained by Beth's conventional background and penchant for thoroughness. Deep down, Oscar knew that Beth would be relentless and the bases would be covered. While a necessary element in the progress of Soul Star, he knew Beth would be an irritant.

Extreme chunking of big challenges into many smaller challenges is an excellent way to design the forecast and the actual accounting database: the myriad chunks covered surface rights, mineral rights, environmental approvals, aboriginal claims, tunnelling, roads, railroads, pipelines, wildlife management, environmental protection, living quarters, social responsibilities, citizen building, democratic initiatives, share ownership, litigation threats, ad infinitum.

A revelation hit Beth: She appointed herself the key person in a complex administrative model that involved small business, big business, government, not-for-profit, international relations, conflict resolution, research, and education—all of this to be done on a cost-effective basis with transparent integrity and fairness.

Beth started the business plan. She recognized a formal written business plan is the best way to refine the challenges and identify the variables. It would be the skeleton on which she would develop the series of documents that would serve the needs of the variety of participants.

Her gut told her that Soul Star would continue to feel real to those millions of individuals who dedicated so much to Soul Star; her mind saw her as insane.

Chapter 50

Through the years, Lex worked his way through college, received a PhD in sociology, and specialized in dysfunctional youngsters. Simon Fraser University asked him to search out new approaches to deal with troubled youth. Every learned article he read replowed old ground. Not one new line of thought emerged. He might fail. Little failures are effective but monumental failures must not be tolerated.

Lex bought an old Volkswagen Westphalia camper and headed up the Alaska Highway. He followed the route the American soldiers beat to Alaska. He'd heard the top of the world highway in Alaska, just beyond Dawson City, constituted the eighty-ninth wonder of the world. Lex observed the Mile Zero Post in Dawson Creek, the Trutch Mountain scenery, the obese woman emerge from the Liard Hot Springs, the moderate climate in Anchorage, the salmon run south of Fairbanks, the gold rush remnants in the Yukon, the top of the world highway, the clear skies, and the brisk chill in the air. But no sociological revelations crossed his path.

He sauntered south through the Yukon and happened into a coffee shop in Watson Lake. Every table was occupied. A waitress said, "Please follow me. I bet George will welcome a visitor to his table."

The waitress said, "George, would you allow a traveler to sit with you for dinner?"

George stood and smiled. "Hi, I'm George Zhong; please have dinner with me. Here in rural BC, dinner is at noon, supper is the evening meal."

"I'm pleased to meet you, George. Lex Thorn. Thanks for your hospitality."

"Where're you headed?"

“I'm on my way back from Alaska. I’m a university professor with a project that has me flummoxed, so I took a notion to go somewhere new.”

“What’s your project?”

“I specialize in troubled youngsters. Breakthrough insights have been nonexistent for several years and I agreed to find a new approach. Massive failure is not in my lexicon but I’m close, because I don’t have a thread to follow.”

George considered Lex’s explanation. “I’m a specialized farmer here in Watson Lake. I raise vegetables, fruit, and flowers in a climate not suited to warm weather crops. I’m a consultant on a project that’s under construction across northern Canada. My task is to help each village of about three hundred people raise vegetables, fruit, and flowers right in the villages and as cost effectively as possible.”

“What kind of project is this?” asked Lex.

“Will you promise not to laugh when I tell you?”

“Okay, I promise.”

“A tunnel from southwest of Whitehorse near the Pacific coast to Bersimis in the mouth of the St. Lawrence. The tailings from the tunnel are used to build a surface road, railroad, pipeline, and townhouses across Canada. The project’s called Soul Star.”

Lex absorbed all this. “Are you serious?”

“Yeah, I'm serious.”

“What’s the genesis of this idea?”

“Funny you should ask; I suspect you’ve tripped on the solution to your university project. A visionary named Brett Larson wants a viable alternative to the welfare system in Canada. He believes small villages provide the best environment for people who lose their way in life. He looked for a way for these people to earn a livelihood. If you stick around for a few dinners and suppers, I expect we’ll both learn a bunch.”

Lex hesitated. Warm weather crops grown in a dumb place and a huge project so bizarre that Lex couldn’t quite bring himself to believe it.

George sensed Lex's concerns. "You told me that you didn't accept monumental failures but you teeter on the edge of monumental stupidity. My wife, Cindy, is a teacher here in Watson Lake. We both long for new perspectives in a place where PhDs are rare. Let me call her and see if she'll encourage you to stay with us for a few days. We'll let you sleep in a real bed adjacent to a real bathroom instead of that tin tent."

Cindy asked George to put Lex on the phone. She invited Lex to spend a few days with them. Lex agreed and landed in a center of ideas and goodwill that regenerated his enthusiasm.

Chapter 51

Back at Simon Fraser University, Lex bubbled with ideas. He lined up meetings with Brett Larson, Oats Wolfe, One Page de Lona, Thompson Miller, Beth Ragouski, and Rosie Savard. He assimilated the Soul Star ideas and put those ideas into the framework of existing sociology models and jargon.

He realized Soul Star provided a variety of Petri dishes, each one influenced by the individuals, the climate, the wildlife, the aboriginal influences, the money, the players, and the geography.

Lex designed a private university to be built along the Soul Star line with unique experiences for university students committed to individual responsibility and willing to study in the north. He saw value in many disciplines in the midst of a unique world-scale project.

Chapter 52

Lex searched through aerial photos. With something over 4,000 kilometers to choose from, he wanted to find the right valley for his university. He got in his Westphalia and headed for the Alaska Highway. He drove to Watson Lake and chartered a plane. He and the pilot flew east; both men watched for the valley and checked the location in degrees of longitude and latitude. Lex asked the pilot to fly over the site from several directions. With no place to land nearby, the explorers flew back to Watson Lake.

Lex discussed his vision with the pilot. He mentioned his disappointment with the surrounding environment.

The pilot, who never spent an hour in a university lecture hall, asked, "Do you want the students to see the north or a suburban oasis? Should a university touch on reality here and there?"

By the time Lex drove back to the lower mainland, he decided that UIRIT University would emerge in the Stoddart Creek valley.

Chapter 53

Wolfgang Schneider nursed a glass of beer in a hotel in Toronto. His mind wandered through the implications of a major German company involved in a segment of Soul Star. His week in Canada yielded a barrage of information. Thompson Miller met him at the Toronto airport and escorted him to a private plane that flew them north of Toronto to the Soul Star right-of-way and then west to the Pacific Ocean. Wolfgang anticipated a Lear jet but Soul Star chartered a prop plane. The scenery, audacity of the project, and depth of commitment of the principals intrigued Wolfgang.

Some weeks earlier, the Board of Kunz Fast Iron Works instructed Wolfgang to develop an inspiring merchandising plan. The consultants, retained by Kunz Fast, left him unconvinced. Exploratory meetings with four firms yielded no inspiration.

One Friday evening, Wolfgang and his wife shared a meal in a little restaurant in the south of France. Wolfgang overheard fellow diners talk of a university project in northern Canada.

Wolfgang approached the table. "Excuse me; I'm Wolfgang Schneider, President of Kunz Fast Iron Works in Hamburg, Germany. I overheard a little of your conversation about the university project in Canada and I suspect we would support it. Would you and your guest join my wife and me for a drink after dinner?"

Lex hesitated. "My friend leaves for the airport in forty-five minutes. After I see him off, I'll be happy to meet with you."

His dinner guest, a world-renowned authority on youth psychology, was amused by the unsolicited interest of a business executive who overheard snippets of the Soul Star conversation.

When Lex joined Wolfgang and Greta at their table, Wolfgang explained his mandate and fruitless quest. Lex told the story of his Simon Fraser University project, trip to Alaska, and discovery of Soul Star. He described his UIRIT University idea on Stoddard Creek. Greta excused herself and went back to the hotel room. Wolfgang and Lex talked until the hotel staff asked them to leave so the restaurant could close. As they parted, Lex recognized an opportunity to further youth research and Soul Star progress.

Wolfgang's imagination raced. Instead of going to bed, he walked along the beach.

How does Lex Thorn, UIRIT University, and Soul Star integrate with Kunz Fast Iron Work goals?

Greta awakened to find Wolfgang missing. She wondered about a mugging. But, she also recognized that Wolfgang walked alone to think through issues. She hurried into clothes and looked in the open coffee shop in the hotel and then outside. She headed to the beach, walked to the end in one direction, then headed in the other direction. She came upon an outdoor café; there she found Wolfgang oblivious to the world.

"It's good that you're alive."

"I'm sorry, Greta. Ideas enthused me and I knew I couldn't sleep. So, I walked along the beach and lost track of time. When the sun came up, I realized I'd walked the night away but I didn't want to disturb your sleep so I stopped here for coffee. I should've gone back to the hotel to let you know. Please forgive me."

She turned back toward the hotel. "Some romantic weekend this turned out to be."

"Will you have breakfast with me? I know I'm wrong and I apologize. The project for Kunz Fast has challenged me for weeks and I believe I've found a solution. Please listen to my plan and critique it and then I promise to be the romantic from ten o'clock this morning through to Sunday evening's return to Hamburg."

"This better be good or the romance won't be."

"Did you notice the ease with which Lex allowed events to evolve without extensive intervention by any authorities? He expects individual responsibility to be dominant, not just a concept to be talked about and ignored. The plan that I've designed goes like this: Kunz Fast will agree to fund one section of Soul Star. We'll choose the closest section to Lex's university that's still available. From that involvement, we'll learn many lessons from Soul Star and the Canadian culture. We'll fund a chair at the university that'll encourage the study of European approaches to business bureaucracy and individual responsibility and we'll seek out projects in every municipality in Germany where we'll demonstrate the power of individual enterprise in ways that will illuminate German structural weaknesses in non-confrontational ways. This will be the Kunz Fast program—and it'll be a success. I know it will."

Greta thought about Wolfgang's proposals. "What kind of projects will you fund in Germany?"

"I envision a selected Kunz Fast employee whose task will be to go around to every municipal authority and ask them to identify the site in their municipality that's the worst challenge for their administration. It might be a slum, a contaminated site, a derelict bridge, any defined site.

"Kunz Fast will utilize our youth development program to change that site into one that will show visitors what can be done with financial responsibility and the power of individual enterprise and responsibility. Kunz Fast will share responsibility for the project but it'll expect that the participants in the project will assess the issues, design the solution, receive appropriate approvals, find funds, and execute the development. Because no government investment will be expected, there'll be a commercial aspect to the projects so that investors may be recompensed by the success of the project.

"We'll use our expertise and influence to encourage the municipal authorities to provide definitive approval, or rejection with specific identification of reasons for rejection, after submission of the plans.

"Kunz Fast will have rights to every aspect of the project and will use those rights to enhance the youth development approach, the reduction of bureaucracy, the reputation of the municipality, and the reputation of Kunz Fast. At the German federal government level, Kunz Fast will negotiate guidelines, which will optimize the net benefits of the project within the confines of federal laws and policies."

Greta sat back. "Whew, this is a massive commitment for Kunz Fast. Do you think the directors will commit money to your dreams?"

"They asked me to develop an inspirational program for the company. I believe I've done it. Besides, it's difficult to judge the effectiveness of promotional campaigns. Why don't we use our budget to develop thousands of young people, improve blight throughout the country, improve the German business climate, and make Kunz Fast a household name in a positive manner?"

Greta smiled. "You amaze and inspire. Now, let's put that adrenaline to use."

Chapter 54

A middle-aged woman, well dressed, walked into the Tim Horton's on 108th Street. As she walked through the outer door, she noticed a young girl who stood between the outer and inner doors. She walked past the girl then looked back at a face of despair. "Are you all right?"

Her lip trembled. "I left home and have no place to go."

"Please come with me and have a chair. I'll get some coffee so we can talk."

The girl hesitated. She did not know this lady, and did not expect any favours from a stranger. But her gut let her follow the lady to a table.

"Why did you leave home?"

"Nobody understands me."

"I have an appointment with a friend. I dropped in for a coffee to drink on my way to her place. Let me phone her." She said, "Sarah, I'll be delayed for an hour or so; I've met a young lady who needs help."

Then the lady said to the girl, "Please come to the counter and we'll get you something to eat and drink. You might like hot chocolate or some other drink and breakfast. My name is Chrissie Harris. Tell me a little of what's happened."

"My name's Krista Wallace. I left home in a rage last night. When I asked a friend to let me stay with her, she refused." Tears brimmed her eyes.

"Oh, Krista, that's rough. How'd you get through the night?"

"Dawn came. I walked some more, further away from home. Before you arrived, I saw this Tim Horton's. I came through the outer door, but I didn't want to go in and be told to leave. I didn't want to spend my money in case I needed it later. That's when you stopped to talk to me. I thank you for that."

"Do you think your mom is worried about you?"

Krista nodded.

"What's your mom's name and phone number?"

Chrissie called. A man answered.

Christie said, "Is Tara there, please?"

"No. Can I get her a message?"

"I'm Chrissie Harris. I'm in a Tim Horton's coffee shop with Krista. We're worried that Tara doesn't know where Krista's at or that she's okay."

"She's looked all night for Tara. She's got her cell phone; I'll give you the number, and I'll give you time to phone her but I'll tell her that Krista's found and safe."

"Thank you. Krista will be okay."

When Tara answered the phone, Chrissie said, "I'm Chrissie Harris. I'm in a Tim Horton's coffee shop with Krista. She's okay. Please go back home. I'll drive her home as soon as we finish our coffee and hot chocolate."

Chrissie turned to Krista. "Krista, tell me about your life."

"Fifteen years ago, my father left my mom. I stayed with Mom. She worked a day job and a night job, but I knew she was bitter and unhappy. Much of that affected how I viewed the world. My dad moved away from town and some of the day-to-day animosity went with him. My mom dated; unfamiliar men showed up. Sometimes these guys criticized me. Sometimes Mom would side with them and sometimes she would side with me but I saw myself as an unloved inconvenience. Then mom met my stepdad; they married. Their sons capture most of their attention. My views and need for attention go unnoticed, or criticized. I don't feel I have a place to call home. Sissy devastated me when she turned me away. I never guessed my best friend would turn on me."

Krista stopped. Tears rolled down Chrissie's cheeks.

Chrissie swept the crumbs off the table. "I have two children, a boy and a girl. They're grown now and have their own families. When teenagers, they experienced some frustrations but our family struggled through. They grew out of those teenage troubles. Now, they're well-adjusted. I want to help you but I know you must decide that you're responsible for your own life. I don't know if you will decide to do that ever, and I don't know if you will decide today, but I'm certain that you have the capability to go forward and make a happy life for yourself. You can also choose to be a joy to your mom."

"I don't know what to do or to where to start."

"Well, let's get you home. If you want, I'll be your friend. Perhaps we can find a path for you to follow."

When they got to Krista's home, Krista asked Chrissie to come with her and meet her family.

Tara came to the door and opened her arms to hug Krista. Tara looked to Chrissie and mouthed, "Thank you."

Krista turned. "Mom, this is Chrissie Harris."

Tara extended a hand. "Thank you for helping Krista. I've been worried sick all night. Krista and I have much to talk about. Thanks, again."

"You're welcome. I hope the two of you can find your way. Goodbye."

Tara closed the door. "What possessed you to wander the streets all night?"

"I feel so alone. I know you care about me, but your focus is on the boys and Larry. I sort of understand, but I need more. Then Sissy turned me away."

As they walked into the kitchen, Larry replaced the coffee pot. "Krista, you're selfish. Your mom has been up all night."

Krista opened her mouth but stifled a retort.

Tara stepped forward. "Larry, no more."

Chapter 55

Two weeks later, Tara told Krista to cancel her campout because Larry wanted Tara to go with him on a trip to Las Vegas and Krista would watch the boys.

"Why are Larry and the friggin' boys more important than me?"

"Don't talk to me in that tone, young lady. You live here, you will contribute."

Saturday morning, the boys watched cartoons on TV. Krista found Chrissie's number and called her.

"Chrissie, this is Krista. Can we talk?"

"Of course; what's the matter?"

"My mom took off with Larry and left me with the boys. I cancelled a campout planned with my friend, Josephine."

"Did you tell her how you felt?"

"Yes, but she didn't listen."

"I follow news stories about a project in northern Canada where the management provides an alternative to the welfare state for people who have lost their way and want to make a fresh start in a new environment. I kept some articles. I'd like you to go through them and see if you think this might be a way for you to get a fresh start."

"I don't know if I can leave home for good, if I can make my own way, if I can be responsible."

"It's okay to be frightened but it's not okay to give up. I'll drop the articles off for you to read."

When Chrissie arrived, Krista invited her in to meet the boys and offered her coffee.

Krista opened the folder and read the news of Soul Star. Articles described the motivation for the Soul Star project, the Healthy Habitats Ribbons & Jewels project, the mining school, the pioneer conditions, the Good Person Act. Some criticized the project.

Could I thrive in an environment like Soul Star?

She put the folder aside and got the boys to their soccer games.

Chapter 56

Several weeks went by in relative calm.

Krista's final basketball game day arrived. That afternoon, Larry phoned Tara to say he planned to go with some friends to a lacrosse game. Tara tried to change Larry's mind so she could go watch Krista play. Larry refused. Tara tried to find a baby sitter on short notice on a school night. No luck. When Krista got home from school, Tara told her what happened.

"Did you tell him how important this is for me?"

"Yes."

"Do you see why I feel left out?"

"Yes. I'm sorry, Krista."

"I will make changes."

"What kind of changes?"

"I have to find a place where I'm as important as the individuals around me."

"You know I love you."

"Yes, I know but you have mixed obligations. I'm the one who has to go."

"Oh, Krista, what're you thinking?"

"I've heard about the Soul Star project in the north. I'm going to look into it."

"Krista, no, that'll be a rough crowd, you won't get a proper education, your life will be in shambles in just a few months."

"But it'll be the shambles that I make. I've got to do my homework before the game."

The next evening, Krista got out the Soul Star folder. She looked under Soul Star in the Edmonton phone book. She found no number. She phoned 411 and asked for the Soul Star project in northern Canada.

The operator said, "I have a number for the Thunder Bay head office and a number for the Calgary office."

Krista said, "Please give me the Calgary number."

The next day, Krista phoned Soul Star from school at a period break. A lady answered. Krista described her circumstances.

The lady said, "We have an alliance with a firm in Edmonton that helps us locate and sign up young people to work on Soul Star. I'll give you the name and number of the person you can talk to."

Krista wrote down the name and number.

Do I feel okay with this? Should I phone this person in Edmonton? I don't know. In the last two weeks have I ever been happy? I don't think so. There've been many times when I existed and times when I got along with Mom, Larry, and my stepbrothers but I don't think I've been happy in the last two weeks...or the last two years. What do I see in the next two weeks, or the next two months, or the next two years that will make me happy? I don't see anything. If that's my circumstance and if the Soul Star project appears to be a fresh start, why wouldn't I do that?

Krista phoned and talked to a man who agreed to come and visit with her and Tara.

The man described Soul Star and the Gronson Fjord section. He described the investor group that happened to be a company from Norway and the young Norwegian manager, Per Aasie, who got partway through university and then decided he wanted a real job, so he took on the management of the Gronson Fjord section. Gronson Fjord needed all kinds of workers: miners, teachers, and service providers for the Recreation Center.

Then he described the Good Person Act and the expectations for individual responsibility by all villagers; encouragement not to be mixed up in drugs and alcohol and cigarettes.

They talked until suppertime. At the end of the discussion, the man said, "Krista, my expectation is that you'll find satisfaction if you choose to go to the Soul Star project. Once you're there and you see how the village is laid out and what the work is in the tunnel, you can choose from the opportunities. Will you make a commitment to be responsible for yourself from here forward?"

"I have to try."

The man took Krista's phone number and said he'd phone the next morning with instructions for Krista to get to Gronson Fjord and who to report to when she got there.

Chapter 57

Tara sat beside Krista on the couch. "Are you prepared to walk out on us?"

"I'm sorry, Mom. I guess I am."

"Krista, you're loved. I should've communicated with you better. Please forgive me."

Krista went to the office of the trucking firm where she was to wait for a ride up the Alaska Highway to Gronson Fjord.

What will happen to me? How do I trust strangers? I'm leaving all familiar things. This must be like a young person in war-torn Europe embarking on a new life in a new country; an amalgam of apprehension and exhilaration.

The trucker arrived. "Hi, I'm Gus. I understand you'll ride with me to Gronson Fjord."

"Hello, Gus, I'm Krista and I'm anxious to be on my way."

A few miles out of Edmonton, Gus glanced over. "If you could name one famous person as a role model, who would you pick?"

"What, are you my shrink?"

"We have a long trip ahead of us and I have lots of time to sit in silence when I have no travel companion. I've hauled people to Soul Star for a few months now and I've concluded that an unusual question causes meaningful conversations."

"Okay, I choose Michelangelo."

"Well, Krista, that's the first time I've heard that answer. What inspires you about Michelangelo?"

"Well, I start with his skill. Then I think of his determination under difficult conditions. Then I think of his self-study where he dissected cadavers of humans and animals to understand how muscles and tendons work. Then I think of a creative genius dedicated to a life of servitude to the Catholic Church. Through it all, I see a strong, talented, driven individual who accomplished much."

When Krista glanced over at Gus, he looked toward her and smiled. "That's a beautiful answer, Krista! Do you think you'll emulate Michelangelo's traits in your life at Soul Star and beyond?"

"I've mishandled my life so far. I hope I'll do better from here forward."

"I've observed many individuals at Soul Star. Most of them messed up their early lives and look for a fresh start in a supportive environment. For those who try to improve, Soul Star appears to be a winner."

The conversation continued on many fronts for the entire trip. Once they got to the Soul Star right of way, Gus described the various villages they passed and pointed out the variety of approaches that each village employed to build the tunnel and community. Gus radioed ahead. They came to a stop near the Gronson Fjord General Store. Per Aasie greeted Krista.

Chapter 58

"Good morning, Mr. Larson. I'm Gorman Goulash with the Canadian Broadcasting Corporation. I'd like to interview you for a story on Soul Star."

Brett didn't respond.

"Are you there, Mr. Larson?"

"Yes, I'm here. I don't know how to answer a request from an outfit I don't trust."

"Why don't you trust the CBC?"

"I believe that widespread individual responsibility and enterprise is important to every element of society. In my perception, CBC Television has eroded, ridiculed, and maligned every individual and every organization that has tried to reinforce individual responsibility. You pretend you represent Canadian culture but a majority of Canadians believe in individual responsibility. Our form of representative government, combined with government funded and sanctioned institutions, forces collective responsibility on the masses, even though the majority of individuals believe in individual responsibility."

"Would you suggest some examples of cases where you believe that CBC erred?"

"The Carter Commission, Ralph Klein's election in Alberta, the National Energy Program, the start of the Reform Party, the long-gun registry, stop signs."

"When could we meet?"

"Whenever you like."

Chapter 59

Eight weeks later, on a Saturday night, the Montréal Canadiens hosted the Vancouver Canucks. Instead of a second hockey game broadcast from the west, the CBC presented a special program.

The news anchor said, "Good evening, Canadians, from coast to coast to coast. Welcome to this special CBC presentation entitled 'Shared Ethics'. Organizational theory includes the concept of continuous improvement. Tonight, we announce a significant improvement."

A video of Canadians in many urban and rural settings provided background as the narrator continued.

"Our chairman observed there might be disappointment with the CBC's view of fairness in the minds of the silent majority, who seldom make their thoughts apparent to opinion leaders."

A picture of a report filled the screen.

"The Fairness Institute recently published a report which declared the CBC perpetuated unfair bias."

The screen changed to a shot of Brett Larson looking up at a Soul Star symbol.

"In the same time frame, Brett Larson, the founder of the Soul Star tunnel project, indicated he didn't trust the CBC to be fair."

A montage of CBC coverage flashed by.

"While the CBC has been around a long time and we're accustomed to criticism, we decided to review our approach. We undertook a thorough examination of our concepts of ethics and fairness and concluded our approach didn't conform to a code of ethics and fairness acceptable to a large majority of Canadians. We've revised and published a code of ethics and fairness that we will follow. We'll promote this Canadian shared ethic as a worthy model for the entire world."

A picture of a stop sign filled the screen.

"Mr. Larson pointed to the stop sign as a metaphor for unreasonable law and made the point that the CBC never made any effort to lead a discussion of stop sign fairness. We explore the rational use of stop signs in our first segment."

Pictures of many sights along the Soul Star line rolled.

"Our second segment presents the Soul Star tunnel project."

The screen reverted to a picture of the narrator.

"We invite every Canadian to reflect on the CBC's adjusted set of ethics. We feel good tonight. We're confident that most Canadians will endorse our new approach and we assure our many supporters we'll continue to be a messenger for Canadian values. We hope our new code will support a more visible expectation that individual responsibility is a required component in productive lives. Enjoy the presentation and let us know your reactions to this initiative."

Chapter 60

Villagers thrived on Krista Wallace's education programs at Gronson Fjord. She'd shown aptitude from her first days there. The village manager introduced Krista to Cindy Zhong. Cindy recognized Krista's potential and encouraged her to lead the schooling in the village as well as champion education along the entire line. Fourteen months into her role as lead educator, Krista brimmed with enthusiasm.

Today, she presented her ideas for extensive theme parks along the Soul Star route to Cindy Zhong, Thompson Miller, and Hymie Friedenberg.

Krista received the resumes of these three individuals when she received notice that a panel would hear her proposals. As the four individuals settled in the boardroom, Thompson Miller opened the discussion. "We're privileged to have Krista Wallace here to present her education ideas. Krista."

"Thank you for this opportunity. I'm young. I may not have considered all of the implications of what I'm about to propose, but I've considered many and trust that you'll approve these suggestions.

"I am the lead teacher in the village of Gronson Fjord. Our village is blessed with many individuals who have potential. We develop that potential. Our methods are supported by most of the villagers. We put each villager 'in the moment'. This involves farm work, garden work, debates, plays, concerts, field trips, fairness initiatives, and all manner of involvement that gets each villager in the environment covered by the topic.

"I sense that we have an opportunity to create legacy learning opportunities for thousands of students, far into the future, along with experiences for millions of tourists. I propose theme parks be built while Soul Star is built. This will allow students to put themselves in various cultural and era situations for generations to come. I propose four parks located about a thousand kilometers apart along the tunnel route. The four themes would involve an Iron Age Village modeled after Norway's history, a full-fledged Norman castle modeled after England's history, a significant stone wall modeled after the Great Wall of China, and a full-sized pyramid modeled after Egypt's history. We would utilize stones at least as hard to handle as those in the original structures.

"In order for all Soul Star villagers to experience these four theme parks, each village's personnel will move four times. This will allow the people in every village to continue the camaraderie of their own group but experience life in a village somewhat near to each of the four theme parks and then be back at their original village before the project is completed. They'll experience the weather, terrain, and conditions at four places across the nation.

"The surface to tunnel level varies across the country, so the move of village personnel will allow balanced work and challenges that arise with differences in elevation and climate. These theme parks will add to the cost and time required to build Soul Star. I remind you that our vision is to build solid citizens out of rough-cut youth. I know the excitement inherent in projects of this magnitude will yield enthusiastic participation and pride far beyond the marginal costs.

"I propose the villages adjacent to each theme park be funded by the Individual Responsibility Foundation because various ethnic and cultural interests could hijack the theme parks to enhance particular agendas. I prefer the theme parks be Canadian ventures under the control of broad-based Canadian supervision. Once Soul Star and the theme parks are completed, students can continue to teach generations of students and host generations of tourists. If built with the quality and craftsmanship used in medieval times, these theme parks will serve for hundreds of years.

"As an example of the most difficult aspects of my proposal, I imagine how authentic pyramid-sized stones might be cut at tunnel level and placed in the pyramid. I picture a pyramid site where the granite is near the surface so the pyramid foundation should be rock solid, so to speak. The access to the tunnel will be built at a slope that will allow a railroad to be built from the tunnel to the center top of the pyramid so that the stone blocks can be hauled to the correct level of the pyramid on the railroad. At each level, some heavy equipment will be designed to lift and place the stones on that level. I propose to use our diamond saws to cut the proper sized and shaped stones from granite at the tunnel level. I've identified a location where the granite is close to the surface and the pyramid can be built on a dominant knoll where no earthquake has ever been recorded. While the historical pyramids honoured kings, I hope our pyramid will enclose a giant dome; a place for people. Below, we can build a ramp down to a mausoleum in recognition of Egyptian history.

"My friend teases me that this is just the latest pyramid scheme. I hope you'll consider my proposal as much more valid than a dishonest profit scheme.

"Thank you for your attention. I'm prepared to stay until you've had enough."

The three seasoned listeners did not react for a few seconds.

Then Hymie rose and clapped. Cindy and Thompson followed with smiles.

Krista exhaled and smiled. "Thank you," she mouthed.

When the applause subsided, Thompson turned to Hymie. "Well, cheerleader, tell us what you think."

"Krista has thought this through and takes a passionate leadership position. I expect all of the theme parks are feasible, but there'll be many critics. I suggest we appoint an advisory group for each park so lots of creative diversity is brought to bear."

Cindy nodded to Krista. "Thank you, Krista; well done! I agree with the concepts. I don't want the parks to be misdirected by various interest groups, even conventional educators. We must include good techniques without sacrificing the creativity necessary to make each park excel. How might we achieve the right outcome?"

The conversation went on for two hours.

The committee recommended four committees be struck, one for each theme.

A search would be made for the four individuals who would be the champions, one for each theme park. The champions would solicit one-page submissions from around the world. The authors of the submissions would be invited to comment on any aspect of the proposed park: location, climate, design, venues, techniques, upkeep, staff, ownership, tourist accommodations, hospitality, safety, aesthetics, government intervention, and any other topic.

The champion and the committee would assemble all of the submissions and draft a detailed project plan to be vetted to the Soul Star board.

As Thompson left, he reflected upon the magical results that can be achieved by empowered individuals. Krista's vision augured well for thousands. He would use his leadership skills to make sure that Soul Star and the Individual Responsibility Foundation supported the theme parks.

While Thompson didn't know how to cause huge stones to rise to their place in the pyramid, he expected it to happen. He knew that the tomb deep inside the pyramid would not hold the mummified body of Brett Larson but a simple Soul Star, symbol of the eternal strength of the human spirit.

Chapter 61

Beth wondered why a sixty-year-old tackled a ten-year project and why the village carried the Twisted name. Full of questions, Beth showed up at the manager's office. "Good morning, I'm Beth Ragouski."

"Welcome, Beth. I'm Twyla Smithson. I'm pleased to meet our financial steward. What would you like from me?"

"My goals are threefold: one, I want to get to know the key personnel in every village; two, I want to understand why your section performs so well; and three, I want to consider all the good ideas that each village offers so that our entire project is as effective as possible. Those are my official goals, but my unofficial goal is to understand why a woman who appears to be around sixty years of age heads up a project called Twisted that could take you into your seventies."

Twyla grinned. "I think your first two official objectives and your unofficial points of interest can all be answered together. The good ideas line of inquiry should include several other members of our team and a little preparation. I'll try to get that organized for this evening. In the meantime, I'll tell you my story this morning and lead you on a detailed tour of our operations. After noon, I'll leave you time to go wherever you want and strike up conversations with whomever you wish. Please tell each person your name and your role."

"Thank you, can you spare the time?"

"Yes, the crew is supposed to run without me and I'm committed to values evident in Soul Star. I want to enhance the life experiences of every individual who's exposed to Soul Star."

"Thanks, Twyla, fire away."

"I grew up on a mixed farm in northern Ontario. When I graduated with a civil engineering degree, I ended up working in a Calgary construction conglomerate. I met my husband Silas in Calgary. He's part of an entrepreneurial family. Soon, his brother Bart and I went out on our own and built a successful company that contracted out to most of the large construction companies in southern Alberta.

"For thirty years, we operated that business. We brought in one younger family member and three arm's length employees. As the business thrived, Bart went on to other business activities and the relationships that we built started to fray. Petty jealousies, genuine differences of opinion, perceived differences in commitment, perceptions of other family members, and historical instances of unfairness all festered, multiplied, and poisoned relationships.

"I'm the oldest, and I wanted to slow down. I got squeezed out for an unfair share of the spoils, but a drag-'em-out fight would've further poisoned family relationships and worn down our health. I accepted a low price. It yielded remarkable relief from the poisoned atmosphere.

"I took three months off to travel and regain my enthusiasm for business. Silas and I hiked north of Fort St. John, BC, where we met some Indians. They invited us to a noon meal. The conversation happened to touch on the life of Oscar One Page de Lona. The natives enthused about One Page, how he helped them with many legal matters, and how he helped youngsters find meaning on the Soul Star line.

"When I returned from the sabbatical, I looked up Oscar de Lona and suggested I manage this village. It's a gradual slope bearing a twisted mess of deadfall. I walked the designated kilometer and thought about the project. I thought about the many misconceptions that festered in our family business. I thought about the many troubled men who worked on construction sites. I thought about the despair on the faces of youth who got into trouble or ran away from home. I thought about a comfortable retirement complex with no use for my skills and no fulfilment. I thought about spaghetti that is so full of promise one day and a cold, tangled blob the next. Out of it all, I decided to christen the village 'Twisted'. My goal is to make whoever—and whatever—I touch less twisted."

"What did your husband think of this adventure?"

"He resisted. I reminded him of my contribution to our family, how I accommodated his interests and kept the family solid. Now, he's an enthusiastic mentor for the villagers here in Twisted. He shows his range of skills to every villager who exhibits the slightest interest. He works full-time here with responsibility for maintenance and safety throughout the village, with primary attention to the lifts and conveyors that move people and tailings."

"So tell me why you think the Soul Star model works so well."

"There are a multitude of reasons. I believe the essential ingredient is the dysfunctional youth have above-average smarts combined with a contrarian streak that causes them to resist conformity. Soul Star adopts a minimalist set of rules that the most rebellious accept as justifiable. Soul Star demands—and expects—individual responsibility. Soul Star encourages and facilitates initiatives by villagers' to achieve fairness. Soul Star respects every individual."

"That's a beautiful answer."

"Thanks. I hope your tape recorder worked because it sounded pretty good to me, too."

"I'm not the least bit religious but Soul Star's approach causes me to wonder if this isn't a conception of heaven I could endorse. Do you see spiritual elements in the Soul Star project?"

"That struck me as I visited a few villages. I liken the Soul Star vibes with the first impressions one gets in a room, or a town, or a valley where everything feels good. I've talked with hundreds of visitors who express some variation of this theme when they talk of their visits to Soul Star villages."

"Thank you so much; it's been a rich experience. I know you'll arrange a session with key members of your team so I can learn the ideas that make Twisted not so twisted."

"Glad to be of service. See you soon."

Chapter 62

Hartland Slate came to play a league baseball game against the Granite of Gronson Fjord. The manager of Slate approached Glen Aspol, the manager of Granite. "Glen, we have only eight players. It looks like we'll have to forfeit the game."

"We can lend you a player, John. We have twelve players here."

"Are there rules against such an accommodation?"

"I don't know, but our team will honour the results no matter who wins."

"Okay, thanks, Glen. See if one of your players will play against his team."

Glen went to his team members, described the situation, and asked for volunteers. Gary Smallford, a skilled infielder and a good hitter, volunteered.

Slate better be happy with this addition to their team.

Gary Smallford played second base for Slate. In the bottom of the fourth, Granite advanced a runner to third base with two out. The batter popped up just deeper than Gary Smallford. He drifted back and caught the fly to end the inning. As Gary prepared to field the ball, a fan from Gronson Fjord hollered, "Drop the ball, Gary, drop the ball!" The support of the fans indicated the homer instinct trumped the commitment of every individual to always do the right thing.

The umpire watched, thought about the situation, and decided to confront the fan and demonstrate a point to the entire group. He called "time" and walked over to the fan. "I request that you come out to home plate and apologize to everyone for your disregard for Soul Star values."

The fan laughed. "Get lost, you stuffy old fart."

The umpire went first to the manager of Slate and informed him that he wouldn't continue the game until the fan apologized or the captain arrested him under the Good Person Act. John agreed. The umpire approached the manager of Granite and got the same approval from Glen Aspol. He then went out and stood on home plate and addressed the fans: "Ladies and gentlemen, I've requested that the fan who advocated that Gary drop the ball for home team advantage should come here to home plate and apologize."

The fans chanted and criticized the umpire. The team managers walked out and stood with the umpire. Each time the crowd noise subsided, the umpire resumed his speech. Each time, the crowd drowned him out.

The police captain noticed the commotion and proceeded over to the ball diamond. He took in the scene, walked out to the umpire, and asked for clarification. When he understood, he took two steps toward the crowd and raised his hand for silence. In dead calm, he announced, "I'll arrest the offending fan, Corey Sylvester, and escort him out of the park. Each one of you who supported Corey has failed Soul Star's principles. The game will continue once Corey and I have left. I request you conduct yourselves with the fairness and good sportsmanship for which our village and the Soul Star project are respected."

The game went on with a subdued crowd.

The game was tied in the top of the ninth inning. Slate's star singled with two out. Zee Zee moved halfway to second base and taunted the catcher. In the past, whatever the catcher decided to do, Zee Zee would run to the unchosen base. Glen Aspol was fed up with this tactic and decided to teach her a lesson. He called "time," then explained to his catcher how to stop Zee Zee. As play resumed, the first pitch was a ball. Zee Zee went halfway to second base and taunted the catcher. But Zee Zee's strategy collapsed when the catcher kept the ball and trotted out to the pitcher's mound and beyond. Zee Zee's face went pale. She bluffed toward first and took off for second base, straight into the tag of the second baseman, who caught a short flip from the catcher.

In the bottom of the ninth, with the bases loaded for Gronson Fjord and two out, their best hitter came to the plate. On the first pitch, the hitter fouled off to the first-base side. Everyone assumed the play harmless but a streak caught everyone's attention. The catcher discarded his mask and ran. At the last instant, he threw himself headfirst into the chain-link backstop. He came up with the ball and a smile. Blood ran down his face around a flap of skin torn from his forehead and drooping over one eye.

The game added to Soul Star folklore. Discussions went on for days about the umpire's actions. Some supported Corey Sylvester.

Soul Star's opinion leaders took care to reinforce the umpire's message that everyone must strive to do the right thing, every moment, every day.

Zee Zee continued to star in the league, stealing the most bases with conventional tactics. She let her hustle and skill speak for her. Fans admired her and a buzz gripped the crowd every time she got on base.

The formal recognition of the catcher's superlative effort led to the inauguration of the "Beneath the Surface" trophy. The inspiration for the trophy came out of the baseball league but the trophy transcended every sport. Every village annually awarded the "Beneath the Surface" trophy to the villager who best exemplified qualities on which society flourishes. It did not matter how popular, how attractive, how smart, how privileged, how skilled, or how connected an individual might be, the trophy went to the villager who best embraced fundamental qualities with positive exuberance, execution, and citizenship.

Chapter 63

"As Minister of Education, I asked each of you here this morning so we could decide how to proceed with Soul Star issues. Please listen as I play a tape of a series of interviews that took place between Jerry Greismith of our department, Krista Wallace of Gronson Fjord, and five villagers."

He hit the PLAY button.

"Thank you for meeting with me, Ms. Wallace."

"Just call me Krista."

"Okay, Krista. We allege that you're not qualified to lead any education program in this province. I'm here to establish the facts and suggest solutions."

"Do you believe your accreditation and experience in conventional school systems qualifies you to judge the approaches used to teach the Soul Star villagers?" Krista asked.

"Yes."

"Good, because we have special demographics here. Our biggest group represents individuals who slipped through the cracks in their home communities. Our next biggest group includes bright people who chose not to conform to some middle-class ideal. The rest are unique individuals who rejected conventional arrangements. Our villagers represent those individuals that underperform every day in every school in every province in this country. We strive to deliver education in a way that encourages them to be model citizens instead of burdens. We hope for a fair-minded review."

"You don't have to be defensive. I'm here to help."

"That seems unlikely."

"I've brought along a questionnaire that every school in the province completes annually to ensure the school meets provincial standards. Will you complete the questionnaire?" Jerry pressed.

"Yes, but I expect the questionnaire will yield unconventional answers to every question."

"Do you see that as a concern?"

"Yes, I expect your coworkers will lay a plastic template over my answers and count the number of correct answers, run the results through a Ouija board, and decide that our program is different. I tell you now, our program is different."

"Can we do the review and then draw conclusions?"

"That appears to be your process."

"Maybe we can reach a consensus on process."

"I'm game to try. Perhaps we can pursue our mandates with mutual respect and measured tone."

"I can see where we might have different perspectives. How do you suggest we move forward?"

"I suggest you interview three villagers at random and I'll interview two," Krista suggested. "You select the five individuals from a list of all Gronson Fjord villagers. We have a focus group facility equipped with one-way glass for observers. When you interview a villager, one-on-one, I'll observe and listen. When I interview a villager, you'll observe and listen. We'll alternate interviews with you first. I hope the interviews will demonstrate the effectiveness of our program."

"How long can an interview last?"

"As long as the individuals wish to continue."

"What happens if I challenge the assumptions of the program?"

"Most villagers have experienced adversity. I suggest you'll fare best if you treat every individual with respect."

"What should happen after we complete all of the interviews?"

"I expect you'll conclude our programs effectively deal with individuals who have not conformed to the province's perception of normal and I expect you'll have some suggestions to further improve our programs."

"What if I conclude the programs have to be stopped because they don't conform to Alberta policy?" Jerry asked.

"Then you'll reinforce my disgust with blind bureaucracy."

"You're one tough woman."

Krista chuckled. "I'm glad you noticed."

"I believe your approach will work. Let's get your list of villagers and I'll select the interviewees."

The minister of education stopped the tape and inserted another.

"Hello, Kurt, I'm Jerry Greismith. I work with the Provincial Board of Education. Krista Wallace has suggested that I'll learn about village schooling if I visit with you and two other villagers."

"Okay."

"How did you come to be a villager at Gronson Fjord?"

"I turned sixteen and started grade ten in a new high school. A boy and two of his buddies picked on me. I endured torture as those bastards burned my stomach with live cigarettes, locked me in a storage shed, and pretended to set the shed on fire. They built a fire beside the shed and let the smoke blow toward the shed. I thought I'd die. This torment went on from mid-September until December seventh. I remember the day well. I contrived to be noticed by the bully after school."

Kurt laughed bitterly, then continued. "But this time, he learned a lesson. One of his sidekicks walked with him. When the bully came around the corner, I swung my baseball bat as hard as I could. I heard bone splinter and saw his rearranged face as he hit the ground. His sidekick came at me and yelled. I swung again and his leg broke. A motorist slammed on his brakes and ran over. I handed the bat to him and waited. The place swarmed with ambulances, police, schoolteachers, and onlookers. The police charged me with assault with a weapon. I went through court. Individuals who could've noticed my predicament and could've helped me experienced tinges of embarrassment but none stepped forward. I received a criminal record, three years' probation, and saw no one as my friend, especially my parents. I left home and took odd jobs."

"What happened then?"

"With no skill and no direction, I remained unhappy. One day, I lunched in a truck stop with a trucker who I helped load some lumber that spilled in a rollover on a cloverleaf. As we ate, another trucker came by that knew my employer. They chatted and I pieced together that the other guy drove for Soul Star. After he left, I asked my employer about Soul Star and he said he'd ask his friend how to get hold of Soul Star. At seventeen, I ended up at Gronson Fjord. Now I'm nineteen and excited about what I can do."

"You seem to have put the bullies behind you. I can empathize with your predicament but can't condone violence."

"Do you play cards?"

"Yes, sometimes."

"Do you understand that the game requires you to follow the rules of Bridge, Hearts, or Poker?"

"Yes."

"If you are dealt a lousy hand, do you ask your competitors to trade some of their good cards for your poor cards?"

"Of course not."

"So, you play the hand as best you can and lose, right?"

"Yes."

"But you know that your life, your sanity, and your self-respect will be intact after the game, right?"

"Yes."

"Well," Kurt resumed, "I studied my hand and I saw my life, my sanity, and my self-respect in jeopardy. I didn't know how to survive the hand and tilt the game in my favour for future hands. I saw my best card as the baseball bat."

"The ace of clubs, I suppose. How did the bully and his friend make out after your attack?"

"The bully was still in hospital, with restorative surgery, when I last heard about him. I'm quite sure he bullied no students from December seventh until he got out of hospital." Kurt chuckled. "The sidekick got a pin in his leg and wore a cast for a few weeks. I hope his aches and pains are sufficient to remind him to treat every individual with respect."

"So, how did you make arrangements to come to Gronson Fjord?"

"Well, the trucker got me the number for the Soul Star recruiter in Edmonton. He arranged a telephone interview with Hymie Friedenberg in New York. His aunt detonated a grenade that killed three Gestapo soldiers, her parents, and her in a desperate effort to preserve dignity in the face of evil. This put my act of desperation into perspective. The entire Soul Star team insisted I take responsibility for my life from here forward. I committed to sign—and abide by—the Good Person Act."

"What's the Good Person Act?"

"Every villager signs the Good Person Act, which requires us to take responsibility for our actions in every aspect of life."

"How do I get a copy of this Act?"

"Krista will give you a copy."

Jerry paused. "So, how do you get your education?"

"Each villager agrees to stay in Soul Star for ten years. The term is broken into five modules of two years each. I started out in the England module, now I'm in the Egypt module, I'll go to the Norway module next, then the China module and, finally, return to Gronson Fjord. These five modules involve the entire village inhabitants moving four times to be somewhat adjacent to the feature exhibit for each module and end up in the village where we started. We bring rock to the surface as we build the tunnel. This allows us to build structures that symbolize each of our modules. In the Egypt module, we are building a pyramid similar to the ones built in the Middle Ages. Every villager adopts a personality from the year 1000 A.D. through the present. As one personality reaches a notional lifespan, the villager adopts a new personality. We experience some semblance of the knowledge base, technology, living conditions, careers, et cetera through the last thousand years. Each villager chooses a personality, within some guidelines, so that the role has a good chance to resonate. Much of our education revolves around the major module themes and our participation with our fellow villagers. At the end of construction for Soul Star, the villagers will own a piece of four major educational and tourist attractions. We'll have pride in our education and the facilities we helped create."

Papers shuffled through the tape recorder's speakers. "Well, Kurt, I appreciate your explanations. I could discuss this with you for hours. However, I'm scheduled to meet with two other villagers and I'll explore many aspects of the modules with them. Before you go, though, I'd like you to tell me what you think of the education you receive here at Soul Star."

Kurt gathered his thoughts, and when he began again, the smile was obvious in his voice. "Soul Star is special. This environment provides a safe, compassionate place for each of us to grow and learn. Days here are worth years in the schools I attended from kindergarten to grade ten. I can't imagine a better place to learn."

"Thank you, Kurt. Good luck."

"You're welcome, Jerry."

The tape was silent for a moment, then started up with Krista interviewing Sonya.

"Hi, Sonya, how're you doing?"

"I'm fine. Why am I here?"

"We have Jerry Greismith from the Provincial Department of Education with us. He'll assess the effectiveness of our program."

"He's come to the right place."

"Yes, I believe you're right but he doesn't know it yet."

"How do we show him?"

"I suggest you give a quick sketch of your life before you got to Gronson Fjord and then we can talk about your experience with the school here. Jerry will get a transcript of this interview."

"Okay. I spent the first fifteen years of my life on an Indian Reservation near Fort St. John, BC I spent many terrified nights, alone, in our cabin. My father left and Mom was bipolar. She coped by leaving the Reservation. I haven't seen her since my thirteenth birthday. The neighbours watched out for me. I survived. My education failed me. Sometimes we started the year with a good teacher but the teacher always quit before Christmas. I missed school because no one supervised me, and I didn't care anyway. When I turned fourteen, three high school boys raped me. I told the police but they didn't believe me."

Sonya paused. "At fifteen, I moved into Fort St. John and became a hooker. One of the johns brought me food as part payment. After a while, he brought me a drug instead of food. The drug provided temporary release and I wanted more of it. He came to me once a week. He wouldn't tell me the kind of drug. So, one night, I threatened him with a knife. He told me the drug.

"That night, I left Fort St. John and went to Edmonton," Sonya continued. "I got involved with a pimp who kept most of my income but left enough for me to feed my habit but not enough to live in a decent place or eat properly. One night, a contingent of conventioneers showed up. I negotiated with a john and serviced him. When I asked for my money, he told me that his boss would pay. I knew that wouldn't happen so I dressed and put on my lipstick. Then I turned on him, still naked on the bed. My lipstick tube turned into a switchblade. I stabbed him three times in the stomach and said, 'Here's your receipt, in triplicate'. He started to come after me and I said, 'If you want to live, you'll stay quiet, where you are, for three minutes'. Then I left. I knew my way around the hotel and I vanished. A few minutes later, a fellow conventioneer found the man bleeding and bawling."

She paused. "The police pieced the story together and charged me. My story made big news in Fort St. John. Oscar One Page noticed. He came to visit me in jail and asked me if I'd consider Soul Star. The remand center and jail were hell. My drug habit went unsatisfied and my pretty face made other prisoners jealous. When Oscar One Page came for another visit, I told him I'd go to Soul Star. He arranged for me to come to Gronson Fjord as soon as my parole went through. He insisted that I take control of my life. I didn't know what that meant."

"What happened when you got to Gronson Fjord?"

"I roomed with another mess of a girl with a different background. We built our suite, enrolled in school, and worked in the tunnel. When the teacher realized I knew so little about reading, writing, arithmetic, social studies, and all, she designed a program just for me."

"Describe the key pieces of her program."

"She asked me to write a journal. She suggested that I write about my life from as early as I could remember. I could write anything I wanted. She promised that she'd help me write two other versions of my journal. One would be in the exact order that I wrote my original stuff but corrected for grammar, spelling, and politically correct words. Then she said she'd help me put my entire journal into a coherent book with common themes, no duplications, and riveting action."

"Did you like the approach?" Krista asked.

"At first I hated it. I couldn't think how to start my story and I didn't know how to spell or use grammar. But, she helped me figure it out and she told me that my original would provide a benchmark against which I could compare my later versions and also see how my basic thoughts could come alive in the final story."

"How long did you work on the journal?"

"My teacher suggested that I plan on fifty-two stories over one year, one per week. My schedule went okay but then we, over three months, created a novel. My teacher knew about a movie called Sliding Doors in which a woman's life unfolded in two ways—one when she got to the sliding train doors before they closed and one when the sliding doors locked her out of the train. To help me learn about life, my teacher and I debated ten different situations in my life where one person made a decision that could have gone a different way. We imagined what might have happened and how my life might have turned out with different decisions. One of our fantasies became the storyline for one of our drama club plays. In the end, for my novel, we chose the sliding doors event for my life as the day I told Oscar One Page I'd go to Soul Star. We spent most of the rest of the story on my vision of how my life would turn out. We also thought about what might have happened if I chose to ignore Soul Star."

"How did that story play out?"

"Not as bad as many would assume. I concluded that my good looks, skill set, street smarts, and health would have allowed me to mature a bit more, kick the drugs, and become a waitress in a roadside diner. I'd fall in love with a mechanic in the truck stop and become a stay-at-home mom with two normal kids in a midsized city. We all knew it could have turned out much worse."

"What else did you do to further your education in those first fifteen months?"

"I worked a full shift in the tunnel. At first I ran a diamond saw but I found I liked work on the concrete tunnel liner where we poured daily as the tunnel progressed. My teacher got me to calculate many aspects of the project. We did volume calculations, ratios of cement, aggregate, water, hardener, et cetera. We estimated what differences would arise when the raw shape of the tunnel caused us to use less or more liner material. We projected how much rock would be hauled to the surface on our section. We calculated amounts of man-hours, saw blades, food, power, minerals mined, and how many homes would be built along the entire tunnel and hundreds of other aspects of the project. Other villagers, guest speakers, company sponsors, environmentalists, and anybody who provided a perspective helped put this in context. Sometimes, the school arranges debates with the guests, sometimes we have question-and-answer sessions after the presentation, sometimes we have our own debates after the guests leave. All the while, our group is studying a thousand years of history with segments in Britain, Egypt, Norway, and China. We also read a classic book every two months. The books have to come from the same era that is in focus in our thousand years of history work. The classic books are hard for me because most aspects are unfamiliar: the history, the words, the class system, the genteel customs, the strange places on land and sea. I know some things very well, the power of sex, the duplicity of individuals, and the ineptness of bureaucracies."

"Did all this activity drain you?"

"Not drain, it lifted me." It was clear that she was smiling, due to the changed tone in her voice. "My life has meaning. My senses are alive and I have self-worth. Now I believe that I can make a difference in this world. Good and bad things happen daily. I believe I choose better when good and bad situations arise."

"Soul Star's name inspires," Krista said, changing the subject. "You have not mentioned any supernatural influences in your life. How do you feel about your soul and God?"

"You know my personal beliefs are off-limits."

"You're right. But I'd like to hear your perspective."

"I'll comment, but this is off the record and must not affect any education considerations."

"That's fair; I'll get Jerry's commitment to respect your privacy on this matter. Go ahead."

"My Reservation seemed hopeless. The social system included native police, aboriginal supernatural beliefs, and missionaries. When I tried to reconcile religious beliefs with our circumstances, I concluded that religion did not answer our problems; belief in the supernatural did not help and might harm. Ask me again when maggots fill my orifices."

"Do you recognize how articulate you are today?"

"Yes, I know I've come far and I'm blessed."

"Thank you for our time together and for your contributions to Soul Star."

"You're welcome. I hope the spy makes good use of the information."

Krista laughed. "Right on, you're special, Sonya! Take care."

Next, Jerry Greismith did his second interview.

"Good morning, Miss Talisman, I'm Jerry Greismith."

"Good to meet you, Jerry."

"What brought you to Gronson Fjord?"

"Eighteen years old, dissatisfied with life, I looked for an inspiring career. A few weeks into my search, I noticed a newspaper article and it leapt at me. Here I am."

"What did you do prior to Soul Star?

"I grew up in Prince George, BC My dad worked in management for a pulp mill. Mom stayed home with my two younger brothers and me. I caused trouble in school because I was bored. The school authorities often disciplined me."

"Tell me what you did to irritate the authorities," Jerry pressed.

"Well, in grade ten, I noticed our teacher always barged into the room just at the bell to start the period. So I convinced a fellow student to remove the pins from the hinges on the classroom door and leave the door balanced on its hinges. I got the whole class to stand at the front of the classroom at the start of the class. Sure enough, Old Smarty barrelled into the class and the door crashed to the floor. We all cheered. Then, we saw a second man with the teacher. The school superintendent said, 'I'll come back when your students behave with reasonable decorum'. The escapade reached further than I anticipated."

"What discipline followed?"

"The class stonewalled the investigation, so we all served detentions for a week and wrote papers about respect for teachers and school property."

"So what did you learn from this incident?"

"Nothing much."

"Describe your most dramatic prank."

The woman chuckled. "That happened on Valentine's Day of my senior year. I itched to cause excitement so I encouraged all the girls at the school Valentine's dance to go topless. We cooked up a signal for every girl to remove her top and bra when the DJ played Garth Brooks' song, 'The River'. I expected five girls would join me. When Garth sang the second stanza, I pulled my top over my head, undid my bra, and draped it around the neck of my dance partner. Most girls sported bare breasts. Some were left with only panties and shoes. One girl explained, 'I wore a dress, when I took off my top, the bottom came too'."

"I've never heard of such a ridiculous stunt. How did the school handle it?"

"Three sets of parents and half a dozen teacher chaperones appeared stunned, amazed, impressed, outraged, embarrassed, and angry. It made the local news for days. As the instigator, I got kicked out of school four months before graduation. The others got suspended for two weeks."

"So, you did learn from this shameful performance."

"Yes, I learned lots: I have leadership skills, school lessons, presented well, will endure for a lifetime, no boy at that dance will ever forget his almost hands-on experience, and the penalties for brazen, non-criminal activity are inconsequential."

"So, you ended up with no graduation and you call that inconsequential?"

"I graduated," Miss Talisman said. "Once I got kicked out of school, I drove around the province asking to be enrolled in a different high school. Without fail, the principals asked why I got expelled. The first twenty-seven principals told me to move on. I came to a little school where six teachers covered twelve grades. The former principal resigned and the young man who taught grades ten through twelve acted as principal. He laughed when I told my story. He enrolled me in grade twelve so I could write the departmental exams but he loaded me up with extracurricular tasks: the track meet, yearbook, field trips, and a few lesson designs for him and the other teachers to use to inspire the kids to learn. I started school on March seventeenth, a little over a month after my topless adventure."

"How did you design the lessons to help students learn?"

"I put the kids in the middle of the action. The more capable students accepted tougher roles so that every student exceeded prior accomplishments. I included classic literature, dramatic historical events, rebellion against authority, situations attractive to kids with active hormones, and politically incorrect approaches. A few parents ranted and many students took my side in debates that swirled in May and June. The teachers couldn't believe the engaged students.

"The principal scheduled the graduation ceremony for mid-May. But the enthused grade twelve students told the principal they wanted to hold the graduation after the last exam—to make it a true celebration of their graduation. When the principal resisted, the seniors told him they would boycott the graduation. He went through with the mid-May graduation ceremony and dinner. The valedictorian attended because she had made a commitment. She described the ceremony to me. About two-thirds of the parents came to the ceremony even though their own child refused to go. The mayor gave the keynote speech. He presumed the students would bend to authority. He expected most of the grads would attend and crafted his remarks around the superior education system and the need for constant vigilance against disruptive influence—but when he arrived, the principal told him that only the valedictorian had come. The valedictorian said she enjoyed that moment. The mayor addressed the assembly: 'I came here tonight prepared to extol our education system and speak out against disruptive influences such as Terri Talisman. Now, we've lost the respect of our graduates. What are we going to do? I will assist in finding solutions'.

"The principal thanked the mayor and introduced the valedictorian, and she smiled and delivered her address," Terri continued. "When I heard I was going to be interviewed, I found my copy of her speech. Please read it before we go on."

Jerry read the transcript of the speech. It said:

"'Good evening honored guests, parents, teachers, and friends.

"'I believe the teachers and students selected me as valedictorian because I exemplify the qualities admired by our community: dedication, skill, leadership, conformity, and niceness.

"'In many respects, I like who I am but there have been ordinariness in my life that I didn't recognize until April seventh, when I became aware of the best thing that's happened to this town. I became aware of Terri Talisman. She's a star. Do you recognize she brought the students alive in a very few weeks? The teachers are engaged, the students are enthused, parents wonder, and we're all better off than we were when Terri arrived.

"'I'll present my valedictory address on June twenty-ninth, the day the graduates suggested that the ceremony should be held. Even though our principal's brilliant admission of Terri Talisman to our school is appreciated, he ignored our request for a change of graduation day because he's accustomed to force. I hope that every parent, teacher, and civil authority recognizes that real leadership counts. Notice the vacuum when leadership fails. Please come back on June twenty-ninth and witness an inspired graduation ceremony with enthusiastic graduates, front and center. Terri Talisman has gathered sufficient funds to pay for tonight's wasted dinner so the school will not be out-of-pocket for the uneaten food.

"'Tonight, I'm pleased. My fellow students stood behind their request. I would've stayed away tonight if not for my commitment to speak.

"'Goodnight.'

"The audience walked out." Jerry concluded the speech and paused in thought. "How did you find such a rebellious group of students?"

"They're everywhere."

"Well, Miss Talisman, I'll consider your perspective. I wish you well. Thank you."

"You're welcome, Jerry, bye."

Then, Krista Wallace interviewed her second villager.

"Good morning, Charlie, how're you?"

"Mornin', Krista, I'm okay. What's going on?"

"We have a visitor who's interested in our education program. He's selected five villagers to be interviewed. He'll interview three and I'll interview two. We'll record the interviews and compare notes afterwards to see how the programs can be improved."

"Why did he pick me?"

"The luck of the draw, Charlie; I gave him a list of all of the villagers enrolled in our programs without any extra information."

"How come I'm always the one they pick on?" Charlie sighed.

"Why did you come to Gronson Fjord?"

"Frustration."

"Do you remember you agreed to take charge of your life from that day forward?"

"Yes."

"Do you remember our discussion about how good and bad things happen and the way to happiness is to learn how to handle each good thing and each bad thing?"

"Yes, but it's hard."

"Charlie, look at me. Tell me if you have a comfortable home here at Gronson Fjord."

"Yes."

"Do you have reasonable food to eat?"

"Yes."

"Do you have a job you like?"

"Yes."

"Do the people frighten you?"

"No."

"Do you feel you're safe here?"

"Yes."

"Do you believe the teachers and villagers help you deal with your issues?"

"Yes."

"Can you think of a better place for you to be?"

"No."

"Do you understand you have to take responsibility for your reaction to incidents?"

"Yes, but it's hard."

"You've never been in an interview like this before, have you?"

"No."

"So, you believe this is a bad thing, right?"

"Yes." Charlie laughed.

"But you could view it as a good thing, couldn't you?"

"Why would I?"

"So each new thing becomes easier to handle."

"That doesn't make sense."

"Well, let's see if we can make sense of it. This review by the Provincial Board of Education is important to Soul Star and Gronson Fjord. We have excellent ways to teach our villagers but we're different. The bureaucrats could force change upon us. We don't want that. But, if we shrink away and believe the world is picking on us, it will. Instead, we'll present our case as well as we can, we'll defend our programs with vigor, and we'll succeed. I see these interviews as a good thing. We have an opportunity to show what we've accomplished and what we will accomplish. Believe and come alive, Charlie."

"You're amazing."

"It all depends on your perspective. Jerry Greismith views me as an uneducated, incompetent nobody. But, we'll show him. Won't we, Charlie?"

"Yeah, Krista."

Laughing, Krista continued the interview.

"You left home at sixteen, didn't you, Charlie?"

"Yes, my adoptive parents didn't understand me."

"Did you feel like a failure?"

"Yes."

"Did they feel like failures, too?"

"Yes."

"What did you expect to achieve when you left home?"

"I didn't know. I just expected to reduce the unhappiness in me and them."

"Did you?"

"Not at first. I moved to the city and hung out with some street kids. They did petty crime, drugs, vandalism, and graffiti. I stole enough to stay alive but I saw a bleak future in that environment. I decided to end it all so I ran out in front of a pickup truck. I misjudged—the pickup swerved but knocked me unconscious. The driver went to my hospital. When I regained my wits, the young driver waited outside my room. When the nurses allowed him to come in, he asked me why I had done that. I told him of my despair. He listened. He questioned. He seemed to understand. Finally, he said, 'I'm unhappy too. I've lots of advantages but I need more'.

"As I recovered, this driver visited me every day," Charlie continued. "One day, he told me about Soul Star. He'd decided to join up. He asked if I'd go with him. We talked about it and I decided to try it. He thrives here but I struggle."

"Why do you struggle, Charlie?"

"I don't know. I expect so much, then I fall into a funk."

"Do the villagers treat you fairly?"

"Oh, yes. They expect lots from me but they seem to understand when I fall apart."

"How long do you think they'll tolerate your lack of progress?"

"I don't know. They're already edgy with me."

"Do you realize many of us in Gronson Fjord are pulling for you?"

Charlie paused. "Yes, but I still might fail."

"You won't fail unless you decide to fail. I bet you'll decide to succeed and you will succeed. Didn't I see you with a cute little gal from Saskatoon last week?'

"Yes, I'm in love with her but she doesn't trust me."

"Will you show her that you can be trusted?"

"I'll try, but it's so hard."

"Charlie, you've used that line several times. You lie. Stop it. I know that Cecily is a wonderful young woman. You'll do well to pay attention to her and build her respect for you. I promise the rewards will be extraordinary."

"Do you think she'll love me, Krista?"

"Your odds are a lot better if you make yourself loveable. You're worth it, Charlie. Don't let yourself down."

"Did I do okay in this interview, Krista?"

"You did fine, Charlie. You illustrated how Soul Star can work with individuals who haven't yet discovered their worth. You're on the road to success. Don't you dare drive over the white lines! Thanks, Charlie. See you around."

"So long, Krista."

The tape was silent for a minute, then Jerry Greismith did his last interview.

"Hello, Tack. I'm Jerry Greismith."

"Hi."

"What's your last name, Tack?"

"It doesn't matter. I'm just Tack."

"Of course it matters. How do you distinguish all the people with the same first names?"

"Funny Bill is mega rich and his friends have first names like Weird Harold and Fat Albert."

"Oh, you mean Bill Cosby?"

"See, even you can communicate if you pay attention."

"How did you learn about Soul Star, Tack?"

"Rosie told me."

"Who's Rosie?"

"She's my bestest friend in the whole world."

"How did Rosie know about Soul Star?"

"I don't know. All I know is she's a half-breed who went to school in Winnipeg and became a famous environmental leader."

"How did you get the name Tack?"

"I have trouble with speech. Because I'm different, people pick on me. In grade two, an older boy started saying I wasn't the sharpest tack in the box. The other kids laughed but I didn't know what the words meant, so I asked my teacher. She explained. From that day forward, I insisted I'm Tack."

"What do you do here in Gronson Fjord?" Jerry asked, changing the subject.

"I have two jobs. One is lead stagehand and the other is Gronson Fjord ambassador."

"Tell me about your lead stagehand job."

"Brett insists every villager tackles work, school, and life with gusto. We involve every villager in social situations so they feel part of the action. There are lots of plays and I help with the stage props and watch for things that don't seem quite right. Even though my mind plods along, I notice things others don't see. I really, really want each play to be special."

"Do you learn as you help with the plays?"

"Sure I do. When my parents and brothers come to visit, they're happy with the things I'm able to tell them. They used to pretend to be happy. Now they're really, really happy and that makes me really, really happy."

"What about your ambassador's job?"

"We have a Good Person Act at Soul Star. Every villager must obey it. Our villagers come from places where they got away with disobedience. They think they can disobey here too. But Captain doesn't let anyone disobey."

"Who's Captain?"

"His name is Ole and the villagers elected him to be our cop. But we never call him a cop; we call him Captain. Like the captain of a hockey team."

"How do you do your ambassador's job?"

"Well, I told you that I notice things that others don't," Tack answered. "Plus I tell people when they do something they shouldn't. I overheard Arnie say that I'm as simple as a child. I asked Captain what that meant and Captain told me that Arnie and all the other villagers appreciate how honest and natural I am. I'm really, really proud to be ambassador for Gronson Fjord."

"Have you ever made a mistake that caused Captain to punish you?"

"Yes, once."

"What happened?"

"Well, we're not supposed to leave garbage around. One day I noticed a tin lid. Someone left it on the ground, so I picked it up and throwed it as hard as I could. Well, it circled like a bird and landed in a group of children. It hit a little boy's head, above his eye, and blood squirted everywhere as he ran to his mom. She got very upset. Pretty soon everybody agreed with her. I curled up in a corner of Captain's office and wouldn't talk to anyone. When I got hungry and sore, I went home and people didn't talk to me like they used to. I was really, really ashamed."

Jerry quickly asked, "What happened then?"

"Captain said my carelessness hurt little Sammy. Three judges listened as Captain explained what happened. All three judges asked me questions. They told me I got five points against me for 1,100 days. I cried. I count the days until I can have the points removed; 914 days. I really, really want to be perfect. I really, really try to never get any more points."

"Good for you, Tack. Are your parents happy with you here?"

"Yes. They used to be ashamed of me even when they pretended to be proud. Now they brag about me. They're really, really happy. My brothers are really, really happy. And I'm really, really happy."

"Will you leave Gronson Fjord one day?" Jerry asked.

"Never, even a dull Tack will stick when driven hard enough."

Jerry asked, "Are you the comedian in your skits?"

"No, but I am not as really, really dumb as a boy smelling pussy."

The Minister of Education stopped the recorder and spoke to the audience.

"Well, ladies and gentlemen; that's the end of the interviews. Jerry Greismith went back to his office, reviewed the policies of the department and the terms of our collective agreement with the teachers, and concluded that Krista's approach, though superior to anything we've accomplished in decades, did not follow our rules. He drafted the letter, which I'll read to you now.

Ms. Krista Wallace
204, 3583 Soul Star Trail
Gronson Fjord, AB

Thank you for the opportunity to visit Gronson Fjord. While your educational techniques have much to recommend them, I regret to inform you our policy, supported by the Teachers' Association, requires accredited teachers with Bachelor of Education degrees to be in charge of every school. Since you do not have the formal qualifications and you refuse to stand aside to make room for someone with the required formal qualifications, I hereby inform you your school will be closed in fifteen days from the date of this letter.

Should you ignore this letter, I inform you I have received formal authority, and encouragement to issue this letter, from the Minister of Education and the Deputy Minister of Education for the Province of Alberta.

Yours very truly,
Jerry Greismith

"As I understand it, three members of the Teachers' Association, who're here today, filed the complaints that led to Jerry Greismith's visit to Gronson Fjord. Those complaints deserve to be considered. Jerry Greismith assembled evidence the Soul Star educational approaches exceed anything our department has managed in the last forty years, maybe ever. What does he do? He decides some complaints and a policy manual should override Soul Star's remarkable success. I've been asked to approve the letter. I can't. Jerry's letter is an embarrassment to each one of us in this room. What I can do is encourage nominal compliance of Krista Wallace's program and reaffirm that education is the objective not turf protection. Do I make myself clear?"

The deputy minister glanced at the complainants before turning to the minister. "Do you have a proposal to achieve nominal compliance for the Soul Star program?"

"Yes, I believe an accredited teacher who lives in Watson Lake has been involved in the design and implementation of the Soul Star approach. She might accept appointment as the nominal head of the Soul Star school system across the province so the letter of our policies can be maintained while the efforts of Krista Wallace's team can continue to educate Soul Star villagers."

"I'm aware of Cindy Zhong, the teacher in Watson Lake. She's capable."

The minister faced the complainants. "Do the members of the Teachers' Association accept this potential solution?"

The three complainants squirmed, hesitated to speak.

"Do the members of the Teachers' Association accept this potential solution?"

One said, "We must preserve the status of the Provincial Teachers' Association as the sole representative of the teachers in the province. We object to recognition of rogue organizations."

"Even when the rogue organization demonstrates superior educational approaches and results?"

"It's a slippery slope."

"Yes, and you're on it."

"We'll report to our executive; you can expect repercussions."

The minister shrugged. "I've made my decision. If Cindy Zhong will accept this appointment, I'll consider the Soul Star education system in compliance and will confirm that in writing. If the Provincial Teachers' Association chooses to make this contentious, I'll face that head on. This meeting is over."

Chapter 64

One Page twisted his pencil in his ear. "I heard a story on the radio this morning. Two young nuns wanted to attend a rock concert in Montreal. To be sure they got tickets, they waited outside the ticket office through the night until the doors opened the next morning. They got their tickets. The next time he stepped out on the balcony at the Vatican, in three languages and somber tones the Pope said, 'They both woke up with bad habits'."

Beth shook her head. "Oscar, you've just insulted a bunch of the folks who support Soul Star."

"It could've been worse—I could've used a full page."

Brett took a seat at the table. "We used to date nurses at the Grey Nuns' Hospital in Saskatoon. We hoped to get under their habits."

Thompson moved to the end of the table. "Enough, I call this meeting to order, uh, the Grey Nuns."

One Page stopped in his tracks. "Did our learned leader just stoop so low as to kid around with us poor peasants?"

Thompson winced at Oscar's jibe. "A momentary lapse. Let's get on with the matters at hand. We need to reach a consensus on how to manage the challenges threatening the foundations of Soul Star."

Beth said, "I've been concerned interest groups might find common ground and mount enough momentum to kill Soul Star."

Thompson handed out the agenda and some supporting analyses. "I hope we'll develop a plan to work our way through. The first issue is the First Nations claim they have inalienable rights to the corridor in seven different places."

Brett summarized the issues and warned that the First Nations issues could be fatal to Soul Star. He went on to assure the group that every effort would be made to gain consensus. The group approved an approach to solving the First Nations claims.

Thompson suggested a bathroom break. When all returned, he raised the second issue: "There's potential four of the five provincial governments and three territorial governments might change the terms of the permits granted to Soul Star. I expect some provincial legislatures will be persuaded to rescind permits by a combination of environmental lobbies, media coverage, business pressure groups, and fear of change."

Brett described how he lay awake at night wondering if Soul Star would be an appropriate imposition on the land and people. He showed them a draft of a decision tree he'd designed to consider the public interest as it might relate to any issue that could cause government to intervene. He suggested the group appoint Thompson to chair a team including Krista Wallace, Terri Talisman, Cindy Zhong, and Lex Thorn.

Thompson handed out a news clipping from the *Globe And Mail*. "The last issue is the media. Conflict is ideal for the media because it provides fuel for story lines. Relentless criticism makes it difficult to maintain enthusiasm."

Brett motioned for the water pitcher and said, "Notice the possibilities in the comments this morning. As I see it, we can benefit from the media if we harness the tendencies in our favour. We can position the conflict, emphasize the helpful issues, and be civil and fair in all our actions. Do you remember what Rosie told us about the Healthy Habitats' board meeting where Gaston Tribolski suggested ways to manage the fallout from the presentation of the corridor routes? Healthy Habitats asked Tribolski how he would manage passionate positions not accommodated in the route chosen. I think she attributed to Tribolski something like 'We'll lead, we'll be civil, we'll be open to compromise, be transparent and fair, and we'll reach out to advocates of all positions'. I think she also said that Healthy Habitats would be neutral. We won't be neutral because we'll be perceived as driven by our own biases."

Brett suggested Gaston Tribolski be asked to assist Soul Star with media relations.

Thompson put his papers in his briefcase. “Most of the time, I take things in stride. This meeting has been an emotional high for me. My thoughts strayed to the stories of Abraham Lincoln and the adversities of the civil war. He led his team to do right. I believe we’ll lead Canadians to a better place. I feel good. I thank each of you.”

Chapter 65

The Healthy Habitats' First Nations project followed a similar evolution to the Ribbons & Jewels project.

Misconceptions about cultures, variances in vocabulary, approaches to private land ownership, assumptions about savages versus civilized individuals, overt attempts to assimilate, attempts to prevent advocacy, atrocities in residential schools, and government assumptions of superiority encouraged controversy around every aspect of the natives' situations.

The failure of governments to consult with the Indians before decisions were made emerged as the fundamental Indian frustration.

In order to make sense out of the rhetoric and provide balance for Indians and others, Healthy Habitats developed the website so each allegation was identified along with the perceived inequity and the perceived original reason for the rule. A current interpretation of the frustration evolved into a narrative that could be laid to rest by the vast majority of Indian individuals. The existence of individuals who wish to prolong the agony ensured that negative publicity and public protest would continue indefinitely.

Consensus coalesced to the point where provincial and federal negotiators signed individual contracts with every interested native. The federal government arranged for a portable video facility to be available in any accessible location in Canada so natives could sign on live television and the contracts could be simultaneously signed by the Governor General of Canada.

Chapter 66

Jocelyn Morning Clear signed the first treaty settlement on March 18.

Negotiated Treaty Settlement

Between Jocelyn Morning Clear (Morning Clear) and the Dominion of Canada (Canada).
This is the sole documentation of the rights and obligations negotiated between Morning Clear and Canada. There will be no recourse against Canada unless Canada fails to meet the commitments in clauses 2 through 5. Recourse against Morning Clear shall be limited to forfeiture of the quarter section of land cited in clause 4 in the case where forfeiture is ordered and sustained under the Good Persons Act. Where the quarter has been disposed of, forfeiture of net worth equal to the gross proceeds on the disposition of the quarter.

A home trust fund of $100,000 will be established within thirty (30) days of the signature on this document. These funds will be available to pay towards the acquisition, or improvement, of a residence of Morning Clear's choice anywhere in Canada. Samuel J. Johnston is appointed as the mutually acceptable mentor to provide sober second thought on any residence acquisition or improvement choice proposed by Morning Clear and funded by the home trust fund.

A Life Security Plan trust of $346,980 will be established within thirty (30) days of the signature of this document. These funds will be available to Morning Clear as prescribed by the Life Security Plan Act, which came into force on January 1. The amount funded in the Life Security Plan shall be the prescribed amount for Morning Clear who is in her 342nd month since birth.

A quarter section of land, legally described as the SW1/4-XX-YY-WZM (in the municipal district "County of Sun Glow"), containing 159.6 acres, will be registered, clear title, in the name of Morning Clear within thirty days of the signature of this document. The title will include all surface rights and no mineral rights. The tax cost of the quarter will be one dollar in total.

Morning Clear will receive thirty-one education coupons tenderable, at her discretion, at any educational facility in Canada, which provides the education represented by the coupon. Successful completion of any prerequisite course is required before any coupon can be used as valid tender. No transportation, housing, room, board, or reference material will be funded beyond whatever the educational facility provides to the general student population.

Morning Clear shall be bound, from this date forward, by the identical laws applicable to individuals not involved in any Treaty situation.
Morning Clear waives all rights to clauses in the Canadian Charter of Rights and Freedoms save those that are available to every individual in Canada.

Morning Clear waives all claims of any description that are not specified in this document or that are not rights available to every individual in Canada.

Morning Clear pledges to use best efforts to attain and maintain a personal net worth of $100,000 outside of her Life Security Plan, a viable education, and a self-sufficient household within ten years of the date of signature on this document.

Morning Clear pledges to refrain from every act of civil disobedience from this date forward.

____

Jocelyn Morning Clear

____

Harold McIsaac
Governor General of Canada

Dated this 18th day of March.

Chapter 67

Consensus emerged that a monument should be built to recognize the historic solution to aboriginal concerns.

Rosie phoned Brett and asked if she could propose Soul Star build the monument on the Soul Star line. She suggested the monument could be built over one of the valleys along the line so hospitality accommodation could be built in the layers of arches under the monument. She asked if an airport might be near enough to accommodate travel to the monument site by air. Brett complimented Rosie on her proposal and agreed to discuss it with the others so that the Soul Star team could reach a consensus.

Chapter 68

The receptionist ushered Lex Thorn into the office of the BC Minister of Advanced Education, Jack Maudler.

"Good to meet you, Mr. Thorn."

"Thanks for the opportunity, Mr. Maudler."

The two shook hands.

"I'm looking forward to it, Lex. Let's drop the formal dialogue and get to the substance of your proposal. I understand you want to start a university where there are no students and no teachers. Governments have done dumb things in the past so I hope you'll show me why your proposal isn't the dumbest one yet."

"Our hopes match. I'm a tenured professor of sociology at Simon Fraser University. Two summers ago, I searched for a genuine innovation to help troubled young people. I took the summer off and traveled the Alaska Highway to Alaska and back. On the way back, I met a couple in Watson Lake, BC. The husband is George Zhong. He's an immigrant from Sri Lanka who grows vegetables and flowers in Watson Lake. She's Cindy Zhong, a Canadian-born teacher in Watson Lake. George and Cindy are technical advisors for the Soul Star project with which you'll be familiar. I spent a few days with George and Cindy as we explored the philosophies utilized in the Soul Star villages. I decided to champion an educational environment built on individual responsibility. A champion for individual responsibility, in an established university, is about as welcome as a panhandler at a state dinner. So, I found a suitable alternative to pursue my vision."

"How'd you do that?"

"I found a polished director who could navigate various bureaucracies while maintaining a commitment to individual responsibility. Thompson Miller is also president of the Soul Star project. Thompson is organizing the Individual Responsibility Foundation. We intend to raise a base trust fund of one billion dollars. The income from the billion dollars will first keep up with inflation and any excess will be used to fund individual responsibility initiatives and scholarships. We'll continue to raise new funds to pursue our objectives. We won't register as a charity that would permit donors to receive income tax deductions for their donations to the Individual Responsibility Foundation. We want our donors to use their own resources, not governments', to fund the activities of the Foundation."

"This all sounds naïve and hopeless."

"I want to design a university experience that'll be more effective than any of us has yet experienced. More like the original universities where inspired, dedicated individuals yearned for knowledge. To achieve that experience, the university has to be unique—not extravagant—and has to expect lots from students."

"I guess you have ideas in mind to achieve this special university experience."

"Yes, maybe some you'll agree with," Lex said.

"I'm listening."

"Thank you. I have a package that I'll leave with you but I plan to present my vision in regular conversation so that you can interject anytime. I don't think you'll need to take many notes because the package addresses all of the issues that we've identified so far. When a new issue arises, we should both make a note so that we can research and document the resolution. The plan provides 10,000 townhouses that will be available for students, teachers, and support staff. With an average of two people per townhouse, we have homes at economical rates for 20,000 people. The homes are cost-effective because they have geothermal heating and cooling and solar power generated by the solar panels on the road surface.

"Food, clothes, recreation, and entertainment will all be grown, produced, processed, and distributed by the residents with the exception of a few items such as sugar, salt, coffee, tea, and the like," Lex continued. "In short, the residents will be self-sufficient in terms of shelter, food, entertainment, recreation, and local travel. There are large windowless areas under the roadways for the entire length of the tunnel. This space, near the university, is available for storage, laboratories, recreation, concert halls, and any activity that does not require ambient light. We've received approval to build a focal campus building in the shape of a diamond over the cloverleaf and roadways. I've named the university UIRIT—the University of Individual Responsibility and Independent Thought. I pronounce the acronym, 'You're it'.

"I considered some kind of alliance with an established university to allow UIRIT to grant diplomas with immediate stature across Canada and the world. But the UIRIT graduates will be different, so we must build our own reputation. This'll take longer, but it places responsibility on the individuals at this university, where it belongs.

The principle of the university is individual responsibility. This cannot be achieved with government assistance with strings attached because such impositions erode individual responsibility of student, mentor, and staff. Instead, each student will approach the university with a defined goal and suggestions about the resources that will be needed to acquire the knowledge, equipment, and mentor to reach the student's goal. UIRIT will provide capable facilitators to help the student but the responsibility will be on the student all the way through to graduation. It'll be refreshing to be amongst driven individuals who pursue their dreams in an environment free from bureaucracy, rules, and politics."

Lex shrugged. "That's my presentation."

"You seem astute. Yet, you've ventured into the heart of academia with a conservative idea when you already know conventional education is socialistic to a fault. On top of that, you've approached a minister in a province that insists all bureaucrats wear pink on weekends and statutory holidays. Why haven't I thrown you out by now?"

"Because you're smarter than you look." Lex grinned.

"Not many beggars would be brave enough, or stupid enough, to riposte like that."

"I learned a long time ago that wilting violets don't get enough water. I won't wilt."

"I like all this. Let me mull it over for a few days and figure out how I might assist. You may be the instigator who'll benefit all education. Such an outcome suggests the resisters of change will marshal all the negatives. You do know that British Columbia is more than a little miffed that the Soul Star corridor misses BC and hugs the BC border all the way to Alaska. Not every BC resident and politician likes the optics. Let's meet again, here, three weeks from today. I think you and I'll enjoy the ride. If you like my approach enough, I might resign my position and lead your endeavour. My wife will be thrilled to leave Victoria for a place in the Yukon. She might be a bigger challenge than the range of adversaries you'll stir up." Jack chuckled. "Thank you for your vision and courage."

"Thank you, I've enjoyed our meeting."

"See you in three weeks. Goodbye."

Chapter 69

Thompson called the meeting to order. “This group has made decisions on many matters over the life of Soul Star. Today, we focus on one more initiative. Rosie will lead the discussion.”

“Thank you,” Rosie began. “As you’re aware, the internet is abuzz with talk of a consensus monument for the current, positive progress between aboriginal and government factions. It strikes me that Soul Star could provide an assist in the areas of location, amenities, and construction cost. When I raised this with Brett, he saw enough potential wrecks that he wanted the entire Soul Star team to consider any public offer we might make. So, today, I present my ideas and request your approval of the overall plan.”

Thompson turned to Brett. “Brett, perhaps you should outline what you see as the downsides to Soul Star participation.”

“I like Rosie’s proposal and I think we could go through with it. My caution lies in the biases that swirl around aboriginal issues and I see no end in sight. What if we build a monument in the wrong place, in the wrong shape, in the wrong color, or with a door on the wrong side?”

One Page fiddled with his pencil. “We take principled positions and we dare to act. We’ve made differences for youth and we’ve cared for the environment; why shouldn’t we demonstrate our care about aboriginal issues?”

Beth said, “I see the risks that Brett has raised but the message here is so important that we have to find a way to build this monument and manage the downsides.”

One Page gave a fist pump. “It’s too bad this line isn’t a million miles long; we could make an entrepreneur out of Beth.”

Beth leaned forward. “One day, I’ll turn that pencil end-for-end, stick it in your ear, point first, and drive it to the hilt. It won’t hit your brain because something that small will be hard to hit.”

One Page giggled. "Its great fun when I get a reaction."

Thompson tapped his pen on his glass to get their attention. "Okay, you two. Well, Rosie, it seems the game is yours to lose."

"I think about the four historical complexes that Krista championed for the education of our villagers. More recently, we agreed to build a grand courtyard as the centerpiece of UIRIT University. Perhaps we can add two more significant elements along the Soul Star line that will recognize two other elements of importance in Canada, our aboriginal brethren and our environment. I didn't mention the second element to Brett because I wanted him to focus on the monument decision. However, I realize I should outline my complete proposal so that none of us is surprised later.

"I'll mention the other element first," Rosie continued. "The environment is often cast as the loser when the media covers large projects such as pipelines, tar sands, and mines. We've included the environment as a core consideration every step of the way, but how do we catch the imagination of the casual observer when no monument to the environment exists? I propose that we consider a waterfall on the Liard River adjacent to the Soul Star line. I propose to name this waterfall the 'Teeth of the Liard'. I know this is a complete surprise to you. Just be aware.

"Now I turn to the monument. One often hears the expression 'location, location, location' when matters of real estate are discussed. I see this monument as a destination so that the specific location does not matter as much as great amenities, dramatic setting, and usefulness. I believe we can provide great amenities, dramatic setting, and usefulness. Our large cities could match us in these three criteria but the cost of land, construction, and annual operations will be multiples higher than a location along the Soul Star line.

"I've chosen a valley near Thompson, Manitoba for your consideration. It's some distance from the other landmark facilities along the line, it has the Thompson airport nearby, and the valley is picturesque. The vertical drop from the surface of the line to the valley floor will permit a hotel with 2,000 rooms.

"It appears that the most popular monument shape will be the traditional tepee. Unless that changes, I propose that we design a stone tepee that is round in footprint and cone shaped but with scale, perhaps one hundred meters in diameter and one hundred meters high. The tepee would stand over, and be centered on, the Soul Star roadway. It would be visible for long distances in either direction from the roadway and up and down the valley. I propose the tepee be built from the quarried stone from the tunnel and not be sculpted or decorated on the outside due to the extra exposure to erosion and discoloration when water finds its way around obstacles. Perhaps we can polish the outside so that it'll shimmer in the sunshine and stand out in any light. I propose that a row of stones on the inside of the tepee, about seven feet up from the floor, be commissioned, as a sculpture, by every band in the entire country to depict whatever the band decides.

"This tepee space will be the grand room for significant events," Rosie continued. "The vast commercial spaces under the roadway can be designated for museums, traditional long houses, Indian village displays, native language preservation, theatres, whatever integrates with aboriginal culture. I hope that the monument will be named Consensus and will resonate around the world—as does Corcovado in Rio de Janeiro. Annual costs of operation should be as low as they could be anywhere in Canada. Unlimited geothermal heat and ample solar energy should keep utility costs low. Property taxes can be waived by the Soul Star municipality in Manitoba."

Rosie paused. "Those are my initial thoughts on how we might facilitate an impressive monument to aboriginal and government consensus in Canada. I'll be interested in your feedback."

The board discussed the monument until all concerns had been raised.

Then Thompson wrapped up the meeting. "Well, Rosie has launched us on the Consensus monument path and tantalized us with the Teeth of the Liard. Do you have any more surprises for us, Rosie?"

"No, I'm all done. I love you guys. I'll miss this team when Soul Star is completed and we disperse to new adventures."

Brett said, "Hang on a minute. I have a proposal."

Beth groaned. "Don't you ever stop? Can we postpone your idea to another day?"

"Yes, but I sense a monument weariness amongst our group and I want us to be thoughtful about the messages we convey for generations to come. I believe we'll approve seven significant symbols. I hope my latest idea will resonate with each of you."

One Page put his pencil in his pocket. "Why don't we all go for a nightcap and let Brett explain his idea? That way, we'll be aware of feasibility, location, and design on all three ideas."

In the lounge, they pulled two round tables together, ordered drinks, and listened to Brett's suggestion.

"I've designed a symbol for the need to ensure that individual responsibility is always more prevalent than the safety net. It seems to me legislation on helmets, unshovelled sidewalks, seatbelts, work place safety, and the like are all meant to be helpful to the masses, but this continual—and extensive—erosion of individual responsibility is corrosive to society. Many will see my position as 'survival of the fittest' but I don't see the need to be at either extreme. I think individuals can be insulated from outright disasters while most routine eventualities are taken in stride. We already have individuals on both ends of the spectrum: the dependent and the independent. We'll always have those extremes. I'm concerned about the big blob in the middle. I believe tiny nudges toward individual responsibility will yield dividends for society. Likewise, every nudge to insulate individuals from every knock and bruise further drains society."

Thompson stopped chewing on peanuts. "How does this topic integrate with Rosie's proposals?"

"When Rosie told me about her tepee monument idea, I reflected on the possibility the insights demonstrated on Soul Star may not endure in future generations if we fail to provide individual responsibility symbols," Brett said. "When Thompson asked Rosie if more grand ideas would emerge, I sensed our group's tolerance for brilliant new projects may be exhausted. My proposal doesn't integrate. I just want it to be on the table as we explore the monument agenda."

Beth shook her head. "We're building infrastructure on a scale the world has never seen and you still aren't satisfied."

One Page looked up from doodling on his napkin. "We've come a long way with Brett's perceptions. I'd like to hear what he has in mind."

Brett raised his voice a little against the background noise. "What would this group think of a massive teeter-totter symbol where one end is labelled 'taker' and the other end is labelled 'maker'? If the mass of a population is concentrated to the 'taker' end, the weight of the mass pushes the mass toward the 'taker' end and vice versa. This indicates the trend toward laws and rules that protect the masses from every little risk nudges society toward the 'taker' end. I hope we can find ways to nudge individuals toward the 'maker' end; and develop symbols to extol the virtues of that approach."

Rosie said, "What would this taker-maker symbol look like?"

"A glass walkway extends over the Grand Canyon in Arizona. I picture a fulcrum on the edge of a precipice, where the 'maker' end would be heavier and would be over solid ground, in fact and in symbol. The 'taker' end would be extended in mid-air with a deep chasm below. I envision guided tours of the monument where a guide presents a polished version of this discussion so that every guest would feel the sensation on the tenuous end of the taker-maker every time society edges away from individual responsibility. The opposite message is also true; the 'maker' end rests on solid ground so any individual can walk anywhere, and do anything, because the individual is not hobbled by the safety net."

Beth passed the peanut bowl. "What about real risks like a heart attack or the paraplegic aftermath of a car accident?"

“We already have these protections but the disaster safety net is so tangled with the bruised knee safety net; it’ll take years to untangle. It’ll take longer if we don’t start.”

One Page abandoned the sports report on the lounge TV. “Do you have a suggested location for this monument?”

“When Elaine and I travelled in southern Spain, we saw the silhouette of a black bull on the high point of a hill. We could see the bull for a long ways as we drove down the highway. I’m hopeful we can find a dramatic location for the monument so it becomes a landmark for travellers, in either direction, along the Soul Star road.” He shrugged. “I don’t have a specific site in mind.”

Beth said, “All of our other monuments make extensive use of rock. This appears to be a monument that will be built out of strong metals and glass. This’ll be a significant additional cash cost that none of our funders have been informed about. Is that a problem?”

Brett said, “One idea is to start a fund where individuals who have a philosophy built on a foundation of individual responsibility would donate to fund the monument. That way, no entity with an alternative agenda would be in a position to alter the symbolism.”

Beth threw her hands up in defeat. “Why don’t we go tear London to the ground and rebuild it in a logical fashion? It might be faster and easier.”

One Page turned his napkin over and readied his pencil. “Let’s bush for the drinks tab.”

Beth slipped into her jacket. “No way, you championed this little tea party. We’re all an hour older and you’re a few dollars leaner.”

Chapter 70

How can a dam be chosen as an environmental monument when it stands as an intrusion on nature and a barrier to fish swimming upstream?

Rosie considered this question and sought answers. She learned about fish movement technology in university but she sought better solutions. She searched out the lead technicians in successful fish movement in both directions around dams. Then she found an engineer who exhibited careful environmental concerns in dam designs. Rosie arranged a meeting with Joshua Ellingson from Bergen, Norway.

"Thank you for meeting with me, Joshua. How'd you come to be interested in fish movement?"

"My interest in fish movement started in university," Joshua said over a steaming cup of coffee. "A professor sponsored a competition to see who could best explain how fishes get up and down streams where there are natural waterfalls. A beautiful girl thrived in my circle. Juvenile banter led to my rash opinion that I could capture a taste of that girl if I won the fish movement contest. A tad ironic because my reproductive urges impelled my actions like the urges that caused the fish to migrate up the streams."

"The science doesn't matter anymore. Did you get the girl?"

"Sort of; I got the party girl for a date and she got the nerd but few flashy prizes endure and few serious scientists end up with the prom queen. I found a woman in a similar stream to mine. We have two little tadpoles and life is good."

"Okay, back to the fish. How do we build dams that allow fish to migrate as nature intended?"

They discussed the current technology and roughed out a strategy that would lead the world in facilitating fish movement and be a tourist magnet.

Beth gathered her notes. "So how do we build the Teeth of the Liard?"

"You ask a man from a socialistic country where costs are high. I suspect you'll figure out how to build it. I'll join the team and help design the fish passage system. All I want, in payment, is the best fish passage anywhere and a little granite plaque with the inscription, 'Joshua Ellingson designed the fish passage'." He grinned.

"What if the tree huggers ridicule the design?"

"I do the best I can every day. Most tree huggers are better at criticism than solutions. I prefer to help the affected species."

"You might've guessed that my time horizon is twenty-seven seconds. Where do I find the engineer to make sure this dam will stand for centuries and will stay level so that the water runs evenly over all the Teeth of the Liard?"

"I've a friend who designs dams much larger than your dam. I'll call him and see if he'll lend you a young engineer who wants new challenges. My friend and I will make sure the design is sound. You better save room for a couple more plaques."

"Why're you so generous and why do you expect your friends to follow suit?"

"Norway has a rugged coastline, waterfalls, and tunnels. Its citizens are interested in projects that face similar challenges. We've thrived under a model of government that is quite different from the individual responsibility model. We want to learn and contribute. Your initiative provides an entre; we intend to benefit as well as contribute. It'll help the planet."

"Joshua, if we're not already friends; I'm sure we will be. You're a delight. Thank you."

"You're welcome. I'll be in touch."

Chapter 71

Makota grew up a rebel. The only child of influential Japanese parents, he drove too fast, took liberties with girls, and baited authorities. His father mitigated the fallout.

Makota's irresponsibility shamed his father. The strain overcame him.

A loud bang jarred Makota awake. As he tried to interpret what happened, an anguished 'No!' filled the air. Makota discovered his mother in the doorway of the garage. Family shame dripped from the walls and the car. He moved to console his mother. She brushed him away. "See what you've done?"

Without a fixer for his latest brutal attack, Makota landed in prison.

His mother coped; a criminal son in prison and a shamed husband turned to dust.

Makota recognized his mother's plight.

She requested he join the Japanese military and straighten himself out.

When his three-year prison term ended, Makota visited his mother, then joined the Navy.

Chapter 72

Louis LaFlamme drove from Montreal to Quebec City. He checked into his hotel and wondered what tomorrow would bring. He'd agreed to write a piece for *Le Devoir's* religion section. He had snippets of information about Soul Star but nothing caught his full attention. Le Devoir had reached the tentative conclusion that Soul Star rejected God.

Sleep eluded Louis, the thorough reporter, skilled in reporting the heart of stories with an incisiveness that informed and entertained. Foreboding gnawed at him as he rose. He bundled up his clothes, camera, recorder, and laptop and waited for the freight truck driver who agreed to ferry him from Quebec City to the Soul Star village of Saint Simone.

When queried by the driver, Louis provided a synopsis of his assignment.

Louis glanced over to the driver and noticed the tense jaw and the distressed demeanour.

"Did I offend you in some way?"

"Not me, but your mission appears to be a problem for Soul Star. I believe in Soul Star and I want it to succeed."

"Why do you see my mission as a risk to Soul Star? I'm not clear on my mission."

"Brett Larson, the founder of Soul Star, has relied upon the good faith of individuals, companies, and governments to get Soul Star to its present development. I feel certain that an aroused Quebec populace will cause frustration for Soul Star."

Louis pondered this scenario for some time: "Do you believe in God?"

"No."

"I get the impression you grew up in a Catholic home and community. How is it that a French Canadian Roman Catholic truck driver denies belief in God?"

"My mother died of breast cancer before I finished high school. Two years ago, my fiancée died, along with her entire curling team, in a car accident. My dream of a wife and children died with her. I analyzed twenty-five years of Catholicism; God did not fare well. I looked around for some endeavour that would allow my spirit to come alive again." He sighed. "One Sunday morning, a friend called me and asked me to run a freight truck to the north for him. His wife lay in hospital. Rosie Savard was the passenger on that trip. Her story is remarkable but she spent most of the journey as an advocate of Soul Star, its objectives, its methods, its trust, its goodness. When I got back, I phoned Brett Larson and told him a little of my life and my hope he would find a way for me to be involved in Soul Star. We negotiated an arrangement where I would drive freight and passengers from Quebec City to the various villages along the Soul Star line. Our trucks often give rides to vulnerable individuals who've committed to Soul Star but who take a leap of faith that must be honoured every step of the way. Reputable drivers help build trust. I'm dedicated to my job."

"I don't know how my report will develop, so I don't know how you'll fit in to it, but I like you and I'll be extra careful to be fair."

"What's fair to you may be a joke to me."

"If I asked you to read my article before I submit it, would that be meaningful to you?"

The driver looked over at Louis. "Your proposal is fair, but I'm worried I'm not smart enough to protect Soul Star."

"Well, sir, you've gotten more concessions out of me than I thought possible. What's with you? I provide plenty of room for you to respond and you react like a post."

The driver smiled. "I make fewer verbal mistakes when I don't talk at all."

Louis laughed and punched the driver on the shoulder. "We'll be friends."

Louis stayed a full week in Saint Simone, tagged along with a new recruit, accompanied Captain as he made his rounds, sat in classrooms and workshops as rebels became model citizens, studied the Soul Star monument in the center of the Village Square, worked a day with the granite sawing crew, worked a day with the tailings crew, hung around the library, went to social functions, and chatted with everyone that showed the slightest willingness. Louis looked for signs of dysfunction. He remembered vignettes of stories about Mennonite colonies, factories, and small villages where the population represented 150 households and no significant trouble developed. He thought about a bunch of dysfunctional, young people in one place with expectations they would emerge with stability, education, net worth, and happiness. He thought about the handicapped few brought into each village.

Could it work?

Louis went to the library and e-mailed his editor at Le Devoir. "I won't submit my article as scheduled. There're significant facets of this story that can't be researched and put into perspective in the time I allotted. I'll let you know when I have a balanced article."

A prominent lead article in the Religion section of the Sunday edition of Le Devoir read, "SOUL STAR REJECTS GOD." The article weaved a story that incited the populace of Quebec against Soul Star. The CBC picked up the story and splashed it across the country. When Brett caught wind of the story, he telephoned Thompson Miller. Thompson contacted Le Devoir and discovered that a freelance reporter was in Saint Simone.

On Monday morning, Arnie, the trucker, telephoned Brett and told him about his discussion with Louis LaFlamme.

Brett couldn't reconcile the Le Devoir article with the trucker's perspective so he rearranged his schedule for four days and flew to Quebec City. He rode with Arnie and discussed the situation on the way to Saint Simone.

When Brett got to the village, he found Louis LaFlamme in the library.

Brett approached Louis. "Howdy neighbour, I'm Brett Larson."

Louis rose and smiled. “My pleasure, Brett, I’m Louis LaFlamme.”

“I hear Le Devoir has decided Soul Star is a threat to God and all Christian believers.”

“I gave my word that I’d be fair. I sent an e-mail to my editor informing him my article required more time. I’ll show you what I said in the e-mail. Each day, I scan Le Devoir on-line, and I saw the article. The staff pulled together several anecdotal pieces and published an article in line with preconditioned perceptions. When I got here, I was impressed. I wanted to research it so my article would be solid.”

“Do you believe your editor has a sense of fairness?”

“If I didn’t think so, I wouldn’t write for him.”

“Well, you and I have our work cut out for us. Can you spare several hours between now and Wednesday?”

“Certainly. What do you have in mind?”

“Let’s go to the Come Alive Center where we can discuss Soul Star as long as you like.”

Seated in lounge chairs, voice recorder on, and coffee at hand, they talked. Brett described his ideas about alternatives to welfare, genuine help for young folks, the trust that many have shown in Soul Star, the unique individuals that launched Soul Star, the international participation, the UIRIT University at Stoddart Creek, the Good Person Act, the safety aspects of a large project, the chunking of projects into manageable pieces, the reduction of addictions, respect for others, external bureaucracies, and government approvals.

Far into the night, they talked. Brett remembered his trip to Fort St. John to inquire if Oscar One Page would support the project. How they talked till dawn and Brett found a team player. Louis and Brett parted friends. Brett noted the risk Louis represented and Louis recognized the trust Brett placed in him.

When they met for a late breakfast the next morning, Louis asked Brett if they could stand out in the Village Square and talk about the Soul Star monument. Brett explained the ability of every individual, in every village, to look up at the star at the top of the unadorned pole and know that every villager promised to be trustworthy. “Do you know of any other village in the world where every villager has promised to be trustworthy?”

Louis wondered. He couldn’t think of any. He thought of various Amish, Hutterite, Mennonite, and Catholic villages where the locals conformed to religious dogma. But he could not recall whether these kinds of villages ever asked every individual over a given age to promise to be trustworthy. He knew those cultures dealt harsh treatment to those who violated the established norms. The harshness stemmed from an interpretation of God’s will.

Louis recognized a shift in his lifelong beliefs. He could genuflect, recite dogmas, tolerate confessions, baptisms, confirmations, weddings, funerals, Lent, rosary beads, fear, celibacy, saints, infallibility…because all of this fit his comfort zone. Living in the current era, educated in science, familiar with the savagery of the Bible stories, and programmed to obey church hierarchies, Louis ignored the parts of the Catholic approach that his sensibilities couldn’t accept. But even with a trained, investigative mind, he never chose to consider whether reason could, or should, be applied to spiritual aspects. Now, he faced villagers who appeared to him to be admirable in every respect with no need for conventional religion.

Louis gazed seriously at Brett. “Do you believe in God?”

“In most circumstances, I’d answer that question first and explain later. In this case, it may be more productive to finish our whole discussion and then, if you feel it necessary to re-ask your question, I’ll answer.”

Louis contained his killer instinct and waited for Brett to continue.

“You’ll recall the holocaust story made into a movie called *Schindler’s List*. The lawyer who defended Schindler went on to make a lifelong study of what makes people good.” He waved his hands as he spoke. “The answer is elusive. My sense is there are intrinsic qualities in all humans that tell what is right or wrong. I believe this to be conscience. It seems to me that various religious dogmas make it more difficult for individuals to act upon their own conscience but rather encourage them to fall back on the perceptions they have of what the religious answers must be. Most of the young people who join Soul Star have some religion in their upbringing. When they rebel, they often rebel against every symbol of authority in the family. Religious dogmas enter into the rebellion. Soul Star made the decision to downplay the religious aspects of goodness by reliance on a basic sense of fairness and trust acceptable to the vast array of individuals, regardless of their commitment to organized religion."

"How might this concept sound appropriate to a French-Canadian reader of Le Devoir? Most individuals have invested a lifetime in the ambience of the Roman Catholic Church and will not allow secular logic to override belief. Maybe not blind belief but nominal blind belief amended by pre-conditioned resistance to change."

"You've spent ten days with us here. We've laid out our aspirations, our challenges, our methods, and our trust. Arnie told me you agreed to allow him to vet your article before you send it to the editor. Maybe you should write your article now and we'll see what happens."

Louis thought he saw serenity and trust that sent shivers through his body. He wondered how Brett could expect profound trust.

"Arnie will leave after lunch; you can catch a ride with him. Thank you for your consideration." Brett shook hands with Louis and walked away.

The next Sunday the lead article in the religion section of *Le Devoir* read like this:

A BREATH OF FRESH AIR

Two weeks ago, I stepped out of my home in Montréal. A big step, for I landed in the village of Saint Simone on the Soul Star tunnel project. I didn't have a clear assignment but I expected to identify initiatives that might offend the status quo of Le Devoir's readership. I stayed in Saint Simone for ten days. I worked, played, studied, communed, and meditated with a slice of humanity that surprised and charmed me. Let me tell the story.

A visionary by the name of Brett Larson conceived of an alternative to our welfare state. The project itself is the largest the world has ever seen but Larson broke the project into life-sized chunks that could be achieved over ten years by 4,400 villages comprised of 150 households per village. A villager is an individual who has managed to be a misfit in his or her home community; bright, rebellious, mistreated, and misunderstood. Sometimes they authored their own wrecks such as crime, single parenting, drugs, bullying, and laziness. For Larson and the Soul Star brain trust, to count on this type of worker for a world-class project took risk tolerance, some would say, bravado.

Soul Star has made some innovations that would work in the broader community if our cultures would permit. Every individual in Soul Star, from top to bottom, has to decide to be responsible from today forward. What a breath of fresh air.

Every individual makes a pledge to be trustworthy. What a breath of fresh air.

Every villager signs and agrees to honour the Good Person Act. This act requires villagers be individually responsible for every aspect of their lives. A point system, much like the point system for driving infractions, allows the entire village to be aware of the Good Person Act. What a breath of fresh air.

Everyone is treated with respect. Even those who routinely get picked upon by their neighbours are protected from bullying, teasing, and contempt. Individuals with mental and physical traits outside the norm are included and respected to a remarkable degree. What a breath of fresh air.

There is one police person in each village. He's called a captain in the context of a team captain where the police person is part of the team, wants everyone to do well, cooperate, excel, and grow. The captain is a low-key presence in the village. He seldom has incidents to address but all are convinced that he'll be fair when incidents arise. What a breath of fresh air.

Most Christian readers assume a church is integral to any idyllic village. Lo and behold, there's no church per se. Brett Larson explained the majority of the villagers grew up in nominally religious families and communities. When individuals rebelled against authority, they often included the religion of their family as a target for their rebellion. In these circumstances, Soul Star decided to foster a secular, sacred approach to spiritual growth that did not denigrate any religion but focused on goodness in ways that would not violate the norms of any religion but would not rely on any religion for the principles that define goodness. Once the villagers have gained personal stability, functional education, a marketable trade, and a set of social skills appropriate to any community in Canada, they should be ready to adopt, or ignore, any organized religion in the world. What a breath of fresh air.

When I accepted this assignment, I expected to find situations that offend conventional Roman Catholic tenets. I found a massive project, made human by village-sized pieces, which brought out the best in thousands of individuals who had refused to fit into any conventional mould, let alone a Catholic one. Many Christians will see Soul Star villages as prime opportunities to bring the Christian faith to young people. I assure you, the villagers will view such a mission as a breath of stale air.

In my perception, Christians should stand aside and observe this experiment in culture of all kinds, including religion. Perhaps Soul Star has an approach all of us can consider. I came away from Saint Simone with the best contentment I've experienced in my entire life. Indeed, a breath of fresh air.

Chapter 73

The fishing vessel tossed as Janser used his skill to get close enough to the powerless tender. His most reliable crewman threw a grapple that caught the anchor cable. As the winch pulled the tender close, the turbulent sea rammed the vessels together and then snapped the grapple line taught.

Janser's crew maneuvered their overhead crane boom over the tender and lowered a makeshift sling fashioned out of fishing net.

Two men were near the helm of the tender. They caught the sling and one man crawled into the sling. The sling swung as the crew urged the vulnerable package back onto the fishing boat. When they extended the lifesaver again, a child waited.

Sixteen times, the sling made its journey. The sixteenth passenger reported the captain waited but two others had died. Janser decided to risk two heavy ropes for the captain to tie around the bodies. With the help of the crane, the captain steered the bodies out from their places in the cabin.

The sling came back for the captain. He crawled into the sling and prayed that all his passengers in the other tender survived. The vessel rolled seventy degrees and slammed the captain against the crane mast. Crewmembers lowered the captain's limp body and carried him below.

The crew cut the tender adrift and nosed the vessel into the wind.

As dawn lightened the sky, the wind assuaged.

Janser made his way below and checked on the rescued people. The captain lay on the floor in the galley, unconscious. Janser checked his pulse.

The world media featured the dramatic rescue of thirty-seven passengers and crew from two lifeboats along the North Cape.

Janser had persevered when the Norwegian Coast Guard and three commercial ships deemed the conditions too dangerous.

Janser's exploits generated ecstatic reports.

Then, allegations of his crimes at sea emerged.

Chapter 74

Caroline stared at the letter. She wondered if others got a message from the Canada Revenue Agency. It asked her to prove her annual income of $3,500. When she calmed down, she asked her captain what to do. At his suggestion, she called Brett Larson and told him about the letter.

"Well, Caroline, let's see what we can do to make sure you're treated fairly. Don't worry. Email me a copy of the letter. Lots of our villagers may get a similar letter so we must manage our responses well. Leave it with me."

Brett phoned Thompson Miller and Beth Ragouski. They acknowledged they expected a tax inquiry. Brett sent them a copy of Caroline's letter.

Brett called Oscar One Page. One Page listened to the story, thought a while, and said, "I wonder if we can challenge the entire Income Tax Act."

Brett laughed. "What're you smokin'?"

"Seriously, Brett, I've thought for some time the entire Income Tax Act violates the Canadian Charter of Rights and Freedoms."

"When I called you, I described a straightforward issue. Now you've escalated it into a national crisis. Why do I talk to you?"

"Are you getting old, Brett? I thought you might like a challenge."

"I don't mind a challenge but I sure want it to be worthwhile."

"I promise you it'll be worthwhile and I bet we'll win."

"Have you written the one-page justification for this?"

"In my little mind."

"Okay, get it on paper and send it to Thompson Miller, Beth Ragouski, Rosie Savard, and me. You have a reasonable chance of rejection by every one of us."

"Louise has said no to me a few times and we're still sort of friends."

"Which is one of the wonders of the world."

"Goodnight, jerk…I mean Brett."

Chapter 75

Thompson Miller considered Caroline's letter. Beth assured him she could defend the villagers' returns. He pondered One Page's one page; did some wise nugget fester in his proposal? Whatever, Thompson would not be the diplomat that would slam this in the face of the feds.

Beth read the page, crumpled it up, and fired it at the wastebasket. She missed. She swore and wondered once more why she got mixed up with Soul Star. She slammed the door to her office and went home. She couldn't sleep, and when she dozed, she dreamt of the devil's laughter. She recognized the features of several prime ministers. The devil's visages varied as the avarice became more pronounced. The next morning, she trudged into her office. There lay the crumpled paper. She picked it up, smoothed it, and read it again.

Rosie Savard stood on a knoll above the long-deserted trading post. She remembered her mother, her young life on the trap line, her years with the Yudzik family, her Healthy Habitat exploits, and her Soul Star duties. Blessed, gifted, and bored, something must happen. That morning, she made a tentative decision she'd leave Soul Star and go to South America. She hoped to find new challenges.

Rosie got back to her home and read her e-mails, including one from Oscar One Page. Adrenaline surged through her as she recognized the magnitude of the proposal.

Maybe South America would have to wait.

Chapter 76

Part way through dinner, Elaine looked at Brett, who had barely touched his meal. “What's wrong, honey?”

“Do you remember when Hal Eastman sat here and described how we could capture the enthusiasm of young villagers with structured pursuit of fairness?”

“Yes, it was the first time I believed in Soul Star, instead of just you.”

“Well, the biggest kid of all, Oscar One Page, has suggested that Soul Star challenge the fairness of the entire Income Tax Act.”

“How does that have any relevance to Soul Star?”

“That was my initial reaction, but now I have second thoughts.”

“Why?”

“One Page is an effective cheerleader. Our Come Alive messages are successful but Oscar wants to be a visceral influence. In the last several months, Oscar’s activities for Soul Star have lacked excitement. We’ve encouraged the villagers to pursue improvements in fairness. There’ve been many successes but few with widespread impact. Maybe Soul Star can inspire villagers to attempt bigger fairness projects if we show them it can be done.”

“What if you lose?”

“We must not lose—Oscar promises that we won’t lose—and we’ll pursue it well enough that we won’t be embarrassed even if we do lose.”

“It sounds like you’ve already made up your mind. Soul Star already throws rocks 4,000-odd kilometers, now you throw them at the government’s glass house.”

“Do you see merit in my analysis, hon?”

"Yes, I do, but I'm weary. We aren't any younger and Soul Star's been present in our lives for six years already."

Brett paused to consider. "You're right, Elaine. If Soul Star tackles this project, it'll be with a different champion in charge."

"Thank you, Brett. I love you…most of the time." She grinned.

Several days later, Oscar One Page, Thompson Miller, Rosie Savard, Beth Ragouski, and Brett Larson sat around a conference table. They discussed the Income Tax Act challenge from every angle. Thompson Miller said, "This is too big a decision for a vote; we need full-fledged, positive endorsement before we proceed. Does anyone have qualms?"

No one moved to speak.

Thompson Miller turned to Beth. "Beth, we count on you to put the most pessimistic spin on any proposal."

"I like this initiative, a brilliant fairness project, already ninety years past due."

As Beth spoke, Oscar One Page toppled out of his chair and lay on the floor. Everyone rushed to see. One eye opened and a grin spread across his face. "I fainted when Beth said anything positive about anything, let alone about one of my proposals."

Everyone laughed and Beth kicked him in the butt. One Page winced once.

Rosie Savard left that meeting with a mandate to pursue the project through to completion. Oscar One Page would be her primary legal counsel and Thompson Miller, Beth Ragouski, and Brett Larson would be the unpublicized advisory counsel.

Chapter 77

The trial started. After preliminaries, Oscar de Lona commenced his examination of Lester Calhoun, whom the federal government chose as its first defender of the acceptability of the Income Tax Act within the confines of the Canadian Charter of Rights and Freedoms.

One Page stood. “Good morning, Mr. Calhoun. Today, we explore the Canadian Charter of Rights and Freedoms. We’ll interpret the sections from different perspectives but we will search for substance. Are you ready?”

“Yes.”

“Tell me, Mr. Calhoun, what does ‘advantaged’ mean to you?”

Calhoun looked down at the Charter on his table. “Why do you ask? Advantaged doesn’t appear anywhere in the Canadian Charter of Rights and Freedoms.”

“I beg to differ; the letters A D V A N T A G E D appear, in that order, twice in section 15, sub 2.”

“That section says disadvantaged, not advantaged.”

“I realize that, but the principle may be better understood by the opposite of disadvantaged, which I would like to focus on first.”

“Okay.”

“Do you agree that Wayne Gretzky was a talented hockey player?”

“Yes.”

“Did you see him as advantaged?”

“Yes.”

“Does it follow that the Charter requires the Canadian government to treat Wayne Gretzky the same as every other advantaged individual?”

“No.”

"Why do you say no?"

"Higher income individuals have more ability to ameliorate the conditions of disadvantaged individuals and groups. It's fair to tax them more than other lower income advantaged residents."

"Which sections of the charter permit the Canadian government to seize the monetary assets of a minority?"

Calhoun referred to the charter. "Subsection 15, sub 2."

"What words do you rely upon for your answer?"

"Subsection 1 does not preclude any law, program, or activity that has as its object the amelioration of conditions of disadvantaged individuals or groups."

"Does that subsection authorize the seizure of financial assets from a minority?"

Calhoun shifted in his chair. "Not in so many words."

One Page stepped around the table, closer to Calhoun. "Is it possible that it doesn't say it at all?"

"No."

"Well then, please explain how these words cause you to believe that a minority can be forced to fund the programs and activities that have the object of the mitigation of conditions of disadvantaged individuals and/or groups."

Calhoun shrugged. "It's the way it's always been done."

One Page smiled. "So, habitual, illegal government actions are acceptable because they're habitual?"

Calhoun's counsel rose. "Objection."

The judge turned to the court reporter. "Sustained, please strike that question from the record. Mr. de Lona, you will refrain from inflammatory rhetoric."

"Sorry, Your Honour; I'll rephrase. If the Canadian government violates the Canadian Charter of Rights and Freedoms, do you believe that an acceptable outcome would be to perpetuate actions that violate our most basic laws because it's happened before?"

Silence.

"Answer the question," the judge pressed.

Calhoun looked down at the charter and then at his counsel. "No."

"I ask again, does Section 15, sub 2 of the Canadian Charter of Rights and Freedoms authorize the seizure of financial assets of a minority?"

In response to Calhoun's quiet reply, One Page asked him to repeat his answer audibly. "No."

"Are there clauses in the charter that intend to protect every minority from seizure of assets by government?"

"Yes."

"How do you feel about theft, Mr. Calhoun?"

When his counsel didn't object, Calhoun responded, "What do you mean?"

"Well, a teenager goes into a convenience store and steals a chocolate bar. Is that acceptable?"

"No."

"Why not?"

"Because the Criminal Code forbids theft."

One Page raised his voice. "Okay, so three individuals make up an entire community. Two work in the community and one operates the general store. If the two workers independently go into the store and steal a chocolate bar each, that's theft. But, if, before they enter the store, the two workers vote and decide to seize two chocolate bars, that's democracy that's acceptable to the Charter of Rights and Freedoms. Is that your position?"

"Yes, the Canadian government is not bound by the Criminal Code."

One Page held out his hands, palm up. "Isn't that criminal?"

"It's not my call."

"Mr. Calhoun, are you familiar with the Robin Hood story?"

"Yes."

"Would you agree the popular perception is that Robin Hood and his band stole from the rich and gave to the poor?"

"Yes."

"Now consider the same story replicated in Canada where some might observe the Canada Revenue Agency steals from the rich so the federal government can give to the poor. Do you agree with this perception?"

Calhoun sat up straight. "Absolutely not. I find the suggestion distasteful."

"Which suggestion is distasteful: my characterization of the Canada Revenue Agency or the actions of the Canada Revenue Agency?"

"Your allegation offends me and the Canadian government. Canada's government is one of the most respected governments in the world."

"Do you believe any government is respected?"

Calhoun turned to the judge. "Your Honour, do I have to tolerate his baiting?"

The judge removed her glasses. "Mr. Calhoun, I encounter a variety of perceptions and presentation styles. I've found that moderate tolerance for advocacy techniques allows matters to progress smoothly. You might adopt a similar tolerance in these proceedings. Mr. de Lona, please be considerate of Mr. Calhoun's sensitivities."

One Page grinned. "Yes, Your Honour. I wouldn't want to offend the sensitivities of one of Robin's hoods."

Counsel jumped to his feet. "Objection."

The judge raised her voice. "Sustained, strike that from the record and, Mr. de Lona, you'll do well to observe my moderate tolerance guidelines. Please proceed."

"Thank you, Your Honour. Mr. Calhoun, I'll rephrase my proposition with terminology used by the Canadian Charter of Rights and Freedoms. Would you agree with the statement that the Federal Government of Canada repeatedly, through its Canada Revenue Agency, seizes the assets of advantaged individuals and uses it to ameliorate the conditions of the disadvantaged?"

The crowd reaction caused the judge to scan the audience.

Calhoun used the disruption to consider the question. "No."

"So, please help me understand where my proposition is at odds with the facts."

"The Canada Revenue Agency never unreasonably seizes anything."

"Section Eight of the Charter forbids unreasonable search and seizure, correct?"

"Yes."

"What kind of seizure? Would it be an epileptic seizure?"

Calhoun frowned. "No, of course not."

"So, what kind of seizure is addressed in section 8?"

"Well, the seizure of a car or a gun in the hands of a suspected criminal," Calhoun answered.

"Okay, so it's about property such as personal possessions, vehicles, land, money, and all manner of illegally obtained assets?"

"Yes."

"All right; the Canada Revenue Agency gets more money from an advantaged individual than it gets from any other individual. How does it get that money?"

"It collects income tax from that individual."

"And what authority does it use to get this tax?" One Page pressed.

"The Income Tax Act."

"And what protects the individual from the Income Tax Act?"

"Nothing."

"So, we've come to the point where you allege one individual in Canada, the smallest minority we imagine, can have thirty-nine percent of his income taxed away from him no matter how much money is involved. Is that your position?"

"Yes."

One Page approached the witness stand. "Let's turn to Wayne Gretzky's assets when he played professional hockey. With your logic, it'd be fair to cut off thirty-nine percent of Wayne's hockey sticks at the start of every game after the first game in each calendar year. Whenever this travesty caused him to play more like the journeyman hockey players, you'd cut off twenty-six percent of his sticks and, if he couldn't perform at all, you'd cut off thirty-nine percent of Dany Heatley's stick and glue it on to Gretzky's stick, which you demolished a few years before. Do you see how asinine your position is?"

"Your example is not correct. The Canada Revenue Agency collects money, not fractions of non-monetary assets."

"So, hockey sticks used to be made out of trees and money grows on trees so seizing money is fair; is that your position?"

Calhoun addressed the judge. "Your Honour, he twists everything I say."

"Well, Mr. Calhoun, I haven't recognized where Mr. de Lona strayed from the substance of your testimony. Please answer the question."

"No."

"Mr. Calhoun, let's explore whether any clause in the Charter might be expected to protect our advantaged individual. Section 15, sub 1 requires the government to treat individuals equally. Would that give our minority advantaged individual some hope of fair treatment?"

Calhoun leaned forward. "He is treated fairly! He's taxed at thirty-nine percent, the same as every other advantaged individual."

"Do you recall what an algebraic formula looks like, Mr. Calhoun."

"Yes."

"Would you please interpret for me .39a = .39b. What is the logical outcome of that equation?"

"A equals b."

"Alright, so now replace 'a' with the income of Adam and 'b' with income of Bob. Does this require that Adam's income equals Bob's?"

"Yes.

"Nice work, Mr. Calhoun, now explain how the Canadian Charter of Rights and Freedoms might protect our advantaged individual. What clauses would you cite?"

"Sections 8 and 15."

"All right. Section 8 provides the right to be secure from unreasonable seizure of property, correct?"

"Yes."

"And Section 15, sub 1 provides equal protection and equal benefit of the law without discrimination, correct?"

"Yes, subject to Section 15, sub 2 which deals with disadvantaged individuals and groups?"

"I like your interpretation. Now, let's see what happens if we define 'a' and 'b' as the incomes of advantaged individuals. As long as the incomes are equal, the thirty-nine percent tax will be equal. Correct?"

"Not necessarily."

One Page raised his voice. "Why not?"

"Because the Income Tax Act defines many kinds of income and taxes different kinds of income differently."

"Why would the Income Tax Act do that?"

"To encourage saving, homeownership, and many other perceived positive actions."

"Would those motives include gambling and income earned on Indian Reserves?"

"No."

"Then why are gambling winnings and income that is earned on Indian Reserves excluded from taxable income?"

"I don't know about gambling, but Indians earning income on Indian Reserves have some degree of sovereignty."

"So, gambling, which has no apparent social benefit, is a perverse form of discrimination against non-gamblers and this is stated, and encouraged, in the Income Tax Act. Is that true?"

"Yes."

"Are you aware of the apartheid policies that South Africa endured?"

"Yes."

"Is it your understanding that race-based policies are unfair and unacceptable?"

"Yes."

"Then how do you justify the race-based tax policies of the Income Tax Act?"

"I don't know specifically; I believe it arose out of the treaties signed with the Indians."

One Page stepped close to the witness stand and raised his voice. “So, Section 15, sub 1 exists to confuse those of us who can read because official government policy is to discriminate on the basis of race, national or ethnic origin, and color between our Indian citizens and the rest of the population.”

The defence counsel half-rose. “Objection, argumentative.”

“Sustained. Mr. de Lona, you know better than to make such statements.”

“My apologies. I withdraw the assertion. Mr. Calhoun, what kinds of entities are taxed in Canada?”

“I don't know. That’s not my area of expertise.”

One Page returned to his table. “May I help you out a little because I want your explanation for the policies in place and how they fit within the Canadian Charter of Rights and Freedoms? As I understand it, individuals, corporations, and trusts are taxed as separate legal entities whereas partnerships, joint ventures, incorporated societies, and churches are exempt from separate taxation. Why do you believe this situation exists?”

“Accidents of history.”

“What if the accidents are unfair?”

“The Income Tax Act is designed to help achieve fairness.”

“Does it succeed?”

“Yes.”

“You say yes with conviction. Do you know this to be true or do you hope it’s true?”

“I’ve been assured by Counsel that the Income Tax Act achieves fairness.”

“What if Counsel’s wrong?”

“I don’t know.”

“Let's look at an example. Two automobile dealerships earn taxable income of $400,000 in Alberta. One dealership sells cars and utilizes the manufacturer’s floor plan financing. It’s financing and capitalization is well below ten million dollars. The other dealership handles sixty percent as many cars but leases most of the cars to lessees and uses recourse financing. In this case, the dealership has financing and capitalization well over ten million dollars. As a result, the first dealership pays $56,000 in income taxes and the second dealership $100,000 in income taxes. This $44,000 difference appears to citizens as vindictiveness, not fairness, on the part of the Income Tax Act. Which car dealership tax policy would you prefer?"

Calhoun remained silent.

The judge instructed, "Mr. Calhoun, please answer the question."

"The lower taxed dealership," Calhoun muttered.

"As I picture it, the owners of these two car dealerships are advantaged individuals who do not need any amelioration of any disadvantage, yet one dealership is taxed almost double the other one. Can you point out the flaws in the Charter that allows the Income Tax Act to discriminate between these two taxpayers?"

"No."

"Mr. Calhoun, it's been suggested that the Federal Government of Canada is permitted to take any action it chooses against an advantaged individual. Do you believe that suggestion to be true?

"No, certainly not."

"Can you cite any potential federal government actions that are forbidden by Canadian law?"

"Killing, torture, discrimination, detention without legal protection."

"Okay, where is the life of an individual protected?"

"Section 7 of the Canadian Charter of Rights and Freedoms."

"But that's not absolute protection, is it? Doesn't the government have the right to kill an advantaged individual in accordance with fundamental justice?"

"Yes."

"So, what does fundamental justice mean?"

"I believe it means broad consensus amongst the general population on how the legal system should operate."

"Okay, fair enough. Concerning the killing of an advantaged individual, do you believe that the death penalty should apply only to the worst criminal acts?"

"Yes."

"I think you're right. I expect you and I would come to general agreement on torture and detention laws but I expect we differ on discrimination.

"Let's pursue the rights the Canadian government might have to discriminate against any advantaged individual," One Page continued. "I want to dwell on advantaged individuals because our objective here is to protect the advantaged minority, not discriminate against the popular perception of visible and disabled minorities.

"Mr. Calhoun, are you aware of the pig odour law enacted in 1981 and still in place today?"

"Yes."

"Do you believe that law could be enacted today?"

"No."

"I concur. Are you aware of the current initiative to implement a tax on the incidence of sexual intercourse?"

"Yes."

"Do you believe this proposed law will be passed?"

"Yes."

The judge interrupted, "Mr. de Lona, what is the relevance of this line of enquiry? It appears to have no significance to the subject of this trial."

"My point, Your Honour, is that these two programs appear so ludicrous that most citizens would view them as bizarre beyond contemplation. They appear to violate the Canadian Charter of Right and Freedoms in fundamental ways. Yet, the federal government preserves the pig odour law and plans to enact the tax on the incidence of sexual intercourse."

"Thank you, Mr. de Lona, please proceed."

"Thank you, Your Honour. Mr. Calhoun, is this proposed tax on the incidence of sexual intercourse an elaborate hoax designed to feed disinformation to the opposition parties?"

"On the contrary, I've worked on this initiative for months. I see the opportunity to capture statistics so that enterprises will be better able to estimate the number of crock pots that it will sell in Sault St. Marie, thirty years from now."

The crowd stirred.

The judge repositioned her glasses and stared at Calhoun.

No one moved a muscle.

Oscar de Lona refrained from comment.

The defense counsel could not think of a way to lessen the poignancy.

The judge didn't flinch. "We'll adjourn for twenty minutes."

When court reconvened, Oscar de Lona resumed his examination of Calhoun.

"Let's think about the sex tax initiative a bit more. Is the primary reason for the extra tax to replace money spent on municipal infrastructure?"

"Yes, although that'll get lost in the discourse."

"So it can't be justified as a law, program, or activity that has as its objective the amelioration of conditions of disadvantaged individuals or groups."

"It can be justified on that basis because the original money generated for these programs has been spent on infrastructure and services."

"Isn't that dishonest?"

"No, just practical."

One Page looked up from his notes. "So, the Canadian Charter of Rights and Freedoms is a useless document that the federal government can ignore without recourse. Is that true?"

"No, the Charter is required to protect criminals, language rights, and aboriginals' rights," Calhoun answered. "Subsection 15, sub 2 allows the federal government to take unfettered action as long as criminals, language rights, and aboriginals' rights are protected."

One Page looked at Calhoun and waited a couple of seconds. "You don't believe what you just said, do you?"

"Look around you. Smart, educated teenagers are not allowed to vote. Individuals who smoke or drink are taxed at high rates. Some companies are subsidized while others aren't. Massive money is sent to lousy farmers and little or none to productive farmers. Farmers in the west couldn't sell grain outside their province because of the Canadian Wheat Board. We could list similar special rules for days."

"But you don't seem to think the Canadian government is corrupt. Why?"

"We're a nation of accommodators. Wealthy people place less importance on their last dollar and feel blessed with their circumstances in life."

"So, easy marks are preferred targets for theft. Is that your conclusion?"

Calhoun glanced over to his counsel, who didn't react. "No, not okay. Just convenient and acquiescent."

"Is this a variation of the broken window theory where the federal government watches for weak spots and vandalizes those weak spots?"

"The results may look like that, but it's too cynical. Ever-present demands exist for government funds and hundreds of individuals search for ways to raise additional funds."

"This may be the focus of this trial and provide fundamental fairness for every Canadian from here forward. Would you see that as a reasonable outcome?"

"Yes, but I don't see how it could be done."

"There may be many ways but let me propose one and provide you with an opportunity to identify flaws."

"Okay."

"Start with one fundamental fairness principle. That is, no minority individual should be treated worse by any government than any other individual in that jurisdiction. I believe that this principle falls within the Canadian Charter of Rights and Freedoms and it embraces the spirit of that Charter. Do you agree?"

"Maybe. I haven't studied the suggestion."

"One test of this principle, in the area of personal income tax, would be to divide the total personal income tax collected by the federal government by one half of the entire population of the country. Consider that the lower income half of the population might pay no income tax. This would load the entire burden of personal income tax on the higher income half of the population. Do you agree with the example so far?"

"Yes, I follow."

"Now, let's accept that each household can be considered a taxable unit. This would mean that a nuclear, advantaged family of a woman, a man, and two kids could be responsible for four times the individual personal tax limit. Do you follow?"

"Yes."

"Do you see flaws in the proposal?"

"In implementation."

"Let's go to implementation," One Page said. "Each household will calculate its entire federal tax amount on one tax form and remit any amounts not previously remitted, up to the maximum household amount. However, households are now taxed at the federal level by a myriad of systems: import taxes, GST, sin taxes, corporate income taxes in which the household owns shares, and personal income taxes. Rather than cancel these entire taxes at one time, it might be feasible to estimate the actual amount of these myriad taxes paid by advantaged individuals and give them credit for these amounts when each household calculates its annual total tax. Statistics Canada already has hundreds of individuals who could prioritize estimates instead of whatever they do now. Do you agree in principle?"

"I don't know." Calhoun shrugged.

"Did you hear my explanation?"

"Yes but it appeared too simple; there may be considerations that don't come to mind, so I don't know whether I agree or not."

"But don't you think that all the other considerations will cause complexity and unfairness to the advantaged minorities?" One Page pressed.

"Probably."

"Then why complicate the system and make it unfair? The charter is supposed to be fair, is it not?"

"What if people think that the rich are under taxed?"

"Then ask them how they feel about theft. Almost no one wants to be a thief but almost everyone enjoys a free ride. Why not show the free ride as it is, theft?"

The judge interrupted, “Mr. de Lona, why are you designing an entire new revenue system here in a courtroom instead of the House of Commons?”

“Because of a risk you’ll agree with our case but decide that the system would collapse unless the federal government is allowed to pillage at will. I want to demonstrate to you one outcome of this trial could be that most of the complex, unfair systems can be temporarily left in place but with a ceiling to protect every individual from more tax than the majority pays. No disadvantaged person need be threatened by such a decision because the federal government is in a position to collect sufficient income equally from the advantaged majority to support all federal programs designed to ameliorate the conditions of disadvantaged individuals and groups; for any other endeavour, the federal government must treat every individual fairly.”

“You underestimate my resolve to enforce the law, Mr. de Lona.”

“I’m counting on you, Your Honour.” One Page turned back to Calhoun. “Mr. Calhoun, please consider this summary of what’s been proven so far. We’ve submitted a document, Exhibit 6, which lists our analyses of the specific incidences of violations of the Canadian Charter of Rights and Freedoms on each page of the entire Income Tax Act. I represented to this court that Exhibit 6 alleges at least one violation on every page of the Income Tax Act and up to twenty-seven incidences on one page.

“I invited you to select any page that you thought might be the least offensive to the Canadian Charter of Rights and Freedoms,” he continued. “You declined to select such a page. So, I presented you with a new copy of the Income Tax Act I acquired from the publisher.” One Page held up the copy of the Income Tax Act. “So far as I know, no one had previously opened this book. After some hesitation, you agreed to open the book at random and identify the left page for detailed analysis of compliance with the Canadian Charter of Rights and Freedoms.

"You selected a page with seven alleged violations. We discussed each of these incidences in detail and you could not sustain a credible explanation as to how any of the seven incidences could fit into the Canadian Charter of Rights and Freedoms.

"I invited you to get help from your defense team to identify the least offensive page in the entire Income Tax Act. You have not provided a page reference for this court to consider in detail.

"We've reviewed income as defined by the recognized accounting experts in Canada, the members of the Chartered Professional Accountants. We've looked at the array of incomes as defined in the Income Tax Act. In each of the cases, you couldn't sustain a plausible explanation that could position the rule within the Canadian Charter of Rights and Freedoms.

"We've explored what we believe is a reasonable proposition that no individual can be forced to pay more tax than the majority of individuals pays. We acknowledged that households will have obligations to pay the equal amount of tax paid by a majority as long as the household total income is sufficient to reach the maximum tax, even if some of the individuals within the household do not meet the threshold for maximum tax.

"We've demonstrated, beyond doubt, that the Income Tax Act violates the Canadian Charter of Rights and Freedoms in comprehensive ways and must be found ultra vires.

"Mr. Calhoun," he concluded, "have I misrepresented the proven facts in this summary?"

"I don't know."

"You don't know because you didn't explain yourself well enough or because I've summarized the facts, which you've proven, in false terms?"

"I have nothing more to say."

"In that case, Your Honour, I have no more questions of this witness."

The judge turned to defense counsel. "Your witness."

The defense counsel stood. “We have no questions for this witness. We have other witnesses who may interpret the charter in different ways.”

When Mr. Calhoun stepped down, the judge said. “Mr. de Lona, please call your next witness.”

“I don’t wish to call additional witnesses, Your Honour. I rest my case.”

The judge stared at One Page. “Mr. de Lona, you’ve brought before this court a profound case and you rest your case after one witness and two days of court time. Are you sure?”

“I’m sure, Your Honour. I came to this court with a mandate to prove the entire Income Tax Act is ultra vires the Canadian Charter of Rights and Freedoms. The defense has provided its most knowledgeable expert on the Canadian Charter of Rights and Freedoms and that witness has confirmed the entire Income Tax Act violates the Canadian Charter of Rights and Freedoms. I conclude the case is proven beyond a shadow of a doubt. I expect defense counsel to wallow in convoluted arguments and will lead its witnesses to answer ‘yes’ to many questions. The exercise will be pathetic. I expect to dissect and disprove the testimony of every defense witness and reinforce what is already evident; the entire Income Tax Act is ultra vires the Canadian Charter of Rights and Freedoms.”

Chapter 78

The court announced the date the decision would be delivered.

The media dissected the case for several days.

The clerk stepped forward. "Please rise; Madame Lilo Garobaldi presiding."

The judge entered and took her seat. "Please be seated. This is my decision in the matter of Caroline M. Mudrick, as plaintiff, versus Her Majesty the Queen, as defendant."

The judge summarized the allegations and responses and provided her analysis. At the end of her analysis she announced her decision. "I rule that the Income Tax Act of Canada violates the Canadian Charter of Rights and Freedoms in fundamental ways and is declared ultra vires. The federal government is put on notice that no individual shall be taxed at a higher amount than every other individual included in the majority of the population unless that individual provides specific consent. I add these last six words because I see where a transition from the per capita tax to the maximum equal tax should be gradual instead of abrupt. If that occurs, I intend that my ruling will accommodate it. By corollary, no province, territory, county, or municipality shall tax any individual in that jurisdiction at a higher amount than every other individual included in the majority in that jurisdiction unless that individual provides specific consent. Court is adjourned."

The Soul Star group gathered in a hotel suite.

One Page wiped his brow. "What a relief."

Rosie smiled. "You came through. Congratulations."

"I wouldn't have believed it." Beth shook her head.

Thompson hugged Rosie and shook One Page's hand. "Ms. Savard and Mr. de Lona, we're proud of you and recognize your tireless pursuit of this impressive achievement. Thank you."

Brett smiled. *This group has helped establish a grid of Ribbons & Jewels that will benefit Canada forever and will pave the way for other countries to develop similar grids. It has encouraged resolution of the aboriginal issues and now, it's rationalized a tax system of complexity and unfairness that has plagued Canada for a century. This is a good day. Let's make sure we protect the gains and encourage more.*

Brett let the champagne cork pop. "Whatever happens to Soul Star, the contributions made to date are commendable. I don't say often enough how pleased I am that each of you has enriched my life and contributed so much to our country. You are special. Thank you."

Brett handed the bottle to Thompson and gave a thumb up.

Chapter 79

The Portuguese Freighting Company emerged from the shady beginnings of a young pirate, Janser Paramago. The traits that made Janser a successful criminal and a fearless seaman allowed him to meld those traits with conventional business methods and grow his business at an impressive pace. Never interested in the establishment, he poured all his energy into his company.

The phone call caught him by surprise. The Luger carried thirteen years of dust. He checked the action, loaded five new shells from his security guard's cabinet, and strapped on the holster under his rumpled suit.

The black limousine rolled up in front of his office. Janser opened the car door and stepped in.

Will I be alive by hour's end?

The limo drove off. Thirty minutes later, it pulled into the Canadian Embassy in Lisbon. For the first time since the phone call, Janser dared to believe he'd live. The door opened and security personnel waited for Janser to step out and accompany them into the embassy. No security checks. They ushered him into a room furnished with a fireplace, easy chairs, and ocean view.

Two men greeted him: one in military uniform, the other in a business suit.

The suit smiled. "Good morning Mr. Paramago. I'm the Canadian ambassador to Portugal. This is Portugal's Navy commander. Please have a seat."

The ambassador continued. "We have a unique request. Under top-secret conditions, Canada intends to contract the shipment of sensitive cargo in one commercial freighter from Lisbon to Canada. We request that you captain your ship on this mission. The nature of the cargo and the precise dates are secret but it will be in a four-month window in the summer of next year."

Janser studied the ambassador and the commander. He tried to assimilate the information and the anomalies. "I presume my presence is logical, somehow."

"Yes, we selected you as an individual who could be trusted with this mission. Your credentials demand that you accept this assignment."

"And if I refuse?"

"We've prepared a dossier that could fall into the hands of individuals who'd be elated with evidence of your demise. Our assumption is you'll prefer this assignment to the alternatives."

"Your dossier should reveal that I don't respond well to threats," Janser countered.

"It does. You asked a direct question. I gave you a direct answer. I assure you that we want you to accept this assignment and we will, in that case, protect your dossier."

"How much physical risk to my crew, my ship, and my business?"

"Normal maritime risk of a transatlantic voyage. We perceive no unusual risk to you, your crew, your ship, or your business. Post-completion, you'll be permitted, contractually, to exploit any element of the assignment except any inference of force."

"Is this a paid mission?" Janser asked.

"Yes. We request you first calculate the fee you would charge for a conventional commercial round-trip, fully loaded in both directions. When you calculate your estimated gross margin on this assignment, we ask you to triple your estimated gross margin and add that amount to your initial fee with the result you will be expected to earn quadruple your estimated normal gross margin."

"How long do I wait for my money?"

"One quarter cash when you agree to the assignment. One half cash when your ship leaves Lisbon with our cargo. One quarter cash when your ship returns to Lisbon."

“Why is the Navy commander here?”

“Whenever a sovereign country contracts a secret mission on foreign soil, the country must obtain clearance from the host country. Portugal has determined this is a secret marine engagement and has designated the Navy commander as the liaison officer.”

Janser ran a hand through his hair. “Will I ever know the nature of the cargo?”

“Yes.”

“Will I be angry?”

“You’ll be surprised, but not angry.”

“It appears I have no alternative but to accept. Why did you allow me to enter with a loaded Luger under my jacket?’

“Our limousine and tarmac bear sophisticated reconnaissance equipment. We decided that your trust in us should be accepted at face value. While we doubt you would have survived an attack on us, we are aware of your ability to survive in difficult circumstances. Your survival skills are important to this mission.”

“Your answer gives me scarce confidence this mission holds no unusual risk.”

“While we expect the mission will proceed without incident, we want to be assured our precious cargo is in capable hands in case any emergency occurs.”

Chapter 80

The article, written for the environmental lobby organization Green's Good, said:

GREED TURNS GREEN TO GREY

Those of us who care about our environment have learned to expect greedy, big business will ride roughshod over laws dedicated to protect our natural habitat.

The Soul Star tunnel project emerged mysteriously in the north with little media attention and no environmental impact studies.
Thousands of international business giants fund this ghastly scar, which will endure as an embarrassment across our nation. When will our governments wake up to the selfish actions of big business?

The president of this cruel joke is Thompson Miller, a member of a socialite Toronto family that knows its way around government

and business circles in North America.
The visionary in this debacle is Brett Larson, a supposedly retired business executive who pretends to be a shy and innocent farm boy but actually commands the attention and respect of international powerbrokers.

The chief legal counsel is Oscar "One Page" de Lona, who built his reputation on the backs of Beaver Indians around Fort St. John, BC, and now has despicably sold out to big business and abandoned the desperate needs of the people who trusted him.
The chief financial officer, Beth Ragouski, is a formidable forensic accountant who has famously embarrassed individuals in high places to the point where attention by Ragouski will put anybody who is anybody on high alert.

Not satisfied with Canadian-based charlatans, Soul Star has recruited accessories from the United States. Hymie Friedenberg frequently fraternizes with the Soul Star executives. Mr. Friedenberg is rumoured to have manipulated the original owner of an East Coast chain of hotels out of ownership of the empire and is seen as a ruthless, shrewd operator. To demonstrate that no one is too young or too old to fall into the swath of the Soul Star juggernaut, an eighty-year-old miner from the Silver Valley of Idaho took up residence on the Soul Star line, presumably to advise on how best to exploit the mineral riches along the Soul Star route. The Silver Valley demonstrated how to take optimal advantage of the mineral wealth of a region with no care about the people and the environment. We resent the importation of such characters from a country that cares most about the almighty buck.

The Soul Star project will leave debris scattered across forty-four hundred kilometers of pristine land, blind to impacts on wildlife, First Nations' sacred sites, water, forest, air, and habitat of our wildlife.

We plan a massive funeral in Thompson, Manitoba to mourn the loss of so much real and symbolic life as a result of the repugnant actions of a group of greedy, mindless takers. If you have wakened, or waken soon, to the travesty, you are welcome to attend the funeral. Stay tuned for the time and date.

The media thrived on the story. It appeared to help protect the environment, preserve pristine areas, slander big business, and encourage controversy.

When the story surfaced, Brett Larson decided refutation of the allegations would add to the cacophony and prolong the controversy. He called Thompson Miller, Oscar One Page, and Beth Ragouski and discussed the issues at length. They decided to invite CBC Television to live up to its recent commitment to fairness.

When Brett called the chairman of the CBC, he learned the CBC would set the record straight. It planned a six-part miniseries featuring episodes on the Healthy Habitat Society-sponsored Ribbons & Jewels, Soul Star's utilization of the right of way and careful protection of the environment required in that initiative, the scenery aspects of the Soul Star project and other world renowned sites that attract people's enthusiasm, the involvement of big business, the profiles of the Soul Star executives, the education innovations that worked so well, and the alternatives to conventional welfare.

The CBC merchandised the series, put the environmental concerns into context, demonstrated the substance of the Soul Star executives, and highlighted the successful education and welfare initiatives.

After the miniseries, a popular talk show featured the author of the environmental article that sparked the controversy. The author remained belligerent. He confirmed his view that spurious allegations help environmental causes. He claimed big business bought off the CBC.

The talk show host closed the show. "I read the article written by today's guest, I watched the CBC television series, and I toured four Soul Star villages in four provinces. I came away from each village with appreciation for the approaches used by Soul Star to inspire and motivate a slice of our society that holds so much potential but often ends in heartache and tragedy. I hope you recognize the deception perpetrated by today's guest. The environment is important. Trashing responsible social and business leaders with innuendos is immoral. Media personalities often find ways to discount the efforts of competitors. I stand before you today with admiration for the way the CBC has presented the facts about Soul Star and its many alliances.

"I've never made a toast on the show before." The host held his wine glass up. "Today, I feel compelled and thrilled to invite you to join me in a toast to the CBC. Well done, CBC, well done."

Chapter 81

Beth phoned Brett's home. "Hi, Elaine. I've just heard that the US Congress has voted against the Panhandle Rivet. Is Brett around?"

"No, he's gone to the playground with Sherry and the twins."

"Please ask him to call me when he gets home."

"Sure, he should be back in about an hour."

"Okay, bye."

"Bye for now."

Hymie's phone rang. "A nice day isn't it?"

Brett moved the receiver into position. "Good morning, Hymie. What about your goofy government?"

"What's wrong with you?"

"Haven't you heard? Congress voted against the Panhandle Rivet."

"I thought I heard something; it sounded like Kermit saying ribbit, ribbit, but it must have been the Democrats in Washington saying, 'Rivet, Rivet'."

"Don't kid with me. I'm torn up. I thought Alaska assured us the tunnel would be approved. We've got sixty kilometers of tunnel dug under Alaska and it might have a padlock on it by next Tuesday."

"I bought a carload of turkeys on sale, one time; delivery on January second. It turned out that Christmas and New Year had passed and no Thanksgiving loomed for eleven months. It's a good thing the price was right, isn't it?"

"Your wisdom wears on me at the moment."

"As I recall, you called me. Perhaps you should slow down and take it one step at a time."

"Sorry, sometimes the world seems unfair."

"You're one of a very few that can let your vision soar but still adapt to the real world when mere mortals get in your way.

Politicians are as fluid as melted lead. When they cool, they're still malleable. Don't get too big a hate on; tomorrow is a new day, isn't it?"

"Is there some glimmer of strategy in your words?"

"I try to make sense, except when I'm kidding around. I follow politics. We have a dynamic in progress. It seems that the US labour unions have hit upon a ploy to force ocean freight companies to reduce their environmental impact by thirty percent within two years. The Democrats snuggle up to the unions and try to finds ways to make this target believable. Some voice, somewhere in the universe, happened to tell the Democratic House Leader that the Soul Star tunnel across Canada could, conceivably, handle ocean-going vessels and could, conceivably, cut thirty percent of the voyage off the freight in either direction between Asia and Europe. But the messenger put strings on the information. The capability of the tunnel must remain classified for eighteen months. The eighteen-month delay would end about the time the Democrats would need some positive news to bolster their election propaganda in the lead up to the presidential election."

"Do I know the messenger? Do I have permission to thank the messenger or wring his neck?"

"No, your role is to get Thompson Miller to manage a scenario where Alaska pleads its case, the Republicans brag about their support for international cooperation, the Canadian government is appreciative, and the Democrats find some way to explain why they've softened their opposition to the Panhandle Rivet. The Democrats can lead the bill through the Senate and ask the Congress to vote on the improved bill approved by the Republicans and the Democrats. Simple, isn't it?"

"I sometimes question why Soul Star chooses to associate with an offensive, rich, smart-ass Jew from the Bronx. I guess the answer is clear, isn't it? After eleven years, I'm glad I got a chance to use your tagline."

"A few years ago, I questioned why Hymie Friedenberg would be crazy enough to get mixed up in a foreign fantasy. We both decided to take the plunge and I'm glad we did."

"Me too. Thanks, Hymie. We'll see this through."

Chapter 82

Brett's cell phone rang. "Hello."

"Hi, Brett, Thompson here; I received a letter from Quebec; they've rescinded our construction permits. The letter's in French. I'll get it translated. I interpret the letter as insisting we must follow all of Quebec's language laws."

"I thought we negotiated relief from those rules when we got our original permits."

"We did, but Soul Star's profile has caused the Quebec government to insist all laws must be honoured."

"Will you get copies of the translated letter to each of the team members and organize a meeting to see if we can resolve this?"

"Sure."

"Has this been announced to the public?"

"Of course; they arranged media coverage of the delivery to me at the Soul Star office."

The body of the Quebec letter said:

> The Quebec government has reviewed the current French language laws and the preferred laws not yet passed. We reviewed the processes used in the original applications for the entire Soul Star project in Quebec. We determined the concessions granted in those negotiations were not in the public interest of the people of Quebec. Soul Star is hereby notified all approvals are rescinded, construction must cease within forty-eight hours of receipt of this letter, and no new permits will be granted until Soul Star and its affiliated entities comply with all Quebec laws.

We have appointed Marcel Palideau as our liaison person and request that you inform us of your contact person in expectation that Soul Star will choose to comply with Quebec law in order to continue with your project.

Chapter 83

Soul Star management gathered around the conference table in the Chateau Laurier in Ottawa.

Thompson looked around the table. “Thank you, for your presence in our capital to consider the Quebec ultimatum. You have a summary of the rules with which we must comply. Brett has prepared steps we might implement to meet the Quebec demands.”

Beth nodded curtly to One Page. “I expected the right of way and the Indians to be bigger obstacles than Quebec. I guess I’m still not cynical enough.”

One Page removed his pencil from his ear. “Are we in Ottawa because we couldn’t get passports to enter Quebec?”

Rosie dropped her copy of the letter on the table. “My impulse is to run them over, but I guess we need Brett’s two-bits on this fiasco.”

Brett leaned forward and focused on Rosie. “In situations like this, we’ll proceed in measured steps, choosing approaches and messages that’ll be more productive than antagonistic. One principle to remember is whatever happened yesterday has already happened. We’ve landed at this point today. We’ll seek solutions that work for today and for the future. I remember elation at the language concessions in our original permits. Maybe we would’ve been better served by good answers rather than convenient ones.”

Thompson passed papers around. “I prepared an agenda for today’s meeting. Perhaps we can start with the agenda but I recognize many of the issues will spill over any simple list. The first item asks whether Soul Star might be expected to comply with the stated objectives of the Quebec language advocates or just the bare minimum.”

Brett said, "I recognize that each of us would be inclined to comply with current law and ignore the dreams of the revolutionaries. However, I sense we may work better with Quebec if we go the extra mile on some of their initiatives because we choose not to stand and fight; we need to negotiate permits to build infrastructure. Furthermore, our base motivation is to develop character in a multitude of young people. The Quebec revolution may have enough traction in Canada to suggest we should stand aside, do enough to keep our permits, and avoid animosity with the revolutionaries. We've done well with our fairness initiatives. I believe this is one fight we should leave for another day."

One Page raised an arm in mock *Heil, Hitler* fashion. "I saw Brett with a black beret and a red neck scarf and some sort of *Heil, Hitler* salute. A shy and innocent farm boy exposed as a rebel. Let's get out of here while we're still alive."

Laughter lightened the room.

Beth looked at her notes. "Brett, do you suggest we understand the motivations underlying the language agenda and then try to accommodate that expanded mandate?"

"Many of the villagers along the Quebec line are French. It turns out that French families are just as adept as English families in screwing up their kids' psyches. We thought our 'English only' efforts would help all villagers; however, I think we might've underestimated the value of a bunch more bilingual Soul Star advocates in Quebec when the line is completed. We have enough experience in each village to identify the French individuals who're capable leaders. I expect most are already bilingual. Can we find ways to operate the Quebec villages in French and still enhance the villagers' English language skills to the point where they emerge as fluently bilingual?"

Beth asked, "How do we accommodate the label laws for materials and supplies shipped into Quebec from other jurisdictions?"

"I've made some enquiries," Brett said. "The shipments of goods that come into Canada in routine commerce are already obligated to have bilingual labels. There appear to be 'direct order' goods that enter Canada without meeting the label rules. I expect we could arrange staff at Quebec ports of entry, which would permit the attachment of a second label that complies with the Quebec rules even if not required under federal laws. For materials from other parts of Canada, I believe we could arrange some extra attention in the receiving areas of each village to ensure appropriate labels are attached as the materials enter any Quebec village."

Rosie slammed her palm on the table. "I don't believe this. We've worked so hard to simplify and rationalize operations and now we accommodate a bunch of hocus pocus to pacify zealots."

Brett took a deep breath. "I appreciate that sentiment and, mostly, I agree. However, we have a situation that's beyond our control. When you come to a mountain you can't move, you find a way over, around, or through. We can assemble ammunition for a fairness initiative but I haven't found a good citizen way to continue Soul Star across Quebec without compliance with Quebec laws."

Thompson looked toward Brett. "Is there a way to get French individuals in key positions in every village?"

"I believe we'll have to promote some French individuals to the highest posts where we've already granted that role to an individual who is not fluent in French. This is problematic from fundamental fairness and village morale points of view. My proposed solution is to appoint a two-man team with a mandate to attend every Quebec village, and arrange workable solutions for the specific personalities involved in that village. I expect some wrecks will surface but I believe we have to try."

Rosie set down her water glass. "You mentioned a two-man team. Do you have individuals in mind?"

"The Quebec letter requested we provide the name of our liaison person to deal with the Quebec government. I've discussed this with Thompson—he'd be our logical contact. However, he's about as bilingual as the rest of us. I don't believe that an English liaison person is in our best interest. I'd like this group to consider Louis LaFlamme, the freelance writer who wrote the ‘Breath of Fresh Air’ article in Le Devoir, to be our liaison with Quebec. To help achieve balance and fairness, I propose we ask Gaston Tribolski to be the second member of the team handling the personnel issues.”

Brett continued, “I’ve been in touch with Krista Wallace and Cindy Zhong. They’ll develop an approach that will allow the formal education system to be in French but still preserve English language development in many of the social and entertainment initiatives. This’ll take some time and resources but we expect the Quebec government will allow us to continue with the project while we retool the education approach in each Quebec village.”

Beth finished a note in her journal. “What about signage? I understand village signs on roads and shops will have to be in French.”

Brett reached for a page containing the Quebec road sign rules. “Yes, we’ll have to ensure that all signs are in French. It can be a village project that engages a few of our artistic villagers. When it comes to the permanent highway signage, we’ll get professional expertise to ensure the signs are appropriate and permanent.”

Thompson leaned forward. “Are there other issues that need to be addressed?’

When nobody raised any more issues, he continued, “Are we all in agreement on the way we’ll proceed?”

Rosie stood. “No, I’m not happy. Brett has been so high falutin’ about doing the right thing, every day, now we accept a bunch of stupid rules. It looks like my days on Soul Star are over.”

Brett rose from his chair. “Rosie, you’re a wonderful person. Each of us recognizes how precious you are and the effectiveness of your approach. We face a threat to the mandate that Soul Star has set for itself. We’ll address that threat in the best way we can and we’ll continue to act with principle and consideration. The French language is important to people. We’ve pursued solutions to environmental and aboriginal issues with your enthusiastic help. We’ve succeeded where eight generations of our predecessors have failed. Now, we face an emotional issue outside your experience. We'll listen—carefully—to what you have to say, but we ask you to accept the group wisdom, even when it differs from your chosen solution. We've come a long way together and we expect to finish together. Will you climb down off your high horse and give me a hug?"

A smile spread across Rosie's face as she met Brett half way round the table and gave him a big hug.

The others smiled and clapped.

Rosie shrugged. "I'm such a wimp. I can't even handle an old man."

Chapter 84

Elaine, Jacquie, Erika, Sherry and Simone gathered in the Larson home for a 'ladies only' party.

Brett, Jeremy, Michael, Sam, Saul and Solomon went to a baseball game.

A bluff of trees on the west hills of Calgary screened the activities of a man. At 7:30 in the evening, he pressed a button. A precision-strike rocket launched. It penetrated the Larson home. Five seconds later, it vaporized everything and everyone. A fireball flashed.

Neighbours' houses caught fire.

Sirens blared.

After the game, the guys drove back toward the family home. As they neared home, police lights flashed. An officer signalled them to stop.

"Good evening, folks. We're dealing with an incident and have cordoned off the area. It looks like it'll be several hours before you'll be able to enter the area."

Jeremy squeezed the steering wheel. "The rest of our family is at a house party. Isn't there any way to get to them?"

"Sorry, no one's allowed to enter the area."

Jeremy turned the car around and drove back to a strip mall. He called the house on his cell phone. When he got no answer, Brett suggested he call a neighbour. The neighbour seemed reluctant to talk so Jeremy asked him to talk to Brett. When Brett greeted him, the man sobbed audibly. "I'm sorry, Brett, your home has exploded. It's burning. I don't see how anybody in the house could've survived."

Brett dropped the phone. Brett told them what had happened. The rest didn't know what to do.

Sam suggested they could walk through alleys and side streets to get closer. Before they could see the house, police stopped them. Brett insisted that he be allowed to go to his home. When he pushed too hard, the police escorted him to a cruiser.

Jeremy spoke to the police and enquired whether they could take Brett to Jeremy's home. The police requested Jeremy's name and address and told the rest of the family to go there. He would deliver Brett to the address in about an hour.

Had all of the women and Simone been in the house? Are they all dead?

Chapter 85

Three men and two boys trudged back to the car. Jeremy drove to his home and parked on the driveway.

He unlocked the front door and all went into the kitchen.

Sam cuddled the twins. The demeanour of their dad, Jeremy, and Michael disoriented them.

Sam held his sons. "What could have happened? Could it have been a gas leak?"

Jeremy sat on the edge of a chair with his head in his hands. "We'll have to wait but I must phone Jacquie's parents."

The phone rang in Saskatoon, Saskatchewan.

Hazel Ambrose said, "Hello."

"It's Jeremy. There's been an explosion. We think Jacquie and Simone have been killed."

There was a moment of silence on the other end, then a raspy cry came from Hazel's throat. "Oh, no! How could such a thing happen?"

"They had a girls' night at my parents' home this evening. All the guys went to a baseball game. When we got back, the police had cordoned off the area and we couldn't get close. We expect the police to come and tell us more. I've talked to a neighbour who says the home exploded and burned. He doesn't see how anyone inside could have survived."

"What can we do?" Hazel's voice broke.

"I hope you and Bill will drive out tomorrow and stay with me until we understand what happened and find out if anyone survived."

"I'll talk to him now and we'll decide what to do. I'll let you know."

Sam phoned Sherry's parents, who lived on the south side of the city. They didn't answer. Sam left a message: "It's Sam;

we've had a terrible tragedy. Please call me, on my cell, as soon as you get this message."

An hour went by.

It seemed an eternity.

They heard a car close by.

They went to the door.

The policeman and Brett got out of the cruiser.

Brett embraced each of Saul, Solomon, Jeremy, Sam, and Michael.

Jeremy said, "Did they hurt you, Dad?"

"No, son, I'm okay."

The policeman closed the door. "Investigations take time. We keep evidence classified as long as it takes to assemble and prosecute a case. The two most obvious possibilities this evening are a natural gas explosion or some deliberate explosion. Many tragedies are the result of domestic situations. You should prepare yourselves for additional hurt as potential suspects. It's possible that the victims could have been lured or taken from the house. I understand there are eyewitness stories in the public realm. Perhaps you'll get some sense of the nature of this tragedy on TV.

"Trauma is difficult for anyone, especially young children," he continued. "If any of you need a counsellor, please call the number on this card and ask for help. You should decide, soon, how to communicate the impact of this situation to the children. Are you okay for tonight?"

Jeremy prepared to open the door for the policeman to leave. "Yes, we'll be okay. Thanks."

Sam shifted the boys on his lap. "I'm concerned about Saul and Solomon. I'll take them home and get them to sleep. I'll talk to Sherry's parents whenever I catch up to them. I'll watch the coverage on television and try to make sense of this. Will the rest of you come over to my house around eight o'clock tomorrow morning and help me decide what to do?"

Jeremy reached for a hand of Saul and Solomon. "Okay, Sam. Dad, will you and Michael stay here with me tonight? We can watch the coverage and also provide some comfort for each other."

Michael stepped forward. "I'll call my parents and make sure they know what's happened and then I'll decide whether to stay here or go stay with them tonight."

Brett put his arm around Sam's shoulder. "Sam, will you be alright with the boys? Do you want us to come to your home for the night?"

"No, I think I'll be okay; I never contemplated any situation like this but I think I'll survive. Please come over in the morning."

Sam took the boys home and Michael decided to go to his parents' home for the night. He promised to be at Sam's the next morning at 8:00.

Jeremy turned on the television and saw the basement shell of Elaine and Brett's home and neighbours' homes.

Then a reporter interviewed a cyclist. "Sir, I understand you're an eyewitness to aspects of this story."

"I believe I am. I cycled along a trail in west Calgary. I heard an explosion and sensed a whoosh of something in the air. A few seconds later I saw an explosion and a fireball."

"What'd you do then?"

"Well, I stopped to watch for a bit and then I phoned 911 and told them what I saw and heard."

"Then what did you do?"

"I decided to walk up to the bluff of trees where I thought the small explosion came from."

"What did you find there?"

"I suspected this might be a crime scene so I watched for anything unusual. I saw a small meadow in the grove of trees. As I scanned the meadow, I saw a tripod. I walked a little closer and I took a picture with my cell phone."

"What did you do then?"

"I went back to my bike, cycled home, and drove my car to the police station. I showed them the picture and gave them directions to the tripod. They took a copy of the picture, got me to write out a report, lectured me about care around crime scenes, asked me to keep the location confidential until they secured the site, and sent me on my way."

"Thank you."

The reporter summed up the day's events: "The evidence points to a deliberate attack on a private residence with a precision strike rocket causing explosion and fire. We doubt the occupants could have survived the blast. Neighbours' houses have burned but the neighbours are unharmed. Rocket attacks in Calgary. Who would believe it? Our crews will be on this story for several hours; now, back to the studio."

Jeremy looked at his dad, pale and slumped in a chair. "Dad, are you alright?"

"I've caused the death of all the girls in our family."

"What do you mean? Why do you think you're responsible? Are you aware of anyone with this kind of ill will toward you?"

He waved his hand weakly. "I can't think of anyone."

"If this attack happened on the Soul Star line, how would you figure out what happened?"

"Won't the police figure it out?"

"Yes, but they won't share the details with us or anyone in the public."

"Well, I'd call Beth and ask her to help."

"Let's call Beth."

"It's late. We shouldn't bother her tonight."

"Nonsense, Beth'll be offended if you wait."

Jeremy handed Brett the phone. He hesitated a moment and then dialled.

"Hello."

"Hello, Beth, it's Brett. I have terrible news. A bomb has demolished our home and all of our women folk. It looks like Elaine, Jacquie, Erika, Sherry and Simone are dead."

Beth gasped. "Oh, Brett, can it be?"

"The girls organized a ladies night and the guys went to a baseball game. We didn't know until we got back. A witness on TV says he heard an explosion and a whoosh in the air so he searched and found a missile launcher on the hill west of our home."

"Where are you now?"

"I'm at Jeremy's home. He's here with me. Sam took Saul and Solomon home and Michael has gone to his parents for the night."

"Should I come over?" Her voice wavered.

"No, we'll be okay. How do we figure out what happened?"

"I'll watch the news tonight and plan a strategy. I'll call you in the morning. I'll cancel all of the activities Soul Star planned for you and me for the next few days."

"I'll be over at Sam's home by eight tomorrow morning. Maybe wait until about ten and call me on my cell."

"Are you sure all of them were in the house?"

"Not sure, but we think so."

"This is terrible, Brett. I'll drop everything and help you discover what happened."

"Thanks, Beth."

Chapter 86

Beth called Oscar as soon as she got off the phone with Brett.

When Oscar answered, Beth gave him the story as she heard it from Brett.

Oscar said, "Sunday night, supper hour, it's a fluke that Brett and the rest of the guys are alive. Can you think of any suspects?"

"No, Brett's so even-handed; I don't see who might've taken such an aggressive step."

"The police won't release much information. How do we help solve this for Brett and his family?"

"I'll work on it through the night. I'll call Jeremy and Sam and get the names and numbers of Jacquie, Erika, Sherry, and Simone's friends so that we can call them and see when the last time anyone talked to anyone in the house. They're dead or detained or they would've called by now."

"What'll you do?"

I'll call Thompson, Rosie, and Hymie and let them know. We have a detailed listing of the Good Person Act expulsions. I'll try to get that list in the morning. I have a contact at airport security. I'll call him. We'll think of more approaches as we proceed. How terrible for Brett and his family."

Armed with the phone numbers of the friends of the Larson women, Beth called well into the night. No one had talked to any of the Larson women that evening but they agreed to check with others to see if anyone made contact.

Chapter 87

Sam put his boys to bed. Unsettled, they finally slept.

Sam watched the TV coverage.

Who could have done this?

Just before midnight, the phone rang.

Sherry's mom, Ellen, said, "Hello, Sam, what's happened?"

"You won't believe it. Someone bombed my parents' home. We think that Sherry and all the others are dead."

Ellen's reaction was immediate: "Sam, Sam, Sam, no."

"They might have been somewhere else, but we doubt it."

"Where are Saul and Solomon?"

"They're here with me, asleep. I haven't told them anything yet."

"Should we come over and stay with you?"

"No, we'll survive the night. I've asked Dad, Jeremy, and Michael to come over tomorrow morning at eight. Maybe you and Jim could come around seven so that we can talk a little before the rest get here."

"What time did the blast happen? I talked to Sherry around seven-thirty. They were all gathered around the fireplace doing pedicures and manicures. They seemed fine."

"I don't know the time. But please check your cell phone, it might show the time of that call. It might prove that all the girls were there close to the time the missile hit."

Chapter 88

One Page called his airport security contact.

"Hello."

"Hi, Ronnie, this is Oscar de Lona. How're you doin'?"

"It's the middle of the night; how do you think?" He groaned.

"You're in security, everything happens in the middle of the night."

"So what's on your mind?"

"The missile attack hit my friends' home last night. I want to figure out who did it."

"You and a million others. The cops swarmed all over the airport all night."

"What're they looking for?"

"The same thing you are."

"Have they found anything?'

"I'm not sure, they seemed to be focused on the Las Vegas passengers when my shift finished."

"Can I get a copy of the security film for that flight?"

"I doubt it. Most of us want our jobs and release of any tape to an outsider is not apt to improve our prospects."

"I hear you. Let me know if you hear anything helpful. Many thanks."

Chapter 89

Ellen and Jim arrived at seven, the twins still slept. Sam came to the door.

Ellen embraced Sam.

Tears flowed.

Jim swallowed, almost stoic. "I've checked Ellen's phone call with Sherry. It occurred five minutes before the explosion. It seems certain that all are gone."

Ellen said, "Do you have any idea who might've done this?"

Sam shrugged. "No, but it looks like they wanted to kill the entire family. We often gather at Mom and Dad's on Sunday evening. The time seems to indicate a desire for maximum carnage."

"Does your dad have any idea who might be responsible?"

"I don't think so, although he assumes he caused this atrocity."

"What will we say to Saul and Solomon?"

"I've struggled with that. I think we'll have to tell them that Mommy, Grandma, Auntie Jacquie, Auntie Erika, and Simone have all gone to Heaven. They're familiar with straightforward language but this is so extreme."

Sam put out some fruit and made a pot of coffee.

Brett and Jeremy arrived.

Ellen hugged Brett. "Oh, Brett, I'm so sorry; what a tragedy."

Brett continued the embrace. "I feel responsible. It's the worst feeling. Your Sherry, lost for nothing."

Ellen turned to Jeremy. "Jeremy, how terrible, three generations wiped out in an instant." Tears filled her eyes. "Why do people do such things?"

Jim shook hands all around, swallowed, nodded.

Michael arrived.

Brett, Jeremy, and Sam came to Michael and hugged him.

What to say? Erika gone.

The group lapsed into silence, sad, confused, conscious of the others but not motivated to talk.

Jeremy put down his coffee cup. "I think Dad and I'll go back to my home. We'll leave Ellen and Jim here with Sam, Saul, and Solomon. What would you like to do Michael?"

"I'll go to my parents' home. Please let me know any news and include me in memorial planning."

Brett stepped to Michael. "Michael, we'll always consider you family. I'm so sorry this happened to you so early in your life. Please forgive me."

Michael faced Brett. "My association with Erika and her family has been special. I know you blame yourself for what's happened, but I also know how much Erika admired your approach to life. We're all devastated but I remember the advice of a man who often said, 'What happened yesterday has already happened; let's decide to learn from history and make the best of today and tomorrow.' I admire that approach and that man. Can I go before I cry?"

Chapter 90

Brett considered how the family members could deal with grieving over the next couple of days. He decided he would rent a room at the Hyatt. This would allow Jacquie's parents to be with Jeremy and Sherry's parents to be with Sam, Saul, and Solomon. Brett wanted some time to come to grips with all that'd happened. Jeremy and Sam wanted Brett to stay with one of them but Brett prevailed. Jeremy dropped him off at the Hyatt.

Jeremy met Hazel and Bill at the door. Hazel embraced Jeremy. "Is there news?"

Bill shook Jeremy's hand. "Are you okay, Jeremy?"

"The police have released a photo of a person of interest. His name's Paulo Ramirez. Sherry's mom talked to Sherry on the phone a few minutes before the explosion. We think the missile killed them all."

Hazel glared at Jeremy with tear-filled eyes. "We've lost our only daughter and our only grandchild. Our heritage has been wiped out."

Jeremy nodded. "I feel lost and alone. My wife, child, and mother are all dead. My dad feels responsible. This feels pretty rotten right now."

Hazel spat, "You'll get over it. You're just as selfish as your father."

Jeremy looked at his mother-in-law.

Bill put his hand on her arm. "Hazel."

"Men, they're all so ignorant."

Bill turned to Jeremy. "She should calm down. I'm sorry she acts like she does."

Jeremy went for a long walk. When he came back, he suggested, "Bill, take her back home tomorrow morning. She's poison."

Chapter 91

Telephone calls inundated Brett: Beth Ragouski, Thompson Miller, Rosie Savard, Oscar One Page, Hymie Friedenberg, Oats Wolf, Keith Zisemo, Hal Eastman, George Zhong, Scott Shadle, Gord Tempel, Lex Thorn, Krista Wallace, Gorman Goulash, Louis LaFlamme, Jack Yudzik, Hal Eastman, Myrtle Murdoch, Glen Aspol, Gaston Tribolski, Terri Talisman, Per Aaslund, Arnie the truck driver, Calgary construction contacts, and extended family.

Brett appreciated the support but he couldn't shake the sense he'd caused the tragedy.

When the calls petered out, Brett called room service for some supper. He ate a little.

He thought back to Marjie, whose suicide triggered his quest for a star for individuals to follow. *Will I let that star fade? What price does one pay when one leads? Is the price justified? How does one know? What message will I send to Jeremy, who's lost his wife, his daughter, his mother? What message will I send to Sam, who's lost his wife and his mother? Now he's left to carry on with two young sons. What message will I send to Michael, who's lost his fiancé and has expressed his admiration for me?*

The night closed in.

The city calmed.

Brett pondered.

When the sun rose, would he?

Chapter 92

Brett woke with a start. He'd fallen asleep on the hotel sofa. When he got his bearings, he looked at his watch. Seven-thirty in the morning.

The sun did rise. I must too.

Brett phoned Sam. "Are you okay?"

"Yes, I'm okay. Ellen and Jim stayed most of the day. They'll come over about nine o'clock this morning. We told the boys. They don't seem to have comprehended yet."

"Be careful with them, Sam. We don't need more tragedy."

"Yes, Dad, I know. How're you?"

"A tough night, but I'll be okay."

"You sound better. I love you, Dad."

"I know, son, I love you, too."

Brett phoned Jeremy, "Are you okay?"

"Not that great. Hazel and Bill arrived about four. Hazel is bitter beyond words. I told Bill to take her back to Saskatoon. She's pure poison. He apologized for her and promised they'd go home this morning."

"Sorry, Jeremy. She always had a mean streak but she's lost a lot. One can sympathize with her."

"Yes, but she could be human."

"Once they're gone, give me a call. I'll come over and stay with you a few days. We need to decide about a memorial service."

"Are you up for that today?"

"I'm through the worst of it. I feel better this morning."

"You sound a lot better. I'll call you around ten."

"Thanks, son, I love you."

"I love you, too, Dad. Glad your old spirit is back."

Chapter 93

As soon as the 911 call came in with the alleged missile strike, high alert protocols went into effect. This caused all the security camera images at the airport to be saved. Detectives pored over those images through the night. While unlimited possibilities for disguise and deception might occur, the police decided the act itself, and the note left beside the missile launcher, indicated a brazen perpetrator. So they looked for a passenger who might be suspect.

A detective honed in on a man, about thirty, who held a Las Vegas ticket. The detective sensed the guy was on edge, and asked two others to review the tape. One of the two also picked out the guy for more careful scrutiny.

After eight hours of security tapes, the Las Vegas man emerged as the prime target. The police ran the photo through their database. Found no match.

The chief of police reviewed the tape, questioned the detectives, and checked the address before he authorized the publication of the man's photo as a person of interest in the missile attack.

The publication missed the morning papers but dominated the television. The perpetrator carried a ticket in the name of Paul Ramirez. The address was false.

Chapter 94

On Monday evening, Glen and Sally Aspol watched the news. The Larson home bombing dominated along with a photo of Paulo Ramirez.

As the initial shock turned to anger, Glen took a closer look at the photo. "Sally, look at that photo. Isn't that Tom Cairns?"

Sally studied the photo with a furrowed brow. "Yes, that's him. Do you suppose Tom Cairns could've done this?"

"I don't know, but we better let the captain know."

Glen called Ole Tchir. "Hello, Captain, this is Glen Aspol. Have you seen the news this evening?"

"Hi, Glen. No, I just came in from my rounds and haven't turned the television on. What's happened?"

"Well, Brett Larson's home in Calgary has been bombed and it appears all of the women in his family have been killed. Sally and I have identified the man as Tom Cairns."

"Are you serious? Tom Cairns?"

"Yes, I'm serious."

Ole watched the news and phoned the Calgary police.

The detective asked, "How sure are you of the identity of this man?"

Captain said, "The Gronson Fjord village on the Soul Star line evicted Tom Cairns for his part in a conspiracy to conceal a silver find and for threats against Glen and Sally Aspol. Glen and Sally saw the news this evening and called me. All three of us are certain that the man in the photo is Tom Cairns."

"Thank you, Mr. Tchir. We'll take it from here."

Chapter 95

The police considered the accumulated evidence.

Tom Cairns, a former villager on a project championed by Brett Larson.

Travelled under an alias with a false address.

A missile launcher left at the site.

A note left beside the launcher.

Tom Cairns expelled from a Soul Star village; apparent motive.

But how did he acquire a missile and guide it with precision?

Headlines in London, New York, Sydney, and Auckland featured the irony of a missile attack in peaceful Canada. The worldwide warrant for the arrest of Tom Cairns for the murders of four women and one child brought another round of news coverage. Some of the coverage suggested the policies implemented on the Soul Star project could not survive resulting atrocities such as the Calgary bombing.

The Soul Star team considered publically addressing the issues raised in the media but they decided to let the news die down and learn from the spin that could be expected from commentators harbouring different perspectives from those used to build the Soul Star line.

Chapter 96

Ellen and Jim arranged a day with the twins.

Jacquie's parents decided to have a service in Saskatoon for Jacquie and Simone.

Sherry's parents arranged a service for Sherry in Calgary.

Brett, Jeremy, Sam, and Michael gathered at Jeremy's home to plan a memorial that would include all five ladies. They believed each sacrificed life formed part of a common fabric.

Michael held a photo of Erika. "How can we manage a tribute for five individuals that does justice to each but doesn't drag on for hours?"

Sam looked up from a list of friends and relatives. "I suggest a book that we'll assemble and hand out to every individual who attends the memorial. It could have a chapter for each of Mom, Jacquie, Erika, Sherry, and Simone."

Jeremy set aside a photo album. "I like that idea. The book could contain the full tribute for each lady and still allow brief commentary in the service."

A discussion convinced the guys a book could be assembled, polished, and printed in time if the tasks were shared amongst close friends. They decided the probable inconsistent messages would add texture and reflect the differences between the five individuals while still recognizing the context of the Larson family and the Soul Star project. The memorial would be held at Mitford Park. The service would be recorded and broadcast on closed circuit television to every village on the Soul Star line.

Five ladies were chosen to prepare the tributes. The group would decide on songs and hymns.

Chapter 97

Eleanor, Henrietta, Melissa, and Karen all dove into their roles. The variety and depth of the tributes provided texture: sadness, shattered expectations, and emptiness. Bobbi's mother, Samantha, expressed concern about the impact on her young daughter. Samantha met with Jeremy and Brett. "When we first heard Simone died in the explosion, Bobbi and I talked. She said, 'We imagined all kinds of good and scary things. We didn't expect the scary things to happen. Now, a scary thing has happened and my friend is dead. I imagine Simone alone in Heaven. She'll have her mommy, grandma, and aunties, but there'll be nobody her age. She'll go through her whole lifetime with none of her friends beside her.' We talked about that and what we might do to allow Simone's fate to teach life lessons. We've revisited this topic over the last few days. Now, Jeremy has come to me to ask if Bobbi might help with the memorial book and speak at the service. It's an honour, but I must be certain that Bobbi can manage the emotions and discomfort in front of an audience. Can an eleven-year-old handle that?"

Brett said, "We must protect Bobbi. It's possible that this structured element might be better for Bobbi than relative calm with fewer avenues to shed light on her thoughts. Perhaps you and Bobbi can work on the written tribute for the book and then decide whether Bobbi can safely speak at the service. Her imagined picture of Simone with no one her own age will resonate with everyone. It'll be special if Bobbi decides to talk herself, but it'll still be powerful if you decide that you could present for her."

Jeremy shut down his iPad. "Is this too much to ask of Bobbi and you?"

Samantha looked at Jeremy and hesitated. “I don’t know. Can you leave it with me for two days? I’ll talk about it with Bobbi and see what we decide.”

Jeremy nodded. “Thanks. The events are terrible but we have to carry on.”

Samantha headed for the door. “I know. Give me some time.”

Chapter 98

A slight breeze followed the sun in from the southwest.

People streamed into Mitford Park, signed the guest registers, and placed their lawn chairs in a curve around the stage.

Instrumental music played in the background.

The sound volume increased as Frank Mills played "The Music Box Dancer".

The volume raised some more as Michael Jackson sang "Heal the World".

A trumpet sounded *The Bugler's Cry, Taps* and a hush fell over the crowd.

Six ladies walked from the wings and took their places at a podium built for six that dominated the stage.

Ellen turned on her microphone. "Thank you for sharing this day. I'm Ellen Livingstone, Sherry's mother. We've planned a concert of love, inspiration, respect, and music in celebration of the lives of five individuals. Please feel free to applaud at the end of each presentation.

"As you settled into your seats, you heard Michael Jackson singing *'Heal the World'*. That song alerts us to the bad things that happen each day and invites us to do our part to make it better. A tragic incident has brought us here today. We think about the family and friends left to grieve and we share their grief, but we will not break. We will remember, we will learn, we will endure and we will continue to make positive differences.

"When you leave, you'll receive a bound book that contains portraits of, and tributes to, the five ladies we honour today. The book is titled, *Five Tears to Shed; Five Tears to Mend*. Many tears have been shed and more will come. There are many tears in the fabric of the families, in the community and in the world.

We'll all tend to the tears and tears as we press on in spite of all obstacles.

"Onstage is a group of musicians and soloists who'll inspire us in song. After the formal part of this service, we encourage you to stay and visit with the individuals who've lost their mates, mothers, daughters and granddaughter. Each of them will provide a gathering spot along the west side of the grounds. There'll be refreshments. Please visit awhile and reflect on the ideas the ladies beside me will present to you.

"We've arranged for the songs and talks to flow without introductions."

Glen Martin, Simone's uncle, sang, *'You Raise Me Up'*, a song made famous by Josh Grobin.

Eleanor took a deep breath. "My dear friend, Elaine, is dead, killed by a man who wasted his opportunity for a fresh start. Elaine supported Brett's mission to allow young people the opportunity to build good lives through individual responsibility. That mission has been accomplished many times over. We might view Elaine's death as a needless outcome of Brett's determined pursuit of better ways. Brett feels it. Jeremy and Sam feel it. But I wonder. Brett could have retired and let his vision and skill wither. He chose a different path and sought the support of Elaine and other family members. He received that support and the Soul Star project nears completion, eleven years later. Eight years ago, the Gronson Fjord villagers judged the actions of Tom Cairns and found him unworthy. I ask each of you, today, if you lead your life by trying to do the right thing at every moment of every day? Elaine tried to do that. She usually succeeded. Brett's decisions didn't kill Elaine; Tom Cairns did.

"We mourn the loss of a special woman. We know the emptiness that fills many hearts because of it. Now we honor her as we press on and absorb these sad moments. She lifted up her husband, her children, her grandchildren, and her many friends. We can, too. We're thankful to have shared our world with this woman. Rest in peace, my friend."

Ginger Smith, Sherry's friend sang, *'The Climb'*, a song popularized by Miley Cyrus.

Henrietta wiped a tear away and began with a wavering voice, "An only child, Jacquie was raised in a home short on hope, vision, and compassion. After high school, she moved from Saskatoon to Calgary. We became friends. We studied culinary arts at the Southern Alberta Institute of Technology and we got jobs at the Hyatt in downtown Calgary. Jacquie met Jeremy. Their relationship flourished, they married, and Simone arrived. Jacquie built a better household dynamic than the one she endured in her youth. Her commitment to this goal shone through almost every day. Sometimes, she regressed. On those occasions, Jeremy summoned the care and compassion to ride out the storm. After one of these episodes, Jacquie confided in me, 'I'm so thankful Jeremy seems to have the capacity to let me safely vent. I often wonder how he came to be the man he is.' I told her I knew how: he came from a home filled with hope, vision, and compassion.

"Jeremy has lost much: he's lost his wife, his daughter, and his mother. These are huge losses by any measure, but he still comes out a winner. He still has his original heritage but he's lost the heritage he built with Jacquie and Simone. When he recovers from the worst of this sad situation, he has the tools to build again. As we ponder Jacquie's legacy, we grasp the significance of her mission to overcome the many hurts of her youth, to be strong enough to do better herself and to be generous enough to encourage others who have similar missions. Jacquie's quest ended early. Those of us who knew her story will draw inspiration from her example. You did well, Jacquie. We pass your torch to others who continue to face challenges and we'll use your approach to help others. Good bye Jacquie, I love you."

Ginger sang Garth Brooks' song, *'The River'*.

Melissa scanned the audience. "Hello, friends. Erika blessed me with her friendship. Michael found Erika. I saw Erika as a princess: kind, exuberant, smart, outgoing, and beautiful. You could travel the world and not find a more complete package. She died young, many would say needlessly. I wonder about the needless part. Those who are religious may find solace in their superpower's will. Those who rely upon rational thought may find few insights to counter the needless point of view. But I see a reason for random traumatic events. Good and bad things happen to each one of us. Some instinctively know how to thrive on the good and avoid the bad. Most of us struggle a little bit with the bad and don't cherish the good quite as much as we should. Some succumb to the bad and don't recognize how to benefit from the good. In our everyday worlds, we don't think about the goods and the bads in a clear way." Her voice hardened in tone. "However, when some idiot directs a missile at five individuals and vaporizes them all, we notice. When we do notice, we have an opportunity to reflect on the good and bad and decide on better choices. I want to leave you with Erika's bequest. She leaves with a clear message: your life will be rewarded if you thrive on the goods and master how to deal with the bads. She learned this well. It didn't protect her from an ultimate bad but it did benefit her throughout her life. Goodbye, princess; your bequest will benefit millions."

Glen sang, *'Amazing Grace'*.

Karen approached Glen and kissed him before returning to her podium. "Sherry was my friend since kindergarten. I resented Sam when he stole her heart and consumed her time. We recognize the traits of the Larson family that allow so many achievements. Sherry recognized them, too. The difference between Sherry's family and Sam's family is the Larson gift of seizing the moment. Sherry had a good chance in life because she grew up in a family that nourished individual responsibility. But this advantage did not stop a missile. Saul and Solomon, precious twin sons, are here today. They're Sherry's legacy. I know that Sam will nourish them but a widowed father will have challenges. I leave you with the thought that Sherry's first four years with her sons will serve them well. However, she needed more years to grant them her full gift. Please think about Saul and Solomon and Sam in the days and years ahead. While they have many tools already, they are vulnerable. In the absence of Sherry, they must make do. You can help them. Sherry will be thankful."

Ginger sang John Lennon's song, *'Imagine'*.

Bobbi looked down at her mom in the front row. “You can do it,” her mom mouthed.

“Simone and I were friends. We imagined all sorts of things, happy things and scary things. I imagine her alone in Heaven, no one her own age. It might be eons before her friends join her. Now, I imagine how I might be able help others who are still here.

“I asked my mom if she would help me. She cried when she said she would. Then, she suggested that I ask each person at Simone’s service if they would help. I was afraid. Mom assured me that you’d understand and appreciate my idea. I hope you do. I wonder if each one of us would watch for kids who think they’re alone; when we find one we should offer to imagine with them and help them find their way. Simone and I would appreciate that.”

Ginger and Glen sang, *‘What A Wonderful World’*.

Ellen smiled. “Wow, what a wonderful world. That concludes the formal part of the day. Please linger.”

Chapter 99

Makoto Shiryendo spent eighteen years as a rebellious anarchist. His experiences combined with admirable, inherited traits allowed him to emerge as a gifted leader. As Makoto progressed through the military hierarchy, his ability to manage the most difficult of Navy personnel shone through.

When Makoto retired from the Navy, a commercial shipping company recruited him to train and inspire their personnel. Most Japanese shipping executives knew of Makoto's reputation.

The president of Makoto's company mulled over the phone call he received from the Japanese Prime Minister. His own lifetime experiences and Makota's reputation as a rebel, prisoner, Navy officer, and commercial shipping executive led to this request. Makoto must decide whether he would accept the assignment that would require him to work with a Japanese Navy officer in complete secrecy.

Chapter 100

United States intelligence agencies assembled pieces of information. As the weeks went by, senior military personnel perceived the government of Japan had embarked on a mission involving a civilian cargo ship. The president of the United States contemplated the information brought to him by the secretary of defense. A civilian Japanese cargo ship loaded with top-secret cargo headed toward North America. He asked his aide to get the Canadian Prime Minister on the phone.

"Good morning, Mr. President."

"Good morning. I'll get to the point. We have information that a Japanese civilian ship is headed toward North America. It carries secret cargo."

"Yes, Mr. President. We're aware of the mission and we've determined there is no security threat."

"Why have you failed to keep us informed in accordance with the protocols between our countries?"

"The answer is threefold: one, we determined that the mission is benign; two, we wished to observe the capabilities and management of the security agencies on which we rely; and three, we wanted to be the first to know, for a change."

The president said, "I'm disturbed at this breach. Why would Canada jeopardize the respect between our two countries?"

"Mr. President, I've explained that to you. We wish to be good neighbours and allies. I'll instruct our ambassador to brief your select senior personnel. The purpose of the mission and the nature of the cargo are both benign. Canada requests, and demands, no public disclosure of this mission within the next seven days."

Chapter 101

As the project neared completion, Jack Yudzik told Hymie that he wanted to visit a village, get a firsthand feel for the project, and take some photographs. Hymie suggested that he go to Gronson Fjord because he admired the people and the site. As Jack ventured into the village, he asked for Krista Wallace. She met Jack at the general store and led him to the coffee shop where she regaled him with the culture of the place and told him that Glen Aspol would spend the next couple of hours with him. She assured Jack that he'd appreciate his time with Glen.

Glen came over to the table and introduced himself. "Hello, Jack, I'm Glen Aspol. Welcome to Gronson Fjord."

"Good to meet you, Glen. I'm enthused about my visit."

Krista waved as she headed out. "Glen, please show Jack to his room when you finish tonight and, Jack, I'll meet you in the morning here in the coffee shop at seven-thirty."

Glen led Jack out of the coffee shop. "I want to show you a place that means a lot to me."

They walked for a few minutes. Jack already felt at home here in a remote northern village, which he entered an hour before.

The two men walked out onto a stone terrace. Jack stopped. Seven tiers of stone arches curved around a lake shimmering in the evening sun. Jack stood there some minutes, in no rush to end the magic. He took out his camera and snapped a few frames. "These are not professional photos but personal mementos of this magic scene."

Glen sat. "I placed this bench here so I could come and sit at times when I needed a spiritual lift. You're welcome to come here anytime. Enjoy the place, and take pictures as you see fit. When Per Aasie realized these terraces could curve along this man-made lake, he thought of his homeland and his Norwegian mentors and chose to call this village Gronson Fjord. Gronson Fjord has become a poster village for many aspects of the Soul Star project. One of our gems is Krista Wallace, who's led many profound educational innovations."

"How did you and Krista know that this place would strike me so vividly?"

"We seldom host accomplished photographers. We did some research, including talks with Rosie Savard, Hymie Friedenberg, and Myrtle Murdoch, and formed the impression that you'd appreciate this scene."

"I didn't know what to expect. Rosie is driven. I kind of expected she had oversold the good that Soul Star does for so many. I envisioned a ramshackle, temporary village where a bunch of underachievers maintained a modicum of responsibility. The bulk of the media coverage tends to the dramatic, negative aspects of a situation. To come here, see, and feel the commitment to each individual is wonderful."

"Take your time and ask me anything, I have knowledge of this village and the Soul Star project in general. I also have an interest in the social and spiritual nuances that assure the success of Soul Star."

Jack set his camera on the bench. "I'm a simple man. I seldom dwell on social and spiritual issues except where those considerations inspire a specific photograph. Since I've taken a few acclaimed photographs, my subconscious approach may be more spiritual than I perceive."

"You can be as modest as you want, but our research shows a man that has a sense of right and the willpower to persevere that's consistent with the Soul Star culture. Are you a religious man?"

Jack looked at Glen, surprise etched on his face.

"We tend to be direct here. Too many of our villagers failed to discern a realistic path from the garbled messages they received in their first fifteen or twenty years."

"In that light, I'll answer your question. Early on, I formed the impression that belief in God is expected. I don't know how

I got that message. I've chosen to spend little time on the genesis of human life. Evolution fits my sense of things. Supreme Designer and Big Bang theories do nothing for me. I can't imagine an all-knowing, all-powerful God that just happened. Even if I could get over that hurdle, I have profound trouble with a God authoring so much grief. Time and again, my conscience has served me better than the admonitions of the church. I'd say I've been a closet atheist since the Old Testament stories seemed criminal and the explanations seemed irrational."

"Most of the young people in the Soul Star villages rebelled against something, often minor but sometimes significant. We discovered religion formed one of the focal points of rebellion. In order to minimize the impact, Soul Star found ways to downplay specific religious doctrines while concentrating on what makes a person good. We've reached consensus that fear is not the best foundation on which to build a life. This may be a key ingredient to the success of Soul Star. Most rebels have developed ways to combat fear. Our solution involves few rules and predictable consequences. We have one police person in each village. The villagers elect a police officer who's a sociable person who's willing to be visible around the community most of his waking hours. Violent incidents seldom occur."

"Why did you ask me about religion?"

"Two reasons. One, we want to be considerate of visitors; two, we wish to find ways to articulate Soul Star successes so that the wider world might benefit."

"You can practice on me. I should already know more than I do about Soul Star. I hope to shoot some photos that will provide opportunities for dialogue."

"What do you think of these rows of arches along the shore?"

"On an emotional level, I'm entranced; it's a scene I'll never forget. On a practical level, I haven't discerned why they're here."

"The Soul Star team decided each village would grow as much of its own food as possible. They adopted two significant innovations: the pivot wedge, which Frannie Milpak will show you tomorrow, and these arched terraces all along both sides of the line. Every village has terraces where the villagers raise their own vegetables. Soul Star found a mentor for the management of these terraced farms. His name is George Zhong. He and his friend perfected farming under awning, which they called fawning. The idea is to store heat in the rocks during sunny periods that then keep the soil and air warmer at night. In this climate, we've made sure that there are geothermal tubes under all the gardens so that we can extend the growing season well beyond the ninety-five frost-free days that are normal here in conventional farming. George designed terraces on open hillsides with awnings made of canvas with water tubing integrated for strength and also to heat water. Soul Star's innovation has been the use of the rock from the tunnel to build these arched terraces so the roofs are permanent. Soul Star wants to instil craftsmen-like qualities in all of the villagers. They build grand arches wherever practical. The short-term benefits are the fawning terraces, living space for the villagers, and attention to detail on a very large scale. Each village has built arched terraces wherever the surface terrain allows enough height from the natural elevation to the finished elevation of the project surface."

"Are there arches like those almost everywhere under this project?"

"Wherever the elevations permit."

What about the volume of space created by Soul Star?

Jack paused a moment. "What will all this space be used for after the project is done?"

"There are many possibilities. Where the Soul Star line is adjacent to communities, we see the sides used as housing. The interiors can be used for community halls, commercial space for stores, manufacturing plants, car and implement dealerships, curling rinks…you name it. Further away, the exposed terraces may continue to be fawning operations, tourist facilities, hunting and fishing lodges. Where there are wild animal trails and migration routes, the arches are left open for the animals to cross through. We expect manufacturing plants will be attracted to space that is very economical to heat and cool, has massive solar power available on the road surface above, has housing established for large numbers of people, and has lots of surface transportation within a stone's throw of the plant. We expect the Soul Star line will become a vibrant ribbon clear across the country."

"What does Rosie think of all this density in the north?"

"Rosie has been a key player in our designs. Each villager has been encouraged to think about the environment. As we ponder the impact of many people concentrated in one spot, we know that infrastructure is bound to happen. This project has accomplished more than any other area in the world, in density terms, while the environment thrives. As you visit our village, think about environmental concerns and consider what Soul Star has done to address them. I hope you'll be surprised and impressed."

"We started out at the very personal level and branched out to broad environmental and economic issues. Let's get back to Gronson Fjord. There're too many terraces here to raise vegetables for 300 Gronson Fjord villagers."

"For sure, Gronson Fjord happened to have the terrain that allowed the seven tiers of terraces to be built in one spot. This justifies resident expertise for growing flowers and fruits that couldn't be supported in most of the villages. So this is our greenhouse area where special flowers are raised for the entire Soul Star population. It's also home to our research team and hosts George Zhong, our fawning mentor."

"Is there a university nearby?"

"Yes, UIRIT University is northwest of us in the Northwest Territories; we're in Alberta. The university is premised on driven students near a project with scale, innovative methods, proximity to northern wilderness, and examples of alternatives to education and social welfare. The students find their own mentors and pursue their own agenda but with milestones to assure diligent progress. The dam on Stoddart Creek pools this body of water. The dam is just upstream from the university that's built underneath the right of way and stretches across the valley. The dam provides power for the mill that grinds our grain and powers one of our machine shops."

"How do the native Indians fit into the Soul Star fabric?"

"Do you realize how dedicated, maybe even lucky, a native person has to be to excel in the broader community?"

"Yes; my family fostered Rosie for sixteen years. I know some of the hardships her mother endured."

"I use Rosie's story often when native issues arise. She's lucky, her mother's vision combined with your family's contribution. It could've turned out different."

"Do you believe that many experiences, similar to Rosie's, can be achieved?"

"That's one of the messages evident in Soul Star."

"Help me understand how Canada can help natives reach serenity while still finding acceptance in the whole community. I recognize the Healthy Habitats project has allowed many natives to sign Individual Treaty Obligations, but I haven't understood the mission?"

"Soul Star perfected a view of individual responsibility. It has multiple facets but the central tenant is the Good Person Act. This act requires every individual in every element of life to be individually responsible. The rules are minimal and the consequences profound. Concerning our native individuals, this means significant changes in long-established laws and approaches. It means all treaties end, revisions to the Canadian Charter of Rights and Freedoms, abolishment of the Indian Act, and individual responsibility from every individual in Canada, regardless of race, creed, historical arrangements, and petty politics. The transition from our dysfunctional systems to the Soul Star model requires action on multiple fronts. We expect Soul Star will graduate hundreds of champions for change. Each of us can encourage and support initiatives that'll get us there. On an individual basis, natives can take charge of their own situations, much as Young Eagle did. Those of us in positions of influence can speed the transition. A few can cause an epidemic when the few are viral."

"How did you come to be involved in Soul Star, Glen?"

"I grew up in a good family. Slow classes and complacent teachers bored me in school. I played with drugs, ignored sports, disobeyed my parents, resented almost every aspect of life, and became a heavy burden on my family. I thought they deserved better. I didn't understand my unhappiness. One day, a group of us jumped our bikes off a retaining wall in the park near my home. Our parents forbid us and the police warned us, which added to the excitement, of course. One day, I jumped my bike off the wall and landed on the side of a mower. I bounced off the driver, tumbled over the reels of the mower, and landed in a heap. I lay there, winded and sore. The mower driver fell off the mower and lay unconscious; blood spurted from a leg where his foot should have been.

"When I came to, my shoulder ball bulged in my armpit but, otherwise, I seemed to be okay. My parents tended me in hospital. They provided love and support. I let them down. With two years' probation, I quit school and invested six months to raise the net pay that the driver would've earned to age sixty-five. With the money in a trust account, I went to him and his family, handed over the trust cheque, apologized for my stupidity, and promised I'd be a good citizen for the rest of my life. I left the man's home and went to my friend's home. He watched the accident. His parents searched for a solution. His mother said to me, 'I've found a project that may be good for you boys'. I came to Gronson Fjord. He died in a car crash."

"Do you think most of the Soul Star villagers have reformed by the time they get to the project?"

"No, I'd say that most have not reformed. However, they're not permitted to come to the project unless they agree to be individually responsible from that moment forward. In that sense, they've made a big commitment. Some don't live up to it. The Good Person Act assigns a point system to mistakes and weeds out those individuals that won't reform."

"Did you ever receive any points under The Good Person Act?"

"Yes, I agreed to be a co-conspirator in a silver find. My girlfriend, who's now my wife, helped me realize my error and I became the whistleblower. When my points dropped off in 1,100 days, Sally and I received the inaugural 'Good Citizen' designations sponsored by Soul Star."

"Do you think that Soul Star has perfected methods to mentor rebellious youth in broader communities?"

"I think about that. There should be ways to do it but there're also impediments. I think large construction projects could use the same methods as Soul Star. However, the entities involved will have myriad rules in place, human resources, unions, safety, incentives, pay scales, and many more. We need a model where those sorts of rules can be changed. It's probable that much of the developed world won't tolerate the changes required in the Soul Star model. Less developed countries may be a place where Soul Star methods could be implemented to tremendous benefit."

"I'm inclined to agree with your analysis, but I think you should set your sights much higher in the developed world. A few dedicated champions can originate profound change."

"That's true, Jack, but I'm not that champion. I've worked within the structure at Gronson Fjord and I've benefited immensely. Even with my success, I don't have the vision and drive necessary to initiate change. The founders of Soul Star and oodles of our villagers have that potential. I hope you're right about the broadened potential of the Soul Star model all over America, Europe, and beyond."

"I better go to my room, rest, and get ready for a new day of discovery. Thank you so much for this wonderful evening."

"You're welcome. I enjoyed our visit. I hope you get some great photographs."

At breakfast the next morning, Jack told Krista how much he appreciated his first evening in Gronson Fjord. Krista expected Glen and Gronson Fjord would make a good impression but she appreciated Jack's thanks.

"This morning, I'll guide you out to the farm where Frannie will tour you through the farming operations."

"I'm ready."

As they strolled beyond the north edge of the right-of-way, Jack noticed many peculiar tubes with a wire enclosure tagged onto one side of each tube.

"What, pray tell, are those contraptions?"

Krista laughed. "They're pivot wedges. Frannie has worked with the farm for years and she'll explain them to you. Let's find her."

Frannie stepped into view. "Hi, Krista. I see you have Jack with you."

"Yes, Frannie, please meet Jack Yudzik. Jack this is Frannie Milpak."

"Pleased to meet you, Frannie."

Frannie shook his hand. "I'm looking forward to the morning. Krista, I'll get Jack to the coffee shop by dinnertime."

Frannie and Jack walked on.

Jack said, "Please explain these tubes and wire cages to me."

"The Soul Star team decided to be careful about conflict between farming operations and native animal populations. They decided all domestic animals and birds should be fenced in and all wild animals and birds should be fenced out. At the same time, they wanted to optimize the capability of each acre of land under cultivation. Gord Rempel designed a pivot that would utilize one acre of ground and would achieve all the goals defined by Soul Star. Gord perfected these pivot wedges for dairy and beef cattle and let the users design improvements on the fly."

"What's the radius of each pivot?"

"The radius is 148 feet. The distance allows each pivot to catch the corners of one acre, which is 209 feet square. We have the pivots programmed so that adjacent pivots do not arrive at the same corner at the same time."

"What powers the movement of the pivots?"

"The exterior walls and roof of the tubes that you mentioned are solar panels. They provide enough power to move the pivot. Each pivot has a battery that stores energy for power when needed."

"What are the tubes for, other than support for the solar panels?"

"Their primary use is to provide shelter for the animals; protection from sun, rain, snow and wind."

"How many animals can be supported in one pivot?"

"That depends on the species. We have one cow with her calf, two ewes with their lambs, and twenty laying hens. This, combination seems to balance the grass production with the amount the animals eat. There can be variations depending on weather and size of animals."

"How do the animals get bred when they are confined in their pens?"

"That has been one of the challenges. There are sophisticated ways to tell when females are in estrus but we've adopted the old-fashioned way. We've fenced the perimeter of the farm with a reliable game fence. This allows us to turn the bulls, rams, and billy goats loose in the area. When they identify receptive females, we turn the females out to get bred."

"Isn't it kind of cruel to confine the animals in cages like this?"

"We've considered many aspects of segregation. We think our methods may be less ideal than herds in a large pasture when just the social aspects of the species are considered. However, the hierarchy aspects of herds cause some animals to be shunned, disadvantaged, and injured, as the animals compete in the group. Our methods seldom place one animal of one species in a pen. Usually, there are at least mother-offspring pairs that are very natural in any environment. We've observed that most animals are satisfied that other animals of their species are in adjacent pens. In short, we've concluded that the overall welfare of the animals is better in our pivot wedge modules than any other farm arrangement."

"Why do you mix various species in one pen?"

"We've learned that cattle, sheep, goats, and chickens choose to eat different plants and insects with the result that manure is broken down quicker, insect pests are controlled, and no weed is permitted to thrive inside the pivot. Another reason we include sheep, goats, and chickens with cattle is to better balance grass production with consumption."

"How do the animals get water?"

"When the pivots are installed, we plow in a water pipe underground and then plumb it to permit a water bowl in each pen."

"Why don't you have pigs in the pivot pens?"

"Pigs are a challenge." Frannie shrugged. "They root in the soil. This causes mechanical problems with the rotation of the pivots. As a result, we keep our pigs in one of the arches under the right-of-way."

"Do you have problems with squirrels, raccoons, magpies, eagles, gulls, and the like?"

"You'll notice that the top of each pivot pen is closed in with mesh. This prevents wild birds and some small wild animals from hassling the farm animals. We've not designed the pens to protect from smaller animals such as weasels and mice."

"How do the bulk of the villagers learn from the farm?"

"The exposure to the lifecycle and the natural order of things. The obvious effects of selective breeding and its probable support for evolution. Fresh produce from our own gardens, home grown flour, beef, pork, chicken, cheese, sausage, yarn, woollen bats in our quilts, skin rugs on our floors, rawhide bindings on her furniture. The reality of slaughter, gutting, skinning, meat cutting. The repetition of feeding, milking, collecting eggs. The trauma and elation of birth. The insistence of the males. The mothering instincts of the females. The direct connection between animal husbandry and wholesome food for the villages. Various specializations evident on each farm. The responses of animals to fear, weather, noise, and aggression. The damage of foot rot, mastitis, bloating, warbles, horseflies, maggots."

"Okay, I get your drift, but it still seems different than the family farm of sixty years ago. Here, a few are charged with farm responsibilities."

"You have a point. We've developed ways to widen the experience in our villages. Every villager takes turns gathering eggs, milking cows, slaughtering, making sausages, taking grain to the mill for grinding into flour, and gathering garden produce. We have competitions in our fall fair to judge animals for conformation, breed characteristics, size, and gender traits. Our spring celebration involves extensive tours of the newborn farm animals and our Thanksgiving celebrations focus on the farm as a key part of the village experience. Our education program includes modules on each farm endeavour and our Come Alive! center uses farm metaphors to explain enduring truths."

You project enthusiasm for your career here at Soul Star. The Soul Star experience seems to have been thorough in surprising dimensions."

"I'm pleased you see that. I enjoy my job at Gronson Fjord and I appreciate the chance to develop a meaningful approach to life. While you'll find villagers that are superficial in their approach, I guarantee you'll find a high percentage of villagers who know they've been blessed by the approaches that Soul Star has utilized."

"Do you think the villagers recognize the influence that's salvaged dysfunctional lives?"

"I guess the short answer is 'yes', but there're several nuances. Quite a few of the villagers would have come around to useful lives without Soul Star. Brett Larson intended to attract real misfits. For that group, Soul Star is a stellar success. Brett realizes complete villages of his targeted misfits would not have been as successful as what happened. What did happen is the Soul Star adventure attracted a bunch of bored, rebellious young people who yearned for straight answers. They brought a set of traits that help provide peer role models and examples of individual leadership that aren't as prevalent in the true misfits."

"Well, Frannie," Jack began, "I'm a photographer. I'll shoot around the farm but what do you envision as the perfect farm photo?"

"That's easy; it's me beside a beautiful palomino stallion. My hair is combed, my cheeks are rosy, and my boobs are perky. Seriously, I have the article that Myrtle Murdoch published about

Rosie. I admire your photo of Young Eagle. If you photograph the scenery, the workers, the animals, the players, the lovers, the handicapped, and the ordinary, the world will be impressed."

"Thank you, for your compliments and your tour. I appreciate all you've done."

"It's been fun. If you think of other questions or need access to farm places for your photo shoots, just let me know. I better get you over to the coffee shop for dinner. Krista is a real task master, you know."

Chapter 102

A Japanese cargo ship sailed toward North America. It headed for somewhere north of Vancouver Island, near the Alaskan panhandle. While Canada assured the US military about security, the United States managed its own surveillance. Most of the staff expected the ship to dock in Prince Rupert, British Columbia. As darkness fell on June twenty-eighth, the mystery ship adopted a more northerly course. Surveillance personnel and the Pentagon went into high alert. Top command knew the rest of the story.

Then the ship vanished.

Chapter 103

June twenty-ninth, Myrtle Murdoch left her desk to walk home for supper. As she stepped onto the sidewalk, she sensed something. Am I mad? She wasn't the first person to ask that question. She turned back and hurried to the editor.

"Where did you say the CBC would set up for the Canada Day celebration on the Soul Star line?"

"Whispering Pine in Manitoba."

"How can I get there by tomorrow noon?"

"Why do you want to?"

"Because I sense a story."

"Well, charter a plane for the morning. Remember you run a little, local paper, not the New York Times."

"Is the summer student working tonight? I need a researcher."

"No, she has a date. If you want her to work, you better get your hands on her before he does."

Myrtle found Jennifer and requested her help in piecing together filaments of recent stories. Jennifer warmed to the possibilities as her research coalesced. When she met Myrtle at the airstrip the next morning, she carried a binder. "This story will leave a phalanx of Washington Post star informants thinking it was April Fool's Day and they're poised to take a 'Deep Gulp'."

Myrtle laughed and wondered if she should let Jennifer go back to school or chain her to a job this instant.

When Myrtle got to Whispering Pine, she noted the bustle and the electric atmosphere. Tight security around the mouth of the shaft at Whispering Pine caused her to walk north to the next village, ask a few questions, and learn that no strangers could go below ground. Myrtle walked north another kilometer and became the grandmother of a villager. She concocted a story that played well with the villagers' sense of fair play, so they ignored the ban on visitors below ground.

As the elevator hauled her and her convenient grandchild down the shaft, Myrtle asked, "How deep is this shaft?" The elevator slowed at the bottom, and Myrtle's jaw dropped. The implications took her breath away. Her hostess implored her to get back to the surface before detection of their little foray.

Back on the surface, Myrtle phoned her editor. "We have the biggest story this paper will ever break. We must print a special edition and be ready to distribute it within ten minutes of my phone call on July First."

"Are you out of your mind? We don't do special editions; we're a small town weekly."

"Tomorrow, we do a special edition and we'll prove publication preceded the July First gala that's about to catch the attention of the world."

"Yeah, right," said the editor, attuned to the peccadilloes of politicians and miscreants. Maybe he would retire but, in the meantime, his day off evaporated.

Chapter 104

Saturday dawned bright and crisp. Krista Wallace stepped out on the veranda, took a deep breath. At last night's party for the Gronson Fjord villagers, she hugged every individual and wished them well in their futures.

What a grand experience to have accomplished this magnificent project. Four pipelines designed to carry gases, liquids, and solids across our nation, two passenger monorails to carry passengers at speeds up to 300 kilometers per hour, two railroads to carry freight to and from every other rail line in the country; six lanes of highway to permit autobahn speed and efficiency and not one traffic light, intersection, or left turn, in its 4,400-kilometer length, six open-air bicycle lanes and six all-weather bicycle lanes for the entire length of the tunnel, two sixteen foot-wide walking paths, one open air and one all weather, from end to end, the Teeth of the Liard waterfall, the UIRIT grand courtyard, the taker-maker symbol, the tepee monument, and four theme parks built to endure for centuries and featuring Norway, Britain, Egypt, and China, each one a stellar example of what can be accomplished with vision and commitment.

UIRIT University cradled in a verdant valley celebrated the quest for the next breakthroughs in knowledge and responsibility.

The project provided connectivity nodes with every highway, railroad, and pipeline that crossed the Soul Star line. Two hundred and thirteen viable mines launched as a result of mineral deposits found along the line.

All this activity, and infrastructure, impacted the environment. Krista studied how industrial development affected other areas of the world and how such effects could best be managed. She discovered she couldn't justify any aspect of the Soul Star project to those zealots who viewed anything but pristine as obscene. She knew that capitalism would not place enough importance on the environment. The first time she met Brett Larson, a few weeks after she arrived in Gronson Fjord, eighteen years of age, she asked Brett, "How can you live with yourself? You've launched massive development that'll change the north forever."

Brett responded to her with an invitation to meet in the Gronson Fjord library the following day from nine in the morning until the two of them came to a consensus. The meeting adjourned after six hours and reconvened two weeks later.

In the first meeting, Brett reminisced about the shining dot in the water, his vision of the tunnel project to provide an alternative to social welfare, his perception that a small village best suits the individual responsibility model that he believed to be critical to the integration of young people. He told of lying awake at night wondering about the environmental impacts of the project. She remembered Brett talking of the ridicule that Beth Ragouski heaped on him and how she taunted him about draining Lake Athabasca and drowning thousands of Brett's precious misfits. Brett told her of his trip to Fort St. John to meet Oscar One Page de Lona and how One Page grilled him about the risks to the environment and opposition to any large-scale project.

Krista recalled how Brett talked of the ancient developments in China, Egypt, Greece, and Italy. He mentioned the filth and disease of the early industrial cities of Europe; he recalled visiting the slums in Tijuana and Bombay and the favelas in Rio de Janeiro. He knew about the planned cities of Savannah, Brasilia, and Canberra.

Then Brett asked her to think of the places that draw human attention in a neutral or positive way. She remembered discussing the picturesque villages of New England, the wine country of Tuscany, the castles of Europe, the pyramids of Egypt, the Great Wall of China, the walled city of Jerusalem, the Parthenon of Athens, the Coliseum in Rome, and the Mayan ruins of Mexico.

She recalled natural wonders like the waterfalls of the Norwegian fjords, the Grand Canyon, the majestic mountains, the rain forests, and the prairies. Then, Brett startled her with a series of basic questions: "Do individuals live somewhere?" "Do they form colonies?" "Do they impact the environment in the places where they live?" He explained that he came alert one night when these three questions came clear in his mind. Without those answers, Brett said he couldn't see sufficient justification to champion the project.

Once the fundamental justification was clear to Brett, he turned his attention to development without wrecking the surroundings. He mentioned traveling along the highway from Whitehorse to Dawson City and lamenting the grotesque piles of gravel left behind by the gold dredges.

With a focus in mind, Brett encouraged the Healthy Habitat grid system and corridors. That initiative identified five-mile corridors across the country and employed resources to identify the multitude of priorities necessary to balance environmental impact with commercial development. Soul Star followed one of those corridors and enhanced the many requirements specified in the original design. Soul Star recruited Rosie Savard, the champion of the Healthy Habitat project, to help design and implement the criteria that would preserve environmental priorities including the migratory patterns of wild animals. The Soul Star project refined observations about these patterns through the villagers living every kilometer along the route. Villagers observed the activities of the wild animals in the area. Brett concluded the roadway itself would be designed to prevent wild animals on the roadway. Road kill would be a non-issue. He further determined every observed trail and migration route would be preserved by archways at ground level that would not intimidate any animal as it passed under the Soul Star line.

The First Nations people who lived along the Soul Star corridor were exposed to aspects of Canadian commercial enterprise and government. Brett knew Indian history was pitiful for many and improvement lagged. He encouraged the Healthy Habitats' First Nations project and insisted on Soul Star improvements for First Nations individuals and families.

Soul Star developed energy sources much friendlier to the environment than fossil fuels. Soul Star chose solar energy stored in hydrogen cells. Policies would be in place to achieve solar energy at the start of the construction phase and ensure that solar energy emerged as the most economic energy source for all transportation, industrial and residential activity along the route. All housing units were built within the roadway. Self-sufficiency meant crops and pasture along the route. Every village ensured that its pastures and fields took care to manage the topography and vegetation in the vicinity of the village.

Even with the exhilaration of this moment and the extensive efforts to do the right thing, Krista still wondered whether history would embrace Soul Star.

Chapter 105

Terri met Brett, Thompson, Beth, Oscar, Rosie, Oats and Hymie at ten in the morning in the library at Whispering Pine. None of them had been allowed into Whispering Pine for eight weeks.

What had Terri prepared for the celebration?

Terri looked at each guest. “Thank you for the honour of designing this celebration. I’ve integrated key pieces put in place before my appointment. We’ve arranged four venues for the celebration.

“This road surface is the first focal point. It features those large screens that will provide new meaning to the expression, ‘when our ship comes in’. International visitors, villagers and their guests, and the media will all gather on the roadway. Every attendee will join hands as aerial photographs are taken. Here at Whispering Pine, the joining of hands might involve two or three switchbacks because of the extra guests invited to this section.

“Once the initial celebration is finished, I’ll invite the guests to walk to the Exhibit Hall set up under this section of the roadway,” she continued. “Before dinner, the doors will be opened to the last two venues. Each guest will walk through a series of four special sections. Once inside the Fairness Dome, under the pyramid, the guests will be treated to a grand dinner, feature speaker, and finale.

“I want to walk you through the venues so you can help with the celebrations but also experience the third venue as all of our guests will experience it later this afternoon.”

The group followed Terri.

The general layout of the exhibit hall did not surprise them. However, the spaciousness and the subjects covered impressed them all. Terri told them who would man each exhibit and the general topics to be covered. The exhibits stretched down one side of the space. The other side featured tables covered in gingham and fresh flowers in vases, chairs, snacks and non-alcoholic drinks. Walls, covered with 4,400 photos showing many aspects of the Soul Star experience, separated the seating sections.

As the group reached the end of the exhibits, Terri turned. "I hope I've captured many of the messages and innovations that Soul Star has championed. It acknowledges those individuals instrumental in the Soul Star experience and indicates how they've grown along with the millions of villagers."

Brett said, "Can we walk back along the exhibits? I want to absorb as much as I can before the visitors descend on us."

"Sure, Brett. I'll tag along behind and each of you can browse at your own pace."

When all finished browsing and gathered, Thompson said, "This place feels great."

Terri smiled. "I'm glad you like it. Let's move on."

They walked through a revolving door. On the other side: searing heat and blowing sand.

Thirty meters down the path, they came to another revolving door. On the other side: biting cold and blowing snow; blizzard conditions.

Thirty meters down the path they came to another revolving door. On the other side: a cacophony of sounds: shouts, gunshots, explosions, harsh words, fires, and armoured cars. Human figures darted about, some with painted faces, some with bandanas or balaclavas over their faces. All carried weapons: guns, machetes, spears, knives, and axes. Scaffolds, guillotines, razor wires, shackles, and chains littered the area. A chain gang shuffled along. Low-hanging clouds with inscriptions big government, big rules, big business, big unions, big abuses, big advocates, and big trouble. The path, covered in coarse shale, inclined through the heat, the cold, and the treachery zones. As the grouped walked through the treachery zone, the path became easier to walk on, finer shale, then sand, then paving stones.

As the group ventured further forward, they came to a glass wall. Seven yards beyond, a mural depicted many individuals suspended in a net. Heads tipped back with mouths open. Hands held above their heads with palms up. All watched for crumbs that might fall their way. A walkway circled above the net. On the left of the walkway, a man in a business suit held a large basket from which he dropped crumbs to the masses. Another man dressed in liturgical garments stood on the right side of the walkway. He dispensed holy water over the masses. The letters CBC were etched on the stole draped over his shoulders. Six cheerleaders—three on the walkway, two on their shoulders, and one on their shoulders—performed. Their jerseys wore the NDP initials of their school. The caption across the bottom of the mural said, The Natural Outcome of the Taker Mentality.

After the visitors observed the mural, the platform tipped from a pivot point above the mural so that the near end of the platform settled in front of the visitors. When it stopped, flush with the floor, the mural now closed from view, the glass doors opened. With room for fifty visitors, the doors closed and the platform tipped up on the taker end and down on the maker end. A voice on the sound system encouraged the visitors to walk toward the maker end of the platform.

When the glass doors opened, the visitors walked out into an oasis. The path curved alongside a stream fed by a waterfall. With tranquil sounds of the waterfall and stream, clouds gone, sun shining, the path morphed into the smooth tile around the pyramid. Trees grew nearby, grass softened the grounds, birds chirped in the background.

The path led to the door of the dome. Inside the dome, Terri turned. "I hoped for awe as you walked through the extreme natural elements and then the extreme human elements, then the natural outcome of diminished individual responsibility, then the ride on the Taker-Maker to the serenity of the oasis and this dome of fairness. My hope is that each visitor will carry an image in which she survives the eventualities of existence, adopts individual responsibility, and realizes this dome of fairness can be carried, as a virtual dome of fairness around her, for the rest of her life."

When the silence lasted longer than Terri expected, she turned and led the group a few meters into the dome so they could observe the mass of formal dinner tables.

The group waited for Brett to speak. "Terri, this is spectacular. Thank you." He gave a thumb up.

The group applauded.

Thompson pointed back the way they had come. "Is the mural too critical. Will it offend sensible folks?"

"I needed some focal point to fuel controversy and ignite commentary. I think it accurately depicts the results of vanished individual responsibility. I hope most folks will be anxious to step on the Taker-Maker and head for the maker end."

Beth looked toward the middle of the room. "What's that glass enclosure in the middle of the dome?"

"That'll become clear in the grand finale. When I planned this celebration, Brett insisted, 'No pedestal is low enough to make me comfortable'. Tonight, he'll stand on his pedestal deep in the bowels of the earth and he'll shine."

Hymie said, "It's good that Brett finds gems like Terri, isn't it?"

Oscar One Page piped up, "He leaves no top unturned."

Thompson shook Terri's hand. "From the moment I met Brett in my office, the Soul Star project inspired me. The rehearsal of tonight's program is pure joy. Thank you, Terri, and thanks to each of you. This is a magical journey."

Chapter 106

Over 4,400 kilometers, a mass of humanity stirred in celebration. Four million individuals joined hands in a continuous line across a country. At least two individuals from every country in the world, physically and symbolically, joined hands in celebration of a successful project with a minimum of government involvement, corporate excess, labour strife, human tragedy, or mass discontent. The celebrations featured no politicians.

Each of the 4,400 villages elected a representative who rode one of the bullet trains on celebration day. A group of 2,200 rode a bullet train from Baie Comeau to Whispering Pine and another 2,200 rode a bullet train from Whitehorse to Whispering Pine. Each train left a coast at seven in the morning central time on the first of July and arrived in Whispering Pine at three in the afternoon, central time.

Myrtle Murphy, editor of the *Prairie Sentinel*, strolled along the road in Whispering Pine when she heard her name called. She turned.

Rosie waved. “Myrtle, so glad to see you. I didn’t know you’d be here.”

“Hi, Rosie. I sensed a story and I came to see.”

“What’s your impression, so far?”

“I believe I’ve scooped CBC, CTV, BBC, CNN, Fox, and all the rest. I discovered the water in the tunnel and I put two and two together and got a million. The *Prairie Sentinel* has put a special edition together, the first one in its history. My staff will file the stories on the *Canadian Press* newswire ten minutes prior to the public announcement this afternoon. We’ve hired children in Brandon to distribute the special edition and taught them how to merchandise this occasion with enough flair that we’ll be the talk of the world for our five seconds of fame. It feels good.”

"That's fantastic. We'll keep it our little secret for the rest of this celebration. Have you got a seat for dinner tonight?"

"No, I came with no invitation."

"Don't fret; I'll get you a seat and media accreditation. I'll leave the media badge with Glen Aspol at the gate when you enter the evening venue. I'll tell Glen your name and describe you as a persistent old bird with a heart of gold."

"Thanks, I think, and thanks for smoothing my way."

"You're welcome. I'm pleased you're here. Have a wonderful time and represent us well in the Prairie Sentinel."

The news anchor of CBC Television resented his time on location in some mosquito patch in northern Manitoba. As the crews got set up, he prepped for feature coverage of the grand opening of the Soul Star transportation corridor. He imagined this would be a forgettable day.

Then his cell phone rang.

He listened.

He unleashed a torrent of expletives.

Sweat threatened his makeup.

He phoned the director of CBC Television.

Disbelief preceded reality.

The director said, "Report as if we knew all along. Heads will roll over this—probably mine."

Television cameras focused up and down the tunnel. As fog horns sounded, mighty ships slid into view from either direction—two oceangoing vessels, deep in the heart of Canada, a couple thousand kilometers from the Pacific and Atlantic oceans. After the ships came to a stop, bow to bow, the captain of each ship appeared on the gangway and led a procession of pairs of young people, from every country in the world down the gangway, along the red carpet, up the shaft, to the surface where applause welcomed them.

The captains, Makoto of Japan and Janser of Portugal, shook hands.

Janser said, "Interesting voyage, precious cargo, great honour."

Makoto smiled and bowed.

On the screens, two high-speed passenger trains sped into Whispering Pine and stopped. A passenger from every Soul Star village joined the crowd.

A young woman stepped to the podium. As the crowd settled, she spoke.

"Welcome to Soul Star. I'm Terri Talisman and I'm thrilled to host this wonderful occasion. Our program here at Whispering Pine has four elements. First, we'll sing a song that celebrates the Soul Star adventure. This will provide time for aerial photos.

"After the song, we'll enter the Exhibit Hall below us. The exhibits feature many of the approaches, innovations, and achievements that have gone into the Soul Star experience. We marvel at the physical aspects but they're dwarfed by the human aspects. As you peruse the Exhibit Hall, please ponder the scale of growth opportunities available to the villagers and recognize how many young lives have soared with the Soul Star experience. Many of you have observed a young person venture off to an unfamiliar life in Soul Star and wondered whether the decision would turn out well. It has turned out well.

"After passing through the Exhibit Hall, every participant will walk a gauntlet of four segments designed to imprint the challenges we face as individuals and societies and how we yearn to emerge to a serenity that's achievable but not always attained. Serenity can become a reality if each of us leaves this place with a dome of fairness over every aspect of our lives. As you reach the oasis and enter the dome of fairness, relax, ponder, and discuss approaches to life and consider the Soul Star adventure.

"For those celebrants in all the other villages along the line, you'll join hands, be photographed from the air, and sing the Soul Star song. Then you'll go to a dinner that'll include your own program.

"At eight o'clock tonight, every village plus our worldwide audience will view a one hour telecast. The television networks will prepare a composite feature program of today's events.

"Here's our cheerleader to help us learn and sing our special song. Please join hands and sing along."

Everyone can dream real big
Who causes us to give fig?
How do hopeless plans config?
We know how
We chunk it! Chunk it! Chunk it!
Soul Star, who woulda thunk it?

Everyone can hope so high
Who stops hopes from flitting by?
How to tell what parts will fly?
We know how
We chunk it! Chunk it! Chunk it!
Soul Star, who woulda thunk it?

Everyone can learn to trust
Who proves to be wise and just?
How to see beneath the crust?
We know how
We chunk it! Chunk it! Chunk it!
Soul Star, who woulda thunk it?

Everyone might learn to lead
Who reaps most from little seeds?
How do champions do good deeds?
We know how
We chunk it! Chunk it! Chunk it!
Soul Star, who woulda thunk it?

Soul Star

The roar of airplanes pierced the air as airborne cameras recorded the joining of hands along the entire line.

The photographers on the ground took pictures.

Terri stepped up to the podium. “That concludes the celebrations at this location. Please follow the signs to the Exhibit

Hall. There you'll find booths of the Soul Star experience. Visit the folks in the exhibits. They bring hands-on experience and knowledge and they'll be pleased to share their insights with you. There are snacks and drinks and places to sit along the entire hall. This warm weather and sunshine might have brought on a thirst and a need to get off your feet. At six o'clock, we'll open the doors to the dinner venue. There are special effects for you to experience. We'll not start dinner until all have gathered in the Fairness Dome. Thank you, enjoy."

Chapter 107

Myrtle looked around the Exhibit Hall.

I wonder if there're truths and messages I can emphasize to add nuance and emotion that might get lost in the mass media coverage. I wonder what lies in the gauntlet and inside the pyramid.

She walked the length of the Exhibit Hall with no conversation. A plan emerged. She'd dig deeper at each booth. She'd discern and convey elements of each exhibit that wouldn't be mentioned by the media who'd be intent on the basic story, the impact of full-size ships near the center of Canada. Myrtle beat them to that story. Now, she'd add flesh while the big boys assimilated the basics. She went back to the first exhibit and commenced her research.

One large photo labeled Ribbons depicted a section of the Soul Star road, and another labeled Jewels showed a migrating herd of caribou snaking its way under the Soul Star line via a magnificent arch of granite shimmering in the evening sun. An enlargement of the first individual treaty signed by Morning Star and the governor-general of Canada dominated the booth. A mock-up of a future cover for the magazine showed Rosie in Thailand. She planned to live in a country for a month. In that month, she'd suggest approaches that might solve the issues in the country. Rosie would create a feature article for Healthy Habitats with her impressions of the country's challenges and possible solutions. Rosie's bluntness, pertinent experience, and fearless approach would add depth to the articles. Healthy Habitats assigned a seasoned editor to help assure that Rosie would stay within acceptable bounds. Rosie planned to cover ten countries per year, with two months to relax and recuperate. Keith Zisemo and Gaston Tribolski joined the directors of

Healthy Habitat as they discussed aspects of Healthy Habitats approach: the Ribbons & Jewels, aboriginal consensus, and Rosie's new international column.

A low-key exhibit with modest kitchen cupboards, lace curtains, and a table with four chairs. The curtains moved in a breeze. On the table lay the illustrations that Hal Eastman brought to show Brett and Elaine Larson when Brett asked Hal to help attract thousands of young people to the Soul Star project. A photograph of Elaine Larson sat on the kitchen counter. Hal Eastman greeted visitors. When Hal got the opportunity, he described his current focus on university students who come to the UIRIT University with a passion for the arts.

One page, eleven feet high and eight and a half feet wide, stood as the element of the next exhibit. Myrtle stopped to read the entire Good Person Act. The act rang true to the belligerent young people that swarmed to the Soul Star line. It became the glue holding the villages together when conventional wisdom assumed anarchy would prevail. The author of the act, Oscar One Page de Lona, stood nearby with Glen and Sally Aspol to respond to interest shown by guests. Glen and Sally, the first recipients of the good citizen's award, planned to move to Teresoto on the Soul Star line to manage a new plant owned by Kunz Fast Ironworks. Oscar One Page accepted a feature writer role for the Canadian Law Journal. His themes focused on simplicity, fairness, prompt process, and individual responsibility. A fresh breeze for a profession built on complexity, obtuse interpretations of fairness, and slow resolution.

A patch of oats grew in front of a large poster of a badge. An old man stood at the booth. He leaned on a cane.

"Hello, I'm Myrtle Murdoch, owner and editor of the *Prairie Sentinel* newspaper in Minnedosa, Manitoba."

"Pleased to meet you, Myrtle, I'm Oats Wolf. I run the mining school for Soul Star."

"You appear to be older than me. How'd you get involved in this adventure?"

"I assume you've met Brett Larson. His ideas and approach attracted me."

"Where'd you learn your craft?"

"In the silver mines of Idaho."

"How did you end up here?"

"Brett came down to Burke, Idaho to learn about mines. He noticed me and here I am."

"Do you plan to go back to Idaho now that the project is finished?"

"No, I've saved an exquisite piece of granite my students quarried from the school site. I hope to have my ashes buried on a knoll near the school with the granite slab as my headstone."

"You've contemplated death. Is it on your mind?"

"Yes, I've been diagnosed with terminal heart problems. I wanted to outlive Brett so I could have a crack at his epitaph."

"What's the significance of the badge on the poster?"

"Brett teased me about 'rolled oats' and 'oat patch' and other jibes. So, when my students graduate, they each receive a patch for their jackets that's a symbol of their proficiency. There've been so many graduates that I hope, one day, the Oat's Patch will become as recognized as the engineers' iron ring. Of course, that's just an old man's vanity, but it inspires me."

"Will the school continue?"

"Yes, we've developed several qualified instructors. The success of Soul Star is expected to encourage other tunnel projects around the world. We have experience and reputation that should allow the school to continue. I'm proud of the achievements we've made."

"Well, Oats, it's been a pleasure. Thank you for your contributions to this project and this country."

"I'll die happy. So long, Myrtle."

Myrtle moved on to a richly finished booth, walnut wall panels, a circular boardroom table with leather inserts in the top, rich leather chairs, and plush carpet. A distinguished man stood near the table. He chatted with guests.

Myrtle waited for those guests to move on. "What's the significance of this boardroom exhibit?"

Thompson Miller held out his hand. "I'm Thompson Miller."

"I'm pleased to meet you, Thompson; I'm Myrtle Murdoch of the Prairie Sentinel."

"Then you'll know Brett Larson searched out a person to be the public face of Soul Star and a head office location calculated to have as little regional baggage as possible. He chose Thunder Bay for the head office and me as the president. It's nice to receive what we believe to be balanced coverage."

"I've endeavoured to encourage individual responsibility in newsworthy situations. When I find examples, I amplify them."

"Then you'll be impressed with the entry into the dome."

"I'm intrigued. What'll you do now that Soul Star is complete?"

"I'm the head of the UIRIT University Foundation. I intend to ensure UIRIT continues as a true university where the students take individual responsibility for their progress. I expect the business community across the globe will support a foundation for a university focusing on exceptional individuals."

"Isn't that the mandate of every university?"

"On paper yes, but they do what they can to sabotage their mission. They grant tenure, they make departments, they make bureaucracy, they count on government largesse, they use huge lecture halls, they don't know their students, they tolerate teachers' unions, and they publish instead of lead. They should lead every individual to excel. Our students, mentors, and staff are not involved unless they perform at a high level and the students won't graduate unless they have a skill set near the top, in the world, in their chosen field. Beyond that, they'll have real work experience in how to produce in an organization not just know how to get promoted."

"Where will you find these students?"

"They're all over. They get swallowed up in our mediocre schools. Many of them are ruined before they get to grade two. One of our goals is to turn out teachers and educational systems that'll let kids thrive from the moment they start play school."

"I thought you were the smoother and accommodator in Soul Star; your last couple of comments don't square with the pacifier façade."

"My wife's amazed. Soul Star ratcheted up my fervour. Brett Larson's attempts to do the right thing every day led me to see where I facilitated mediocrity and outright dishonesty in the folks I managed. I've decided I'll vary my approach to insist on upright decisions in every situation."

"I wish you all the best, but I've watched quite a few individuals," Myrtle said. "Most of them don't change personalities."

"Fair enough, but stick around the Prairie Sentinel long enough to write more individual responsibility stories."

It looked like a back office fifty years earlier. An old man sat at the desk, his suit and tie functional but not stylish. A photo of a native woman hung on the wall. Myrtle recognized the photo and assumed the man was Hymie Friedenberg.

Hymie greeted Myrtle. "A big day, isn't it?"

"A very big day; I'm Myrtle Murdoch of the Prairie Sentinel newspaper. You might remember me from the article on Rosie Savard."

"Oh, yes, Mrs. Murdoch. Glad to meet you."

"What's the significance of your exhibit?"

"I'm an immigrant from Germany. I thrived in the hospitality industry in the United States. Through a series of events, Jack Yudzik invited me to fund the Oat's Patch school run by Oats Wolf. Since then, I've been part of the management group and have provided some insights and money. It's amusing that the stereotype of a Jew is reinforced by situations like this, isn't it?"

"I've attended many trade shows and I've never noticed such a low key display by venture capitalists. Why is the exhibit set up like this?"

"First, I don't want to be cast as a lender in conventional terms. Second, Soul Star wished to acknowledge the importance of risk capital and to encourage entrepreneurs to find unconventional sources of start-up funds. I doubted the whole adventure until I attended a presentation by the Soul Star leaders and decided to trust my gut rather than rational analysis. That decision is one of the highlights of my life, isn't it?"

"Have you been frustrated by the coverage of Americans in Canada as mentors for the rape of our environment and abuse of our aboriginals?"

"We've learned to live with discrimination, but it hurts when our actual motives support Canadian endeavours. I'm pleased that the Soul Star team has managed to thrive in the face of negative publicity. It's a wonder that Soul Star reached completion, isn't it?"

"Yes, it's a great accomplishment and Canadians should thank you for your help."

"I've received many thanks and I'm content."

"I believe you are advanced in years but you look vibrant and ready for more adventures."

"Thanks. When my good health comes up, my wife says, 'I'm a virgin, you know, my Hyman is still intact.' If she croaks before I do, she can remain her version of a virgin forever. Clever, isn't it?"

Myrtle chuckled. "What will you do now that Soul Star is completed?"

"I've searched out a niece and nephew whose grandparents survived the Nazis in Germany. I plan to travel there and help them and their children get a leg up. Then I'll relax at home in New York and mentor individuals in my circle. Even with many challenges, the world is a wonderful place, isn't it?"

"Yes, Hymie, and I'm thankful you're part of it. Take care."

A photograph, the width of the booth, showed the terraced greenhouses of Gronson Fjord bathed in sun and reflected in the water in front. George invited Myrtle to sit on the bench with them and rest her feet. As she chatted, she learned of the tragedy in Sri Lanka, George's naturalization in Canada, his research with Cal Boychuk, Cindy's role in both of their lives, and the remarkable productivity of flowers, vegetables, fruits, and grains in a climate formerly bereft of local crops. Cal Boychuk, Cindy's fiancé when the three met in Watson Lake, struggled with the long winter seasons; his relationship with Cindy deteriorated; he broke his engagement and moved to Vancouver. He continued to innovate but didn't have the skills to merchandise his innovations. After Cal left, Cindy and George married. With Soul Star completed, George planned a two-year return to Sri Lanka as a mentor for the local farmers to adapt his Canadian innovations to his home country. Cindy would go to Sri Lanka with George and observe the education systems. She didn't know the local language and savoured a time of reduced professional responsibilities. After the sabbatical, George expected to return to Gronson Fjord and mentor horticulturists around the world. Cindy planned to concentrate on educational systems that would improve the chances of youngsters ages three through eighteen.

Myrtle next spotted a set of scaffolds over her head. A large saw with a diamond blade eight feet in diameter was mounted on the scaffold. Myrtle waited to chat with the tall, gaunt man under the scaffold. "Hello, I'm Myrtle Murdoch from the Prairie Sentinel newspaper."

"Hello, Myrtle. I'm Wolfgang Schneider with Kunz Fast Ironworks in Hamburg, Germany."

"What's your display about?"

"Kunz Fast sponsored one section of the Soul Star tunnel. We designed methods to quarry rock. Soul Star quarried much of the rock in sizes and shapes that could be used in stone structures on the surface. To accomplish that, we designed a portable scaffold that would protect the workers from debris and allow large saws to cut blocks of stone in cubes a little over one meter in each dimension. The saws could adapt to the fault lines in the rocks and yield as many useable stones as possible. With refined designs and proven prototypes, we sent our staff over to the Soul Star project to teach the local workers how to build the scaffold. We're thrilled that our designs have been used throughout the project."

"I believe you encouraged your company to use Soul Star as a cornerstone of your worldwide marketing initiatives. Have I got the story straight?"

"Yes, it took a little push for the directors to accept the plan. The execution has gone well and I've been promoted to chief executive officer."

"What do you expect to do now that Soul Star is completed?" Myrtle asked.

"I want to manage Soul Star's obligations to the multitude of stakeholders. In addition, cities built near the ocean, with precipitous geography nearby, can benefit from the utilization of tunnels for roads, trains, and rapid transit. Norwegian cities have developed these approaches and I expect similar initiatives will multiply. I plan to exploit those opportunities for Kunz Fast."

"Why did you decide that a project in northern Canada suited a German company?"

"The capture of the inspiration and spirit of young people. Plus, individual responsibility fits well with successful business. I saw this project as a quantum improvement in expectations for the masses."

"Are you aware that Hymie Friedenberg, a refugee from East Germany, has been influential in the Soul Star project?"

"Yes, I met Mr. Friedenberg and heard about his family's losses at the hands of our leaders. I admire individuals who decide on a path and execute well. He's been successful and maintained an admirable sense of fairness. We can't undo past wrongs but we can make good decisions from today forward. Many individuals carry grudges against past actions but the world will be a better place if we put past sins in context and strive to do better every day."

"I agree. Thank you for all you've done for this project and for Canada."

"I'm thrilled I acted on the opportunity."

A man stood inside a wire cage in the shape of a wedge with a metal tube at the narrow end of the wedge.

Myrtle said, "Is this the modern version of penance in the corner?"

He put his hands together emphatically. "But Teach, I didn't mean no harm."

"Who are you and why're you inside the cage?"

"I'm Gord Rempel. My company's Between Ewe and Me and I designed this pivot system."

"Why?"

"The Soul Star team wanted to raise farm animals along the entire line without contact between wildlife and domestic life. These cages are designed to rotate over enough days that the animals inside the cage can graze on fresh grass throughout the season and the farm animals are protected from predators. The metal tube provides shelter from the elements and provides enough solar energy to power the rotation of the cage."

"Is the design successful?"

"Yes, the pivots are used in twenty-seven countries around the world. They're used to allow more natural habitats for chickens as compared to small cages in big barns. As environmental considerations continue to drive decisions, we expect variations of the pivots will become endemic."

"What'll you work on now that the Soul Star project's finished?'

"The pivots themselves are a business. I've agreed to help design pivots for the dry gorges and valleys in California that are exposed to wildfires. I hope we can develop a system of terraces that'll allow animals to be raised along these stretches of otherwise unusable land so that the fire hazard is reduced and the irrigation system can be designed to carry sufficient water to kill any actual fire that approaches the line of pivots."

"When do they let you out of your pen?"

"When Terri rings the dinner bell." He chuckled.

Four large photographs stood in a semi-circle: a great wall, a castle, a pyramid, and an Iron Age farmstead. Six individuals welcomed guests: Krista Wallace, Kurt Woodson, Sonya Redwing, Charlie Tripp, Terri Talisman, and Tack. They wore coordinated blazers and pants. Eight years prior, the Alberta provincial education officer interviewed them in Gronson Fjord.

Cindy Zhong, armed with her education degree, stepped in as the token head of the Soul Star school system. She delegated Krista Wallace to lead the education of the cohort of youngsters that created challenges for conventional school systems. Kurt Woodson learned to be a talented stone sculptor whose works are placed along the line. Sonya Redwing continued to coordinate the settlement of native families in townhouses along the line with efforts to include enough role models in each village to develop cultures that could allow individuals to grow in aptitude and capability while aboriginal cultural choices could be accommodated for individuals. Sonya's background, experiences, and brushes with the justice system allowed her to be a credible mentor for the women who wished to make better lives for their families. Charlie Tripp, still insecure, remained a bachelor and worked as a lead framer for a homebuilder in southern British Columbia. Krista worked with Charlie enough that he could recognize the limits that could be accommodated by an employer. Many natural, adoptive, and foster parents have agonized over the apparent failures of their charges. Charlie, while no burden on society, was not a success story. Terri Talisman thrived in her own business. Tack's growth would be featured in his dinner speech.

A tall numeral 1 formed the center back of the exhibit. Each side of the exhibit displayed photographs of the grand courtyard, a student's workstation, and a contract. The workstation emphasized the focus on knowledge, not beanies, beers, and bunnies. The one-page contract committed the student and the university to a joint effort to find effective technology to prevent corrosion in petroleum pipelines. The student paid no tuition but he committed to twenty hours per week of work in the department and four hours per week in the university general office. He also committed to find the mentor who would help him learn and innovate. That mentor was not paid by the university. In this case, the student identified a mentor in Dusseldorf, Germany—the retired lead engineer for the largest pipe protection company in Europe. The student, Jeremy Swordski, the German engineer, Hilger Schmidt, and Lex Thorn all stood in front of the exhibit to greet visitors and discuss any topic raised.

Myrtle asked Hilger, "Why do you mentor Jeremy for free?"

"Because I can; I have enough money for my wife and me to live comfortably. My lifelong frustration has been our inability to put pipe in the ground that'll last for centuries. Soul Star has put its pipe near the surface, in dry conditions, but it may corrode from the inside. I've met with Jeremy and I've determined that he might have sufficient mental capacity, drive, and ingenuity to find superlative answers. His search inspires me and I appreciate the UIRIT philosophy; let driven people drive and stay out of the way."

"Do you fund you own travels over here?"

"Yes, UIRIT provides a comfortable suite for me to live in when I'm here and free meals. Every other cost that I incur, I pay for myself."

"Does Jeremy pay you anything?"

"No, Jeremy will fly to Germany every second year as a combined holiday and educational tour. He'll find the funds to get to and from Dusseldorf. My wife and I'll provide places to sleep and eat and tour Jeremy around. Younger members of our family will host Jeremy on some social occasions so he gets a taste of Germany that's hard to get as a regular tourist."

"Can you accept a university that seems so spartan and out of touch with our general perception of universities?"

"I accept, I applaud."

"Well, Mr. Schmidt, you're generous in this role. Thank you."

"My pleasure."

Myrtle turned to one of six interactive computer terminals available for visitors to explore. With ease, a user could select a topic of enquiry and then find one page of information. Pages showed how to perform calculations in calculus, how to find the Milky Way, how to interpret Kwakiutl culture, and most anything one could imagine. These accessible, one-page documents represented the core tool used by every student on the Soul Star line from toddler to PhD. UIRIT had encouraged and developed this database since inception.

Open to the world, much like Wikipedia, experts on any topic refined and expanded the information. Experts on every topic covered assured legitimate and sound information. Alternate theories with any traction were included. UIRIT University encouraged every student to add topics to the database as his or her knowledge reached the pinnacle in that specialty. Proficiency grids allowed any student to progress through playschool, kindergarten, grade school, undergraduate and graduate studies, trade studies and any pursuit in life.

Between each computer terminal stood five posters; each featured a breakthrough already achieved by UIRIT students, mentors, and alumni. Myrtle approached one of the terminals and typed in “gut feel”. She read an explanation consistent with her knowledge but extended to explain the current theories that might explain why gut feel often turns out to be a superlative guide to action or inaction.

Two large stone columns sat with a stone beam across the top. The polished columns and beams showed details beyond the architecture that Myrtle observed along the Soul Star line. As Myrtle walked through the arch, she saw a sign “School for Stone Masons” and photos of students with raw stone, fitted stone, and fancy pieces. Photographs of heavy equipment showed finished pieces lifted into place. The stone masons merged ancient styles and raw materials with modern equipment to achieve structures of appeal with less human labour. Four stonemasons talked about their trade and the challenges presented along the Soul Star line. They designed foundations for crossing deep and shallow water, for protection against frost heaves, for earthquake risks, for water dams and for wetlands. They designed systems for building the pyramid, the Great Wall, the castle, the tepee monument, the UIRIT grand courtyard, the Gronson Fjord terraces, and the Teeth of the Liard waterfall.

Myrtle stepped onto a textured surface. Scott Shadle greeted her and pointed to the floor. “This is a section of solar panel that covers the entire road surface on the Soul Star line,” he explained. “Each panel feeds into an electrical grid that powers all of the local and high speed trains, the industries that will use the space under the roads, the apartments all along the line and the villages, towns, and cities adjacent to the line. It will also feed into the national power grid when transmission infrastructure is built. It provides power for the generation of hydrogen fuel, which is our preferred method to store energy and provide portable power for equipment and transportation."

"Is this stuff strong enough to survive the wear and tear of highway traffic, snow ploughs, and accidents?"

"Yes; the design allows for heavy weight vehicles, the abrasive action of snow ploughs, and the repairs made necessary when accidents rip the surface. Each section is eight feet wide. Notice the forty-five degree angle on the road surface. This prevents vehicle tires from tracking the seams in the panels. The panels lock together and they are pliable enough that they adapt to temperature conditions without the separations you often see in pavement."

"What happens in freezing rain and wet snow conditions?"

"The solar receivers are below the surface. This provides a texture that provides good traction for vehicle tires. We've designed a brush system for snow removal instead of conventional grader blades. The brush bristles are gentler on the entire road surface than grader blades. In extreme snow conditions, we've adapted grader blades to ride above the surface on wheels so that large volumes of snow can be removed and the brushes can follow."

"Why isn't this technology on the front pages every day?"

"Have you discovered human nature? What we have here is a new way to produce electricity. It changes the dynamics in road construction, design, large utilities, federal, provincial, and municipal governments, and vested interests. I believe this technology is a quantum improvement and the world will adapt. Electric cars, windmills, and nuclear power have parallel challenges; all have potential but none have proven acceptable across the world. When Soul Star invited me to help design this technology, experts rejected the viability. Your questions are natural reactions to the reality of roads. Lots of individuals will travel the Soul Star line. Delays will allow us to iron out wrinkles. Even though it works well here, hot climates, heavy rain climates, and extreme traffic conditions might raise new challenges. For the moment, I believe you're standing on the future."

"I've been here two days and I'm impressed with the innovations. What's your impression of the whole endeavour?"

"As a young electrical engineer with a new, independent firm, the Soul Star project came to my attention. I listened to the presentation of Brett Larson and Rosie Savard and became enthused with the vision and scope of their plans. I jumped in. It's been quite a ride. The positive attitudes, the courage, the execution, the ethics, the scale, the growth of so many bright but wayward young folks; are all wonderful."

"You mentioned Rosie Savard. I'm Myrtle Murdoch, editor of the Prairie Sentinel newspaper. I did some articles on Rosie when she became newsworthy at Healthy Habitats. She arranged a media pass for me for this celebration."

"Rosie made me pause when I met her because she's blunt, driven, and uncompromising. However, her passion, humanity, and aggressiveness shines through and people admire her. The world needs a bunch of Rosies. By the way, I'm Scott Shadle, ready to put current in your affairs."

Twelve windows in a crescent, each fitted with an old-fashioned blind pulled open a few inches at the bottom. As Myrtle scanned the windows, she saw words under the blinds: renewable energy, geothermal, hydrogen fuel, construction materials, wildlife protection, wetlands, flood control, growing season, animal harmonization with humans, noise pollution, air pollution, and light and water pollution. Each blind a different shade of green. The sign above the windows read The Shades of Concern for Our Environment. Eight folks manned the booth: a baby in a playpen, a toddler, a six-year-old, a mother, a father, a grandmother, a grandfather, and a great grandmother. As Myrtle chatted with the group, she discovered the mother and father (Carolyn and Gerald Sotheby) worked on Soul Star for most of a decade; they married and raised three children.

When the couple heard news of the exhibits planned for the grand opening, they searched out Terri Talisman and asked if they could provide an environmental innovations exhibit. They also requested their children, parents, and grandmother be part of the group to help visitors realize how important each generation must be.

Enthusiastic about the innovations in solar panels on all of the road surfaces, hydrogen fuels for portable energy, geothermal heat throughout the townhouses, public spaces, and extensive multiple use space under the right of way, the group also emphasised stone as a construction material, the extended expected useful lives of the infrastructure components and the aesthetics of grand public structures.

The other exhibits ignored the elimination of road kill risks for wildlife and for travellers. A twelve-foot vertical stone wall above ground level, except for arches to allow animals to cross the line and for waterways, prevented animals from encroaching on the traffic lanes. Where roadways joined cloverleaves, the interchanges used fences and Texas gates to prevent wildlife access to the roadway. No deer, moose, elk, sheep, goat, bear, or other large animal encroached on the completed Soul Star roadways or railroads.

The farm pivots allowed domestic animals near wildlife without significant friction between wildlife and farmers.

Soul Star supplemented wetlands and water reservoirs with overflow basins designed to hold large amounts of floodwater with controlled dissipation.

The availability of unlimited geothermal heat, innovations in pivot farms, farming under awnings, terraces, and stone greenhouses permitted the local growth of many of the fruits, vegetables, crops, and flowers that are grown in warmer climates. These innovations require less irrigation, refrigeration, transportation, and reduce risk of spoilage.

The maximum grade of one percent on the roads and railways combined with ample capacity reduces traffic noises caused by stop-and-go situations and the extra noise of uphill pulls. The elevated roadway and railway removes the immediacy of the traffic and railway noise from the human activity areas. The low-speed and high-speed transit systems are all enclosed and the wind-noise from the high-speed trains is directed into the tunnels underground for effective noise reduction. The design eliminates the impetus for horns on vehicles and trains because there're three lanes of traffic in each direction with no congestion at any point and the trains have no people or vehicle interactions to necessitate use of the train bells and horns.

All industrial activities are planned to be housed in the vast spaces under the right of way and the activities are required to mitigate any kind of pollution before it leaves the facility's bounds.

Sewage plants in each village are all kept at a level that releases potable water. No business is allowed to serve foods in disposable packages and no store is permitted to sell disposable containers. The Soul Star culture has been built on reusable dishes, cutlery, and containers.

There're no streetlights anywhere on the Soul Star line.

The Good Person Act encourages safety from criminals, bullies, drunks, and youth. Every individual of any age, gender, race, sexual orientation, or noticeable trait is deemed to be safe everywhere. There are no locks on public places and individual households seldom lock their doors. Individual responsibility applies to the entire population. In such an environment, darkness does not breed paranoia. The sheer magnificence of the night sky, the northern lights, and the solitude that comes from the absence of artificial light is evident along the line.

The four large pipelines are contained in troughs that will catch any spills and sensors have been installed everywhere to alert operators to leaks. The only uncontrolled spills would occur in the wake of an earthquake or major explosion.

Pedestrian and cycle paths are included throughout the line, both outdoor and sheltered.

No landfill sites are permitted. Any garbage that is generated must be recycled; no throwaways.

Myrtle had her voice recorder on as she walked through the exhibits. She heard so much and so many interpretations that she wanted to record some impressions before dinner. She found a quiet corner in the refreshment area and dictated as many thoughts as came to mind. Her report was due, in final form, by

4:00 AM. By the time she recorded her thoughts, the doors to dinner opened.

Myrtle visited with the individuals she encountered as she made her way to the gate. "Are you Glen Aspol? Rosie Savard promised to leave a media badge for me."

"So glad to meet you, Myrtle. Many of us at Gronson Fjord enjoyed your articles on Rosie's exploits at Healthy Habitats and other coverage of Soul Star activities. It's nice to get genuine encouragement. By the way, I'm supposed to recognize you as a persistent old bird with a heart of gold. That seems a little harsh."

Myrtle laughed. "Rosie's no diplomat. Besides, her description is accurate."

"Enjoy the evening."

Myrtle ventured into the gauntlet. She paid attention to Terri's remarks. Myrtle identified with the hot, arid climate and the blizzard conditions, but the scale and diversity of the human treachery depicted in a thirty-meter space surprised her. A few thousand years of cruelty and force recapped in a confined space. Myrtle slowed down; she wanted to allow herself time to absorb the elements of the exhibit. Other visitors brushed by her, perhaps not yet cognizant of the significance of the symbols. When Myrtle saw the mural, experienced the Taker-Maker, and emerged into the serenity of the creek, trees, grass, and birds of the grounds around the pyramid, she admired the acuity of the design. She needed to talk with the originator of this display.

Brilliant, absolutely brilliant. Loose girdle Myrtle, I thought I'd seen and heard everything, but these folks have shocked me twice in two days!

Myrtle found a bench along the stream and pondered all she'd witnessed in the last three days. She ranked the highs in her life: her wakening sexuality, her wedding, her first child, her launch of her own business, and now, her recognition of Soul Star's spirit.

Chapter 108

The lights dimmed. When they brightened, Terri stood at the podium.

"If your emotions are taut and your body feels drained, you may now enjoy a fine dinner in relative calm. I encourage you to reflect on the exhibits, the gauntlet and the Taker-Maker. We hope the idea of a dome of fairness, which you can carry with you for the rest of your life, will serve you well. We've chosen not to say grace before dinner. Our feature speaker focuses on the management of our souls and we're sure you'll leave here more conscious of your soul than you imagined. We want to thank those inspired individuals whose vision, tenacity, courage, and spirit brought the dream to fruition. We're thrilled with the growth each of us has accomplished in our time with Soul Star. Our featured speaker is an example but we have thousands of well-rounded citizens who've benefited from the lucky affiliation with Soul Star. Enjoy your dinner. Bon appetit."

The lights dimmed and returned. Terri stood at the podium.

"Ladies and gentlemen, you're about to hear a remarkable message. Please welcome…Taaaaaaaaaaaaaack!"

Tack rose from his chair near the platform, walked to the podium with his peculiar gait, kissed Terri, and looked out over the vast crowd.

"Howdy folks; welcome to this milestone celebration. Much notice will be paid to physical achievements, and they're impressive. But Brett Larson's vision focused on the lives of the participants. That's the theme of my talk today.

"You've heard the expression rags to riches. My story is clumsy to capable. During my journey, a soul management model emerged.

"Most of you are aware of the approaches of organized religions. Where individual villagers embraced any religion, Soul

Star provided a rich venue designed to leave room for attention to the soul. However, a majority of the villagers either rejected religion or ignored it. This situation existed up and down the Soul Star line.

"Many thought I was mentally handicapped. Schoolmates teased me with the refrain, 'Not the sharpest tack in the box'. I asked my teacher what it meant. She cried when she explained. I went by Tack from that day forward.

"Three individuals were accepted in Gronson Fjord on the basis of some handicap: mine, a slowness to respond in casual banter. Krista Wallace protected me from too much teasing. She helped me get two jobs in the village: ambassador and assistant stage manager. These insightful positions put me in the loop of many of the petty conflicts that surfaced amongst individuals and let me learn from the foibles enacted on the stage. I came to realize I understood the range of issues before me but I couldn't process the information quickly enough for me to respond in a normal way. I told Glen Aspol. His eyes lit up. He took me to find Krista Wallace.

"I studied the tenets and protocols of the religions. I gleaned the human nature aspects from religious doctrines and celebrations and I tried these ideas out in my work as ambassador and assistant stage manager.

"One aspect of the established religions is the structured sermon. I concluded the sermons relied on religious doctrines beyond the understanding (maybe belief) of the listeners. The sermons lacked flair. I determined two things from this observation. My speeches would not exceed the listeners' credibility and I would learn to be a capable public speaker.

"To help me bring structure to my soul-enriching journey, I started a recipe box. I like the metaphor of the meal as a core avenue for soul enrichment. I decided to develop ingredients, flavours, seasonings, leavening agents, and other aspects of food and drink that could be the elements of the recipes for the soul that could become parts of everyday meals of the villagers and the focal points for those celebratory meals that form important days in our lives.

"The established religions have usurped almost every word that could provide meaning to my perceived role. Minister, pastor, shepherd, ad infinitum are identified with one or more religions to the point they don't reflect my journey. I came up with busboy. I couldn't think of a single religious entity that used busboy in any context, let alone to describe their leaders. My perception of a mentor for each individual's soul enriching journey is to be alert and anticipate the partaker's requirements. In our journeys, we often ignore our souls until we're desperate. Then we discover we have limited skills with soul enriching tools. In a family situation, parents are motivated to instil culture, habit, and approach in each child. In religious families, church attendance, prayer, table grace, Sunday School, holy days, and the like are endemic in the child's upbringing. In more secular families, attention to the soul is much more libertarian, almost to the point of dismissal. I want to be the busboy who brings soul enriching tools to the table whenever an individual notices a need but otherwise go unnoticed.

"Because your busboy may not be handy when your soul wants help, you could develop your own recipe box that contains the recipes that help you make your way through your current troubles.

"What might your recipe box hold?

"Could it be the protagonist Jack Reacher in Lee Child's novels? Jack is a nomad who carries a toothbrush and little else. He has an approach to life. He finds situations and he fixes them with more gusto than most of us attempt. If you think about Jack Reacher, you might discover some recipes for your soul. Could it be Henry David Thoreau on Walden Pond? He asked about the quests that most of us pursue without consideration of the burdens our pursuits place on our souls. Could it be Dolly Parton with her coat of many colors, so meaningful to her but ridiculed by her peers? Could it be the Power of One as described by Bryce Courtenay? Could it be the serenity of a walk through the woods where the birds, insects, and animals thrive with apparently little trauma in their thoughts? Could it be Enya's mellow tones? Could it be Gary Fjellgaard, ten years old and barefoot?

"The available recipes are endless. You might launch a quest to assemble your recipes. Your best chance is in a family committed to each member's quest. Your next best chance is a personal decision from here forward. The next best chances are serendipitous. If serendipity is your friend, study the Soul Star project.

"If your family situation did not provide an adequate set of recipes, my hope is that you'll decide, today, to develop one. If you do, I believe one path would be to adopt the ordinary meal as the vehicle to build a little structure into your quest. You might think of each meal as a peace meal—P-E-A-C-E meal. I like words and I try to use them in unusual ways. We all know the expression piecemeal but we don't think of a meal in terms of inner peace. But you could think in those terms and I suggest the effort would be rewarded. Most of us have been in situations where table grace is said before a private or public meal. In North America, the table grace has focused on Christian approaches. More recently, public table graces have become less specific about Christian traditions and more inclusive of non-Christian participants. The table grace concept provides an opportunity to develop the individual soul's recipe box and to suggest a secular recipe that might fuel discussion throughout the meal. With a little practice, this approach might become an inclusive entre for each participant.

"We're thrilled that each of you has joined us as we celebrate the achievements of Soul Star," he continued. "The recipes are everywhere present along this wonderful line. They can be refined and applied anywhere in the world.

"Early in my time at Gronson Fjord, a girl in the village entranced me. She accepted me as a friend but she did not see me as a worthy life mate. Glen Aspol suggested that I figure out how to appeal to Vicki in every aspect of life. I figured it out. Vicki and I are married and we have one thumbtack underfoot and another one on the assembly line."

Tack smiled. “I leave you now, the happiest tack in the box.”

As the applause receded, Terri strode to the podium, kissed Tack, and addressed the crowd.

“Often, the end of the featured speech is the end of the formalities. Tonight is different. Under this pyramid, consistent with the tombs of ancient Egyptian kings, we built a chamber similar to a mausoleum. This chamber has been fitted with three elements that are unique to Soul Star. First, in a small basin of water, shines a bright speck of light that recognizes Brett Larson’s original inspiration for the Soul Star effort. The water is circulated, filtered, and replaced to ensure it remains fresh, crystal clear, and worthy of its reflection of the founder.

“Second, a time capsule is embedded in the floor. The inscription instructs that the time capsule be opened on July 1, one thousand years from now. The capsule contains a cornucopia of artefacts. The one I want to feature tonight is the original Soul Star that Brett Larson designed, constructed, and placed on a tall pole in the center of the Oat’s Patch village where Oats Wolf launched the training of the miners.

“The third element is the source of a laser beam that will shortly be lit by Brett Larson. The beam of light will shine straight up through a hole in the rock and through the floor in the center of this dome and it will light a special crystal Soul Star that will refract the light around this dome in perpetuity. Brett Larson is reluctant to stand in any spotlight. He prefers to let achievements speak for themselves. I insisted Brett cooperate with me in this special moment. We have placed cameras in the chamber so that Brett’s moment in the spotlight can be viewed live on the screens in this dome, in every village along the line and around the world. Brett, if you’re ready, please begin.”

Images of Brett Larson with five other individuals filled the screens.

He looked into the faces of all the others, then he looked into the camera. “The six individuals at this podium are the sole survivors of the Larson family devastated by a missile which killed our mates, mothers, daughters, sister, aunts, and granddaughter. I continue to feel responsible for their deaths. I’ve concluded the only rational action is to learn from events—try to do the right thing every moment and continue to lead. I invite each of you to build a rich life driven by dreams, fuelled with passion, tempered with individual responsibility, and leavened with goodwill."

He pressed a button on a remote. A brilliant white laser beam flashed to the highest part of the dome and lit the crystal star.

"I hope this beam of light will shine on your star and lead you to your preferred destination. Thank you. Enjoy the journey. Goodnight."

Further the Journey

My website www.VillageSource.net is dedicated to group sourcing solutions to important issues. To help generate discussion, I write a periodic blog and invite responses. My hope is that we can, together, refine meaningful solutions.

If you know someone who's interested in good answers, please encourage them to read Tunnel Vision and add perspectives to the issues.

If your book club chooses the novel, I wrote a blog on www.VillageSource.net entitled "Book Club Ideas." It suggests potential explorations on individual responsibility, good persons, characterization, and innovation.

Connect with me online:

My blog: http://www.VillageSource.net

Facebook: http://www.facebook.com/VillageSourceDotNet

Twitter: http://www.twitter.com/@DaveAmonson

I encourage you to follow me on Facebook and Twitter. You can follow by clicking on the appropriate boxes on my website. Each of my blogs on www.VillageSource.net provides an opportunity to comment on the particular blog. This is effective because the comments are sorted with the original blog. If you wish to contact me privately, my email is (my nickname and last name with no spaces)@VillageSource.net.

About the Author

Dave Amonson grew up on a small mixed farm in northeastern British Columbia. He is the middle of five children born to Jennie and Percy Amonson. After high school, Dave worked in geophysical exploration for five years before attending the University of Calgary. He earned a B. Comm. Accounting major with distinction and articled with Arthur Andersen & Co. He co-founded ALW Partners LLP, Chartered Accountants in 1979 and continues as a partner in that firm.

Always interested in supporting his communities, Dave has served on multiple committees for accounting, community, and political organizations. In 2001, Dave was honored by his peers with a Fellow Chartered Accountant designation.

In 2003, Dave published a free book entitled Towards Improving Canada. That book is available, free, as an e-book on any platform and is available in print for $14.99 at Amazon.com.

In 2015, he published his first novel, Tunnel Vision. He's currently working on revisions to Towards Improving Canada by extending its applicability to any place on earth. The new version is called The Village Cafe. Watch for it in the fall of 2015.

Dave lives with his wife Bernadette in Cochrane, Alberta. His children and grandchildren live in Calgary.

Other Dimensions

Belief
Consensus
Community (Village)
Constitution
Democracy
Education
Engagement
Environment
Fairness
Family
First Nations
Good Persons
Harvest
Justice
Life Security
Myth
Power
Property Rights
Public Interest
Rational Laws
Reason
Respect
Ribbons & Jewels
Soul
Taker-Maker
Taxation
Trust
Villager Philosophy

All of these topics can be explored on www.VillageSource.net

Contact the Author

My preferred communication, with you, is through the comment area following each blog on www.VillageSource.net. This allows me to pay attention to one flow of communications without developing substantial administrative infrastructure.

See the information under the preceding caption Further the Journey.

Made in the USA
Charleston, SC
14 February 2017